The Shilling Doctor

The Shilling Doctor

DIANE COSGROVE

ORION

First published in Great Britain in 2004 by Orion Books
an imprint of The Orion Publishing Group
Orion House, 5 Upper St Martin's Lane, London WC2H 9EA

A CIP catalogue record for this book is available
from the British Library

ISBN (hardback) 0 75285 222 1
ISBN (trade paperback) 0 75285 223 x

Typeset at The Spartan Press Ltd,
Lymington, Hants

Printed in Great Britain by Clays Ltd, St Ives plc

www.orionbooks.co.uk

To Margaret Boyle, who would
make a wonderful mother-in-law
if only her son would get round
to it . . .

ACKNOWLEDGEMENTS

Thanks to Elizabeth Wright, Kate Mills, Nicky Jeanes and Hugh Lamb for their unflinching support.

Chapter 1

Waverley Station was noisy with the shouts of the guards, the rhythmic thundering of the engines and the constant movement of people as they made their way towards their platforms and carriages. Jeannie wove a path through the mass, struggling with her bags as they caught on coats and legs. Eventually she admitted defeat at a painted wrought-iron pillar, and slumped against it. She put down her carpet-bag and her new black case, its shiny brass clasp advertising that, like its owner, it had yet to earn its keep. Jeannie leaned back on her heels, and tried to hum the tune they had been playing at the party last night, when she and the rest of her classmates had said goodbye to each other and to Edinburgh University, but it had gone from her head. Instead she tapped her foot in time to an imaginary jazz beat, and coloured at the memory of her first attempt at the Charleston.

Suddenly, her gloved hands flew to her lips. She had scrubbed them but they were still stained with red lipstick. She glanced round, hoping no one had noticed. But of course no one had. A few women, in crushed velvet and fur collars, were defiantly wearing their lipstick in the early afternoon – not even Fiona had the courage to do that, thought Jeannie, and she didn't care what anyone thought of her. Mainly because, when Fiona was in the room, men lost the ability to think and just gazed in admiration.

Jeannie heard a whistle and craned her neck just in time to

see the Flying Scotsman arrive at the platform, smoke pouring from its funnel.

'Someone, quick!' a young man shouted, as his companion, an elderly man dressed incongruously in a white linen suit with a cashmere overcoat slung over skinny shoulders, staggered against him and fell to the ground, his eyes closed.

'Let me past.' Jeannie pushed through the crowd, who had been watching curiously, until she reached the two men. She got down on her knees, heedless of the fine wool of her long grey skirt.

'Temperature's raised.' She touched the old man's damp forehead with her long fingers. 'Can you open your eyes?'

'He was feeling unwell on the ship,' the young man added, 'but he thought it was the food.'

Jeannie took hold of the patient's wrist. 'Where have you come from?' she asked, as she took his pulse. 'Put your coat under his head.'

'India,' the young man replied, as he made a makeshift pillow and placed it on the ground. 'We docked this morning. He had been complaining of a headache.'

'It may just be the change in temperature, but he's had plenty of time to adjust,' she said. 'Or perhaps a malarial attack. It's common in India.'

'I don't know,' the man replied. 'I only met him on board. But he told me he had been there for some considerable time.'

'Excuse me,' a male voice said behind her. 'I can take over now.'

'I have it in hand.' Jeannie looked up to see a middle-aged man with a girth that betrayed its debt to the finest eating establishments in Edinburgh.

'I'm a doctor,' the man returned easily. 'Now, let's get this gentleman away from here.' He gestured and two porters ran to him.

'Perhaps I can help.' Jeannie lifted the unconscious man's head and placed it on the overcoat.

'I doubt it, my dear,' the doctor said, as a groan escaped from the inert body.

'I'm a doctor too,' she insisted.

'Put him onto a baggage trolley and take him somewhere I can attend to him,' the doctor told the porters. 'No need for you to trouble yourself any longer.' He smiled at Jeannie. 'He's in safe hands now.'

The two men lifted the man on to a trolley and began to push it toward the concourse.

'I'd like—' she began, but the doctor put out a hand to stop her.

'A gentleman needs a real doctor,' he said testily. 'Someone who knows what he's doing.' He turned and followed the porters.

Jeannie stood up and saw that the crowd was now observing her with the same curiosity that they had stared at the old man. Awkwardly, she picked up her carpet-bag and black medical bag, then walked up the platform towards the front of the train. 'I'll show you,' she muttered to herself. 'I'll show you all.'

The train had soon left Edinburgh behind, crossing over the River Forth by the starkly handsome rail bridge. Jeannie watched inky waves pounding the small island in the firth far beneath them. There was a depressing relentlessness about them. No matter how man tried, he could never tame the sea. Once again Jeannie recalled the events at the station. She'd met doctors like him before, men who were not prepared to give her a chance but, rather, preferred to keep her in a place they had defined for her. A place her father had never accepted. He hadn't brought Jeannie up to be a housewife: from the start he had taken her to his workshops, shown her his experiments in engineering and expected her to give opinions as freely as her brother. If only he was with her now, to convince her that she had to keep going in spite of men like that doctor.

As the train pulled into Kirkcaldy station, Jeannie stuck her head out of the window, holding on to her hat, and got a face full of soot that mingled with the familiar stink of the town's linoleum works. But it was worth it for her first sight of home. She wiped her face with her handkerchief, then ducked back into the carriage to gather up her bags. She opened the door and jumped out almost before the train had stopped, and waved frantically at the minister.

She caught sight of her reflection in the carriage window, pushed her dark red hair back under her hat and stepped out to meet her cousin.

'Look at you!' The Reverend Innes Macdonald's pale angular face was smiling. 'You look the same as you always did! My little cousin.' He could look her straight in the eye as they were the same height.

Jeannie made a face. 'Except now I'm a respected professional.'

'I can't believe you're a doctor.' Innes shook his prematurely balding head in disbelief. 'I've never met a female one before.'

'Trust me, plenty of people at the university thought women shouldn't be doctors.'

'You'll make the best lady doctor in Fife.' He patted her cheek. 'Come on, we'll get you back to the house and settled in.'

'Did you manage to make any appointments for me?' She picked up her bags, and strode along a little in front of him.

'I've been too busy, but now you're back you'll be able to take care of the household. Needs a woman's touch, after all this time.' He looked cautiously at her.

'But I don't know how to do that. I've been studying medicine, not housekeeping.'

'That doesn't mean ignoring your more ladylike duties. Perhaps Fiona can help. Give her something to occupy her days. She's shown little inclination for it, but it isn't her house, is it?' He hastened to keep up with Jeannie's long, confident stride.

'I'm sure I'll pick it up. Watch that step!'

'I'm right next to you, Jeannie, you don't have to shout,' he said, as he went down the step to where a square black car was parked.

'You could have fallen down,' she returned, as Innes stowed the luggage in the boot. 'Don't worry, I'll drive. Got to get back in the saddle, as they say.' She marched round to the front of the car and sat in the driver's seat before the three dials that were the only adornment on the walnut-panelled dashboard. 'If you think I'm going to hit anything, do tell me.'

Innes's smile became a grimace. 'It's not your driving that's the problem,' he sighed, 'it's your hearing.'

Jeannie drove along the bumpy, half-made road, away from the dirt and grime of Kirkcaldy to the elegance of Kinross. The road was busy with horse-drawn carts and delivery boys on bicycles. It was still a farming area, but many landowners left the hard work to farm managers and tenants, preferring the delights of tennis and golf. Kinross had an affluent, superior atmosphere, rather like those who lived there.

The Crossley crunched up the wide driveway, past the lush green foliage of the bushes that shielded the wide green lawn from the sun and passers-by. Jeannie hauled on the brake and looked at the high ivy-covered house, each pale stone storey balanced almost precariously on top of the next. It contrasted sharply with the other farmhouses in the district, which were wide and low. It had originally been the millhouse, but as the area had prospered a larger, more modern residence had been built. When Jeannie's grandfather had died, it had passed to her uncle Gordon, a rash, adventurous man. After disastrous business decisions, which Jeannie suspected might have been taken at a card table, her widowed father Ian had purchased it from him. She had grown up there, in a family of men, her father and uncle, her brother Kyle, and two cousins, Hamish and Innes. She had climbed trees and fished, ridden to hounds and shot game in the wooded hills. Which made it seem even more strange that Innes was expecting her to have acquired the skill involved in running a household. Still, she thought, as she stood in front of the house, she had a lifetime in which to acquire them. She gazed at the fading wisteria, which curled round the narrow sills, and smiled.

Innes and Jeannie entered by the familiar heavy mahogany front door, the painted dragons curling round the windows. The narrow hallway was just as it had always been, the old settle still near the door, the floor tiles at angles, the dark wooden staircase ahead.

'I'll get these up to your room,' Innes said quickly, and picked up her bags. 'Not much space here.'

'Why don't you just leave it for Beecham?' she asked.

'We let him go,' Innes said quickly. 'Fiona spent so much time with her family and I was here on my own so there was so little for him to do.' He smiled tightly.

The house was clean, but the shiny wood had dulled and the curtains and fabrics hung without their previous crisp, starched smartness. Jeannie felt a catch in her throat. She walked up the narrow passageway to the drawing room and opened the door.

'Thank God you're here, Jeannie.' Fiona Macdonald rose from her chair, martini glass in hand. 'It's been a nightmare with no female company. So difficult to organise my day.' She kissed the air next to Jeannie's cheek and Jeannie smelt heady scent and face powder. 'Innes has been such a Tartar about Hamish. Insisted he came home,' she hissed to prevent Innes hearing. 'Hamish isn't well enough.'

'We can help him together.' She looked at Hamish's beautiful wife and felt a wave of jealousy surge inside her. Fiona's dark hair was cut in a glossy Eton crop, emphasising her delicate, almost elfin features; her bias-cut day dress flattered her fashionably boyish figure.

'Why don't you unpack? There's a dance at the tennis club tonight that I simply must be at. I'm not spending any more time cooped up in this prison – I shall go completely insane.' She smiled sweetly and left the room.

Jeannie glanced at Innes, who shrugged and went over to the drinks tray, where Fiona's empty glass glinted in the afternoon sunlight. 'Well, I suppose it's over the yardarm somewhere in the Empire.' He picked up the half-empty decanter.

'I'm tired. I've been travelling all day and all I want is dinner and a long soak in the tub, not go to a dance.'

'It's just Fiona's way of welcoming you,' consoled Innes. 'She rarely gets out. She lost her husband to the war – Hamish is just a shell of what he once was.'

'How bad is he? Really.' Jeannie asked.

Innes took a deep breath. 'There are days when he seems fine, and others when he won't go out, almost as if he was terrified of what he might find. Just sits in the conservatory with his dictionaries. I don't know why he can't pull himself together. He wasn't even injured.'

'He was. Just not in a way you can see it.' Jeannie sprang to Hamish's defence.

'He isn't a man any more,' Innes burst out. 'You'll see, Jeannie.'

'It's been over three years now, Innes,' she said gently. 'He must have made some improvement. I saw him at Christmas before he left the sanatorium and he was nervous, but not unduly so.'

'He's unpredictable, but he suffers less than when he first came home.' Innes spread his hands. 'I'm glad you're back, Jeannie. You two were always close and Hamish needs his friends.'

'Does he know I'm here now?'

'I told him, but he can be terribly forgetful. Apparently it's because of the medication.' Innes looked at his watch. 'Got to go. Duty call to one of my parishioners before the dance. I promised Fiona I'd be there,' he ended lamely, and kissed her cheek. 'You're in your old room. I thought it would help you feel at home.'

Jeannie headed for her room. When she was younger she'd shared it with Kyle, but as they had grown up, he had moved in to the next room.

She opened the door and at once saw the old oak tree that reached past the window. When they were children Hamish had taught her and Kyle to climb it. Once, at night, Kyle had dared her to go to the top and she'd done it, but couldn't find a way back. Hamish had climbed up and brought her down. He'd always been her protector. And now it was her turn: she would guide Hamish back to himself.

There wasn't time for dinner before the dance, so she bathed and put on a silky long-line dress that she knew didn't suit her. It made her shapely hips and bosom look matronly. It was the kind of dress that suited Fiona, but as it was extremely fashionable Jeannie had put aside her reservations and bought it. It was only since Hamish had married Fiona that Jeannie had noticed the difference between her functional dress and well-scrubbed complexion, and Fiona's *haute couture* and paint. She had asked her new female cousin for advice, then plucked and filed, swapped her sensible lace-up shoes for narrow high heels that made her toes burn, and bought the dresses everyone admired. But she felt like a carthorse that had blundered into a paddock full of thoroughbreds. Even her red hair was long where everyone else's was short. No matter how hard she tried, Jeannie couldn't turn herself into a social butterfly, the kind of woman who caught an eligible husband. She looked at herself in the mirror, all lumps and creases, gave a grim smile and went downstairs.

Fiona, of course, was *Vogue* perfect. 'Make sure he doesn't drink, Jeannie,' she said, as she checked her appearance in the enormous gilt mirror in the hall. 'It makes him worse.'

'Innes?' Jeannie asked incredulously.

'No, silly,' Fiona chided. 'Hamish. He doesn't usually come with us to the club, but tonight Innes insisted. You can sit with him, he doesn't dance any more.' Jeannie walked into the parlour and found a gaunt man, prematurely lined and aged. Hamish had been once handsome, the gregarious crown prince of the tennis club – in fact if he hadn't been her cousin, Jeannie would have called him a bit of a rake. But now, his clothes hanging off him, red hair dull, green eyes watery and wary, she could hardly recognise him as the same person.

'Hamish?' Jeannie walked slowly towards him.

'Hello, Jeannie.' He smiled. 'Glad you could make it.'

'I've come to stay, Hamish,' she said softly, 'so I'll be here with you now. Just like it used to be.'

'It'll never be the way it was,' he said wistfully, 'but since this is how I am now, there was no point wasting any more money on treatment so . . .'

He was so still, she thought. Hamish didn't sit: he stood up, entertained them all with *risqué* tales, his hands filling in what polite society wouldn't allow him to say. 'Do you go out much?' Jeannie couldn't help but wonder what his old friends at the club thought of him.

'Occasionally. We don't get many visitors here, which suits me, but Fiona needs her friends.'

'What about *your* friends?' she said carefully.

'Didn't you hear?' He raised a bitter smile. 'There was a war and they all died. Except me, of course, and Angus. But the devil looks after his own, as they say.'

'Well, tonight if you get tired and want to come home, just tell me.' She patted his arm.

By the time Innes was able to escape from his parish duties, the dance was in full swing. The tennis club was busy, its high, gilded ceiling echoing to the strains of the resident band. As they walked along the hallway, soft soles and high heels sounding on the elegant tiled floor, Jeannie's heart sank. How many evenings had she spent propping up one of the marble pillars, making conversation with elderly friends of her parents

9

while the others danced the night away? And now, with every family having lost a son, it would be even worse. She caught the eye of a few people walking past and nodded a greeting to them. And she saw the wary glances they returned in Hamish's direction.

'Damn.' Fiona stamped her tiny foot. 'Now we'll be stuck at the back with the old fogies. No one sits there. And why do they never have a guest band? We'll be listening to "Eine Kleine Nachtmusik" all night now. Why they can't play jazz?'

'We always sat there – well, Hamish and Kyle were beside the band, fighting off all the women.' As they were about to sit down, Fiona gave a shriek and ran off in the direction of friends, well-groomed men in dinner jackets and women who chatted with wild, affected hand gestures designed to show off their elegant painted nails or ivory cigarette-holders.

'She hasn't been here for a while,' Innes said. 'Probably got a lot to catch up on. My goodness,' he said, with surprise. 'Julian Balliol is here. I must pay my respects. If the word is true and he's moving into the area, he'll be requiring spiritual guidance.'

'Thou shall not covet thy parishioners' wealth,' Jeannie murmured, and raised her eyebrows at Hamish, who forced a smile in return. The chairs were still upholstered in red velvet, but the wood was painted a garish gold and the red was a cheap scarlet rather than the old, rich claret.

A waiter came over with some sherry and they sat in silence as the band played the Merry Widow waltz. Fiona was being whirled round the dance-floor by a man in a dinner jacket.

'Just sit and watch the people, Hamish.' She put her hand on his. 'If you feel tired just tell me.'

'I should enjoy getting out,' Hamish muttered.

Jeannie snorted. 'I always feel like I'm in the wrong pond.'

'We can go riding,' Hamish said. 'I can show you the best places to go. Fiona doesn't like riding.'

'You know how much I do, Hamish,' Jeannie said. 'You taught me, after all.' She watched him digest the information.

'What else do you like doing?' Her attention was caught by the Hendersons who walked past with their plain, wholesome daughter.

'Crosswords, dictionaries and jigsaw puzzles.' He grimaced, slightly bashfully.

Now Jeannie understood Innes's remark about dictionaries. 'I can't do crosswords,' she said, as she smiled politely at the family. 'I can never understand the clues.'

'I'll teach you.'

'I'd like that,' she said gently, 'if you've the patience.'

Then Hamish smiled, and she saw a sliver of the man he had once been. 'I'd like it, Jeannie,' he said. 'I'd like it very much.' He glanced round the room, at the people dancing, chatting and enjoying themselves. 'I'd like to go home now, please.'

'I'll tell Innes.'

'This is my crossword book.' They were sitting on wrought-iron furniture in the leafy conservatory under enormous potted palms. The others were still at the dance. Hamish brought out a large portfolio and handed it to her, brushing a heavy banana leaf out of her way.

Jeannie looked through it. It contained hours of work, all meticulously written in Hamish's tiny hand. 'You make up your own?' she said admiringly. 'That's really good, Hamish.'

'Fiona thinks it's childish.' He looked at her nervously.

'How do you feel when you finish one?' She drew her finger over a hand-drawn grid.

Hamish sighed. 'Like I've done something important.' His eyes fixed on her pleadingly. 'I know it sounds pathetic, but it makes me feel like a man.'

'What's wrong with achieving something?' she asked gently.

'Because it means nothing, does it?' he snapped. 'It isn't important.'

'It's important to you, Hamish.' She put her hand over his.

For a long minute Hamish stared at the table. 'I never

thought I'd end up like this, Jeannie,' he said softly. 'If a friend of mine had been in this state, I'd have made a polite excuse and resolved never to see him again.' Their eyes met in silent acknowledgement of what had happened at the club.

'Would you rather have been Kyle?'

Hamish gave a wry laugh. 'They asked me that when I was in Craiglockhart. And I had to admit that I wasn't brave enough even to contemplate it. I'd rather be a live coward than a dead hero like your brother.' He exhaled loudly. 'It's getting late, I'll leave you. Goodnight.' He got up, bent to kiss her cheek, then walked out of the conservatory and back into the house.

Jeannie continued to sit at the table. Kyle had gone, but so had Hamish. They had both died, in their own way. And perhaps they all had to accept it.

Chapter 2

Jeannie took a deep breath as she stood on the well-scrubbed granite steps that led to Gordon MacLeod's surgery. The street was broad and leafy with elm trees, and the townhouses gleamed from the attention of housemaids and butlers. She checked her tiny pocket watch, which had been a matriculation gift from Kyle. It was ten o'clock, the time for which she had made her appointment. The kind of advice she wanted from Gordon MacLeod didn't involve medication. And she felt a degree of shame that she had lacked the courage to tell him so when she had requested an interview.

'Eugenia Macdonald.' Dr MacLeod was waiting for her in the hallway of the private house he used as his surgery. As always, he wore a carefully trimmed pencil moustache and smelt strongly of lemon pomade. He held out his hand to shake hers, and Jeannie's eyes were drawn to the less than discreet signet ring, the opal cufflinks and the gold pocket watch. He still wore more jewellery than most women – and she'd always found its glint curiously distracting from whatever indignity he was subjecting her to.

The black and white floor tiles in the hall were the same as those in her own home, and there was an eclectic selection of parasols, umbrellas, shooting- and walking-sticks in the umbrella-stand. 'To what do we owe the pleasure?' He ushered her into the pale cream day room, dominated by its inordinately high ceiling and heavy leather armchairs.

'I am sorry to turn up on your doorstep without an ailment, Dr MacLeod,' Jeannie smiled broadly, 'but there are a few things I would like to discuss with you.'

'Of course. Cup of tea?' Gordon MacLeod smiled with real pleasure as he rang for his housekeeper. 'I heard you were back from Edinburgh.'

'Just finished my medical degree,' she began, with a sense of relief that he had brought it up.

'A lady doctor! Never had one in these parts.' He looked at her warily. 'Are you here to look for a position?'

'Well, you know I'm from a respectable background.' Jeannie smiled. 'I'd be available to start immediately.'

'I can't offer you one,' he told her regretfully.

'I came third in my class.' Her hopes were crumbling.

'My patients are traditional. They would not take kindly to a person such as yourself.' He was staring smoothly into her eyebrows, as he was wont to do when breaking bad news.

'But what if I took the ladies?'

'I have been treating ladies for years.' Dr MacLeod stared over her shoulder towards a small bookcase that held a few leatherbound medical books. 'I treated you, and you never made any complaint.'

'But, Dr MacLeod,' she protested, 'I'm a good doctor.'

'Maybe in Edinburgh or Glasgow, or even England, but, Miss Macdonald, I cannot see you ever being a doctor in Kinross. We are country people here, and don't take kindly to city ideas. Ah, here is our tea.'

With that, he turned to other matters, and Jeannie realised that he was not going to change his mind.

It was late when she arrived home and found Hamish in the conservatory working through the *Scotsman* crossword. 'Busy day?' he asked.

'Trying to get a job.' She grimaced. 'For some reason the

elderly matrons of Kinross are shocked that I might want to doctor them.'

'Well, I don't think I'd want a lady doctor,' Hamish told her mildly.

'But, Hamish, why not?' Disappointed that he hadn't supported her, Jeannie whirled to face him.

'Well,' he chewed his lip awkwardly, 'there might be things I wouldn't want to discuss with a lady. And, certainly, I would not be examined by her.'

'But at Craiglockhart you undressed in front of nurses for medicals,' Jeannie reminded him.

'That's different. A nurse is, well, rather like the nanny you had as a child.' Hamish put down the newspaper and stood up. 'But you hand over your whole life to a doctor, you tell him things you wouldn't tell your closest friend, and it seems disrespectful to do that to a woman. I wouldn't want you knowing all about my plumbing. What if I saw you in the club or, worse still, found myself drawn to you?'

'Hamish, those are ridiculous objections,' Jeannie told him. 'You'd happily have a female nurse undress you, yet you wouldn't want her to look at you. You wouldn't want to talk about your bodily functions in case you embarrassed me – and you'd worry in case you fell in love with me?' She laughed. 'I've seen plenty of men without their clothes on, and I regard them as a set of symptoms.'

'My objections may seem hardly worth considering to you, Jeannie,' Hamish returned, 'but they might mean the world to others.'

As the weeks and interviews with local doctors yielded nothing more than polite enquiries after the tutors at medical school, Jeannie was beginning to wonder if Hamish might have a point. Perhaps change was difficult to bring about in a place like Kinross. But it was odd: St Andrews wasn't far away and lady doctors had trained there for years. Part of her wished she had stayed in Edinburgh and tucked herself away in a laboratory, experimenting.

To escape her worries, Jeannie went riding and let the wind blow away the cobwebs. Hamish usually joined her as he was alone in the afternoons, Innes at work in his parish and Fiona undertaking social duties.

'I haven't enjoyed myself so much in ages,' Jeannie said, as they walked back into the house, tired and exhilarated after an afternoon ride. 'We could get some horses of our own at Perth sales.' She glanced behind her and snorted with laughter at the two sets of muddy footprints they had left on the tiles. 'Those riding-school horses aren't as good as having your own.'

'Hamish, thank goodness!' Fiona rushed up to her husband. 'Where did you go?'

'Riding with Jeannie,' Hamish said, and smiled, his face untroubled and serene.

'It was wonderful to get out again,' Jeannie said, as she watched Fiona nestle into Hamish's arms. Now that Fiona was flaunting herself, Hamish would forget she was there.

'Don't you disappear without telling anyone,' Fiona said to him, and thumped his chest. 'We were about to call the police.'

Jeannie's stomach churned. Calm down, she told herself. He's her husband, not yours. 'We were only riding,' she said apologetically, 'not robbing a bank.'

'He's hardly left the house since he came back,' Fiona said sharply. 'When I got home and you weren't there, I was frantic with worry.' She reached up and kissed Hamish's nose.

'Perhaps if you came with us?'

'I don't ride, and Hamish hasn't for years.' Fiona linked arms with her husband and walked away with him. Hamish bent and kissed the side of her head.

Jeannie threw down her crop and stalked into the drawing-room for a large whisky. Fiona was treating him like a child.

And Jeannie had known what she was doing in taking him riding: Hamish had been her family for far longer than he had been Fiona's husband. And she was a doctor! She wouldn't risk him in a dangerous situation! But there was no point in being jealous: Fiona was family too.

'Never mind,' said Innes, as she poked at her porridge another unsuccessful week later. 'You can join the committee in charge of raising money for kirk boilers. And the ladies' tennis tournament starts soon. You could put your name down. Give you something to do.'

'Yes,' she replied sarcastically. 'If I hit a few well-placed balls perhaps I can get myself a few patients.'

'You are joking, aren't you?'

For some reason the look on Innes's face cheered her all morning.

A few days later Jeannie dressed in her whites and went off to the tennis club. Fiona was there, talking with some friends, but Jeannie didn't feel like gossiping so she went outside to look for someone to play and saw Margaret Carmichael walk in, brown hair shining with health.

'Jeannie!' Margaret cried, and hurried over, tall and slim in her white linen dress. 'I heard you were back. I sent a letter only today inviting you for lunch. It seems like for ever since we had a proper chat.'

'Margaret!' Jeannie embraced her friend. 'I was just on my way to find someone to play.'

'I have a lesson booked, but I'll cancel it. So, what's my bridesmaid doing now? Any handsome men on the horizon?'

'Fighting them off as you can see!' Jeannie grinned and waved her racquet in the air. 'Let's get a court.'

'Marvellous game,' Margaret said, as they shook hands after the match. 'Maybe one day I'll manage to beat you.'

'Any time you want to practise . . .' Jeannie swept at the air with her racquet. 'Are you going in for the tournament?'

'Don't think I'll have time. Now that I'm back, Daddy thinks I'm here to run his household for him. And I'm still trying to get our new home in order.' They sat down at one of the tables and a waiter came over and took their order. 'But won't you be busy working?'

'Can't get a position.' She sighed.

The waiter brought them a large jug of Pimm's.

'Are you that bad?'

'Trouble is, Margaret, I'm not a member of their little-boys club.' Jeannie made a face. 'It seems that that is an essential requirement for being a doctor in Fife.'

'I could have a word with Daddy,' Margaret began. 'He can be wonderfully persuasive.'

'Would you?' Jeannie said eagerly. 'Innes won't help. He thinks I should stay at home and keep Hamish company.'

'It's Fiona he should be telling that to. You'd think she was widowed the way she's been carrying on. I swear she's one of the worst flirts I've ever seen,' Margaret said.

'Really? I always thought she was one of the best.' Jeannie chuckled. 'I never could copy that way she has of wrapping a man round her little finger.'

'You're more of a wrestle-them-into-the-ground type of girl.' Margaret laughed into her drink. 'But cheer up, I'll see what Daddy has to say about your work.' She smiled. 'Oh, look, there's Kirsty McLellan. She'll be a good doubles partner for you.'

'But you and I have always been double partners.'

'You mean you've always saved me from complete disgrace,' Margaret said. 'Kirsty's a much better player than I am. You deserve better than me.'

'I like playing with you.' Jeannie couldn't understand why Margaret seemed so unwilling to partner her.

Margaret hesitated, then bent forward. 'I haven't played for ages. The situation is rather delicate at home – relations between Daddy and Angus are rather strained and taking up all my time.' Jeannie tried to protest, but Margaret stopped her. 'It's nothing to worry about, just a little awkward. Kirsty!' She waved prettily at the woman who had just walked in. 'Looks as if you'll finally have some competition. Jeannie's back.'

Kirsty slipped elegantly between the tables and chairs. She wore a navy blue dress with a heavy white collar, which gave her a jaunty, girlish air. 'Hello, Margaret, Jeannie,' she said, and sat down with them. 'How are you both? Practising for the tournament?'

'A little, but I'm mainly catching up with all the news,' Jeannie replied, and picked up her glass.

Kirsty grimaced, showing even white teeth, and smoothed her dress over her knees. 'But we haven't been doing anything exciting, Jeannie,' she said. 'All I've done is go dancing, play tennis and marry, like everyone else. You're the one who's done something different.'

'How is Arthur?' Margaret asked.

'Making lists!' Kirsty turned to Jeannie. 'We're off to India to his family's jute factory in a few months. Just for a few years till his younger brother is old enough.' She sighed. 'Every day he comes home from work and tells me something else that has to be done before we leave.' She shook her head. 'I'm thankful I don't have any children to organise yet. The climate is brutal there, too fierce for them. Even my fur coat has been dispatched to Jenners in Edinburgh for storage as the hot sun would ruin it. But I'll have time to compete in the tournament.'

'Are you looking for a partner?' Jeannie said casually. 'Because mine has declined to compete.' She grinned at Margaret.

'You know I'd love to play with you, Jeanie,' Kirsty replied, 'but you must promise to let me hit the ball occasionally.'

'Just because you're leaving,' Jeannie teased.

'That'll do for me,' Kirsty said.

*

That weekend Jeannie, in her unflattering new dress, walked into the club. She stopped and chatted to some old friends, then headed into the main sitting area. There, she saw Margaret, with her father and her handsome husband Angus, Hamish's old friend from university.

'Hello, stranger,' Angus said, as he walked over to her. He was rakishly handsome in a well-cut black dinner suit that emphasised his strong shoulders and long body. 'Haven't seen you for almost a year.'

'Every time I came home, you were in Glasgow.' For some reason, when Angus spoke to her, Jeannie always found herself strangely pleased but embarrassed, so that inevitably she blushed.

'Well, I've known you and Margaret long enough to realise that when you two get together everyone else is ignored.' Angus's brown eyes crinkled as he said it. Then he looked down and laughed quietly to himself. 'I see Hamish is in tonight.' He waved and Hamish joined them with Innes.

'Angus, it's good to see you,' he said. 'I didn't know you were back in town. How are your parents? It's been a long time since I've spoken to them.'

'They're fine, but Glasgow life didn't suit Margaret.' Angus raised his hands in mock-exasperation. 'So now I'm stuck with all you Fifers. That's what I get for going to St Andrews with reprobates like you rather than sensible Glaswegians like myself.'

'What are you doing?'

Angus glanced at his father-in-law, who seemed pre-occupied.

'Setting up my own practice, working as solicitor for small firms in the area.' Again, he looked quickly at his wife's father. 'Didn't want to live off the old man, you know.'

'I thought Margaret said you moved back in January,' Jeannie said.

Angus shook his head. 'No, she spent a lot of time here, but I was finishing off business in Glasgow then.'

'You must come up to the house,' Jeannie said. 'Hamish is there most days.'

'Yes, Angus, that would be pleasant,' Hamish said, with a flash of the enthusiasm that was now out of character for him.

Angus nodded absent-mindedly. 'I'll try old boy. What are you doing now?' He stumbled over the words.

Hamish looked down. 'Not a great deal,' he said slowly, 'but since Jeannie came home I've been riding.'

Angus murmured something and moved away. Innes glared after him. 'Didn't have much to say for himself,' he said sharply.

'He's got people to see,' Hamish replied.

'Course he has,' Innes retorted. 'That's probably why he hasn't come to visit you in the last six months.'

'Innes,' Jeannie said warningly.

'Of course.' Innes's lips pursed. 'You've been friends for years, he's just been busy.'

When Jeannie looked towards the Fleming table, Sir Justin beckoned to her. A Celtic bear of a man, with a neatly trimmed beard and heavy build, he was imposing even when he was sitting down.

'Well, Eugenia,' he said loudly, 'I hear you're looking for a job.'

Jeannie caught Margaret's eye. Her friend smiled, then looked away.

'Yes.' She smiled broadly.

'I was talking to Gordon MacLeod,' he continued. 'He's looking for someone to do some doctoring for him.' He smiled. 'I gave him your name.'

'And?'

'He'll speak to you later. Actually,' Sir Justin raised his hand, 'he's just come in.'

Gordon MacLeod walked over and greeted, first, Sir Justin, then the others.

'We were just talking about you,' Sir Justin said. 'Telling young Eugenia that you need a bit of help with your work.'

'Yes, Sir Justin,' Gordon MacLeod said, in a rather stilted way. 'I was meaning to get in contact with you, Eugenia. I will be needing someone, after all. That is, if you're still available?'

Jeannie had to stifle her emotions. She had a position! 'I can start on Monday,' she returned.

'Fine, we'll see you then.' Dr MacLeod nodded. 'Let's hope that all my patients are as welcoming as Sir Justin is.' His voice held a quiet irony.

'And don't think I'm letting you anywhere near me!' Sir Justin chortled.

The doctor raised his eyebrows.

Chapter 3

It was with barely contained excitement that Jeannie went to Gordon MacLeod's surgery the following Monday. She stopped to look at the brass plaque outside the surgery with his name and qualifications etched on it in black. She made a resolution to order an identical one, then took a deep breath and went in.

'Jeannie!' Gordon smiled. 'Come in and I'll introduce you.'

Jeannie met the nurse, the receptionist and a visiting pharmacist who all seemed bemused: they weren't used to doctors in grey skirts.

'Ma'am,' Nurse Soutar said respectfully, as she stared at Jeannie's hand. In her book women didn't shake hands. But women didn't become doctors either: if they were so inclined they became nursing sisters, or helped in university laboratories. Eventually she shook it rather limply.

'Don't call me "ma'am",' Jeannie told her politely. 'You can address me as "Doctor".'

Nurse Soutar looked fearfully at Gordon, who nodded in silent agreement.

'A lady doctor.' Mr Beaton, the pharmacist, eyed her with barely concealed amusement. 'Haven't had one of those here before.'

Over the last six years, Jeannie had become remarkably immune to feeling unwanted. 'Well, I'm here now and ready to do my duty.' She had to force herself not to gabble. This was not the time to show her excitement.

'Let me show you your consulting room.' Gordon MacLeod ushered her towards a door.

As she saw her room Jeannie inhaled sharply. The walls were pale eau-de-Nil with silk curtains over a large window that looked out over an airy green courtyard. There was a day-bed for the patients to be examined on, a large mahogany desk for her to sit at, and an armchair.

'Our patients are accustomed to a certain amount of comfort,' Dr MacLeod informed her.

He went on to outline the various procedures they had, then told her where they kept the patients' notes and mentioned a few of the more problematic ones. 'I'm out on my rounds now. Thought I'd throw you in at the deep end!' He closed his bag and left Jeannie in her lovely new consulting room.

The first patient walked in.

'Good morning.' Jeannie smiled at the middle-aged man standing in front of her.

'I wanted to see the doctor,' he said.

'I'm Dr Macdonald, Dr MacLeod's new junior. Take a seat.' She gestured to the chair at the other side of the beautifully polished desk.

The man hesitated. His hand went to the watch he wore on a chain over his yellow checked waistcoat. He pursed his thin lips, then licked them. 'I'll wait for Dr MacLeod. He knows me.' He walked out.

Jeannie sighed, but she'd almost expected it. The door opened again and a well-dressed woman walked in.

'I wanted to see a doctor, not a nurse,' she said petulantly.

She was no more than Jeannie's age and vaguely familiar, dressed in sensible country tweeds. Jeannie suspected she had seen her at the horse sales. 'I am a doctor.' But it was no use: the woman stared at her, then left.

This was repeated five more times. The only person willing to see her was a woman with an ingrown toenail. A nurse's job.

'It'll get better.' Gordon MacLeod said, when he came in from his rounds. 'They're just not used to the idea of a lady doctor.'

But it didn't. When it was her turn to go on the rounds she cured people simply by knocking at the door: they refused to see her and the maids shut the door apologetically. When she arrived back at the surgery, Gordon met her with the news that some of the patients had already contacted him by telephone or by hurriedly written note, to tell him that Jeannie was not their idea of a doctor.

On one day in particular she went home and sat in her room, watching the old oak tree shifting in the wind. She'd been under no illusions that when she came to work here she'd have a hard time getting people to accept that a woman could be as skilled as a man. But Gordon MacLeod's patients were middle class, and some of the women worked. If only they'd give her a chance she could prove herself, she knew she could.

For the next three weeks, she turned up doggedly at the surgery, only to find patients had begun to request Dr MacLeod. After four weeks, she had lanced three boils and confirmed two pregnancies, but that was all.

'Jeannie, can I talk to you?' Gordon asked, as she peered at a skin sample through his microscope.

'Of course.' She followed him to his office.

'Jeannie, I don't know how to put it nicely so I'll just spit it out.' He looked down at his elegant carved desk. 'My patients are an old-fashioned lot. Our experiment isn't working as well as I hoped.'

'Experiment?' Jeannie looked at him in surprise. 'I'm not an experiment, Gordon, I'm as well qualified as your junior was last year.'

'Look at these.' Gordon picked up a sheaf of papers that lay before him on the desk and handed them to her. 'These are all people who have told me they do not wish you to treat them under any circumstances. My workload is getting larger, and I cannot cope with it alone. Having you here is now putting my own reputation in jeopardy.'

'When do you want me to go?' Jeannie took a deep breath.

'If there was any other way, Jeannie, I would have kept you. I have someone starting next week.'

Jeannie nodded, trying to appear calm and collected. To burst into tears now would only confirm Gordon's suspicion that women weren't stable enough to be doctors. 'I'll take my leave, then.' She stood up and shook his hand. 'Would you have let me treat you?'

'I think you're a competent doctor, my dear,' he said. He looked down. 'I have a colleague who works at the hospital in Pathhead, which might be more suitable for someone like yourself.'

'Will you give me an introduction?' She was unable to keep the desperation out of her voice.

'Of course. And I wish you the best of luck.'

With the rest of the afternoon free, but unwilling to admit defeat by going home early and facing her family, she drifted into Perth with the vague intention of whiling away an hour or so looking at scarves and gloves, anything that might improve the awful dress. She wandered through McEwens's department store, staring at the rows of long chiffon scarves and elegant clips in silver and gold, and wished that it was late enough to go home without arousing suspicion.

'Didn't expect to see you here,' a voice said in her ear.

It was Kirsty, in a maroon velvet coat and a cloche hat that framed her glum expression. She picked up a lemon scarf from a polished wooden drawer, then dropped it.

'Ready for the match, Kirsty?' Jeannie said.

'I'm afraid we'll have to scratch,' Kirsty murmured. 'I can't play. My health . . .' She tailed off as an assistant glided over to them.

'Never mind.' Jeannie bit back her disappointment. She was good at tennis, and to lose, without even a fair fight, was galling. She needed to win – she wanted proof that she could still do something. 'I hope you feel better soon.'

'I won't be, not for ages, if ever. Oh, Jeannie!' Kirsty burst out. 'I'm in a certain condition and it couldn't have happened at a worse time!'

The assistant's severe pincurls shot round, then discretion took over and she busied herself with a drawer of evening gloves. People didn't usually have outbursts over ladies' accessories: it happened over children's school uniforms.

Jeannie took in her words. From her glossy brown curls to her solid pony build, Kirsty was a sensible woman, not the type to become upset over nothing. 'But it's wonderful news,' she said.

'I've got to sail to India, and the journey takes three months! It's winter here, but the child will be born in a foreign country – and my mother won't be there. The heat is merciless in the summer – to escape it you have to go on tour, to the hills. There's a saying that you always lose one on tour. I never gave it much thought, but now . . . Now I've realised that the one you might lose on tour isn't a button on your shoe, it's a child!' She pressed her lips together. 'I'd hoped we could have a few carefree years – you live like a king out there – and when we came back we'd have a family. If we're held up by bad weather, God knows where it will be born!'

'Don't worry about this now,' Jeannie said, as she patted Kirsty's arm.' You can't change what hasn't happened yet. I'm sure that everything will be fine. Perhaps you can dock in Africa, and once your confinement is over . . .'

'I don't want to dock in Africa and have my child in some dirty, God-forsaken foreign country,' Kirsty hissed. 'I want to have it at home with my mother and sister, the midwife and the doctor there.'

'Can't you delay your sailing?' Jeannie asked quietly.

'No, Arthur must be there, and I cannot face making the journey without him. My place is at his side – I'd be letting him down if I wasn't there.' Her hands were covering her eyes now, but tears squeezed out from beneath them. 'Why did I have to let myself down like this?'

'It's only natural, Kirsty.' Jeannie put an arm round her waist. 'Now, why don't I take you home and you can have a nice cup of tea and put your feet up?'

'You're so practical, Jeannie,' Kirsty mumbled, as Jeannie led her away from the club to her car. 'Just like Arthur. He says everything will work out in the end, but I'm scared.'

Jeannie took Kirsty to her home just outside Perth, then began the drive back to her own house. Kirsty was right to be concerned about travelling while pregnant, particularly when there was a real possibility that she would have her baby on board. And all the diseases to which her child would be exposed in India were a threat to it even before it was born. Evidently Kirsty hadn't read that book by Dr Stopes? Jeannie had seen it mentioned in medical publications and knew it contained advice on avoiding pregnancy. But Kirsty was a respectable married woman who wouldn't wish to buy a scandalous book like *Married Love*.

Later, as Jeannie sat in the drawing room, lingering over the *Courier*, it must have dawned on Hamish that, for once, she hadn't been playing tennis. 'Ought I to wish you luck for tomorrow,' he said worriedly, clutching a dictionary, 'since you aren't playing today?'

'I'm not competing any more,' she said sorrowfully. 'I think my time for winning anything is over.'

'Oh, Jeannie.' He stood up and took her hands. 'You sound like me.' He rubbed her long slim fingers. 'Don't let it grind you down. I did and now I can't shake it off. I'll never be able to.'

'Oh, you will, Hamish,' she protested, but Hamish shrugged.

'I've tried so hard to make the nightmares go away.' He

looked towards the french windows. 'But I can't forget that I left men in trenches where they died. I told them lies and half-truths that we were gaining land when all the time the enemy were nearing. I let good men die because I made them trust me when I didn't deserve their trust. When I abused it. And Fiona and I are paying for it.'

'Oh, Hamish.' Suddenly all her problems faded. 'You *are* getting better. One day at a time.'

'I'm treading water, have been for over a year now. I can't even remember what I was like before.' His gaze was taken by a rabbit bouncing along the grass. 'I can't even remember if I was the kind of person I would want to be.'

Jeannie stared at him, trying to remember. What had he been like? He had made her laugh, and she could remember him laughing over the broken heart of yet another young woman. How he would arrive at home on a Sunday morning as the rest of the family were leaving for church, his eyes dull and his mood short. How he would spend money recklessly, with little consequence. And how he had joked about riding his horse to the recruiting office in Perth to save Britain from the Hun.

'You were my favourite cousin,' she whispered, with a hint of a sob in her voice. 'You still are.'

'Even like this?'

She nodded. 'You care more than you did before, Hamish,' she said tenderly. 'And that's a good thing. We should all care more.'

It was almost a week later when Jeannie gripped her handbag in both hands, got out of the cab and went into the grey hospital building. The door was opened for her by a porter, who eyed her curiously but didn't ask her what she was doing.

Jeannie studied the maze of corridors that led off in all directions. Everyone seemed to have somewhere to go. And she sniffed the wonderful clean smell of carbolic that pervaded the air, the linen and the people. She belonged there. Following the instructions she had been given, Jeannie followed a trail of nurses carrying files and samples until she reached the laboratories. She knocked on a door. 'Dr Martin?' She held out her hand as she walked into a room that contained three desks and a wall of wooden shelves and drawers.

A tall, bespectacled man nodded. 'I am he.' He looked her up and down. 'Miss Macdonald, I presume.'

'I have my medical degree,' she told him defensively.

'I know you do, my dear,' he replied. 'And what experience do you have of epidemiology?'

'I was co-opted into helping during the Spanish influenza epidemic.'

'Along with every other medical student in Europe. What clinical experience do you have?'

'I gained some during my training,' she continued.

'My work is studying the effects of waterborne disease.' He looked at his watch. 'And I need not tell you that that means visits to rather unsavoury places.' He looked at her keenly. 'Do you have any research experience?'

'Not yet, but I'm aware of that and willing to learn.'

'Would you go into a sewer? You'll get more than your feet wet, you know.'

Jeannie bridled. 'I am aware that, as a doctor, my clothing must occasionally be sacrificed.'

Dr Martin chuckled. 'You will be working mainly in slums, which I don't think you're used to.'

'Were you accustomed to going into slums before your work took you there?' she asked tightly.

'What I'm willing to do and what I would ask a woman to do are two different things, my dear.'

Jeannie sat back and considered him. He had already made up his mind, she knew that. 'Dr Martin, when you look at me, what do you see?' she asked quietly. 'A doctor or a woman?'

'I see a gentlewoman. Someone who should not be bothering herself with these matters. They should be left to men. We are more robust, more able to sacrifice our sensibilities to undertake the job in hand.'

'I'm surprised you didn't bring out the hoary old chestnut that I cannot do the job because my brain is smaller than a man's,' she said. 'What would have happened to this country if women hadn't put their hands to the tiller in the last war? We were good enough then.'

'Not to serve as field doctors.'

'And how many men died as a result of that attitude?' she demanded. 'How many men could I have saved if I and others like me had been allowed to sign up and work in field hospitals? Would an unconscious man really have cared that he had been operated on by a woman?' She stopped, cursing herself for her outburst.

'You have spirit and undoubted intelligence,' Dr Martin said quietly, 'but it is untested.' He thought for a moment. 'Get some experience, real experience working with real people, and then I might consider you. But at the moment—'

'I can't get experience because no one will let me practise!' she burst out.

'I doubt you understand what you're letting yourself in for,' he said softly. 'Perhaps that is what you require Miss – Dr Macdonald,' he corrected himself. 'Some experience. And not just of medicine.'

'Experience that I do not think I'll be gaining here,' she said curtly. 'Goodbye, Dr Martin, it's unfortunate that I've taken up so much of your valuable time.'

'Jim Smillie,' he said, 'has a surgery in Back Street. A more apt name for the place I couldn't imagine. You'd get plenty of life experience there.'

'And how would I persuade him that I wasn't too much of a lady to work there?' she retorted.

'Go and see him.' He smiled. 'He'll offer you a position, I can guarantee it. Whether or not you'll want to take the job is another matter.'

As Jeannie left the room, she walked past a young man waiting outside.

'What's he like?' he asked nervously, as he fiddled with his tie.

'You won't have a problem,' she said, and strode out of the hospital into the crisp autumn air, which was tinged with linseed pouring from the factory chimneys and seawater. Then she stopped. She could go home and go riding or play tennis and forget about yet another disappointment. Be the woman everyone thought she should be. Or she could turn round and be the woman she wanted to be. She stepped into the muddy road, narrowly avoiding a queue of delivery carts, laden with linen and medical supplies.

'Can you tell me how I get to Back Street, please?' she said to a driver, who was watering his horse at a deep trough.

The man looked her up and down. 'Aye, lass,' he said warily. 'But do you really want to go there? You don't belong in that part of town.'

Jeannie smiled grimly. 'I most certainly do.'

Chapter 4

The streets around the hospital were busy with carts going back and forth, laden with boxes. Then, as she moved further down the hill, she saw more men lingering on street corners, as if they were waiting for something but had no idea when it would arrive. The women seemed busier, pushing prams filled with washing or children, scrubbing the steps, elbows working rhythmically. But despite their Herculean efforts the houses were dirty, with one family piled on top of the other. Some didn't even have net curtains – however did they find any privacy?

Eventually she came to Back Street. The houses were tenements, with one court that looked like a warehouse. But these were not well-kept tenements: the houses were filthy, with steps that had not been cleaned in a month of Sundays, railings that had been sawn off to make tanks during the last war and never replaced. And at the bottom of the door there was a simple wooden sign, not a brass one. Two words were written on it: *Charity Doctor*.

She walked in, and saw a crowd of people, with the smell of damp and poverty on them. The room was low, with only furred grey plaster on the walls. A few old women sat on orange boxes, while children, pale, with runny noses, wandered about shivering or sweating. Some were holding buff envelopes, but just as many were not.

'Next!' A middle-aged man, with a full Viking beard, came

into the room with a stethoscope round his neck. He was dressed in working clothes, his sleeves rolled up to his elbows.

'Are you the doctor?' Jeannie tried to push past the people who had gathered around him.

'Aye, lass. You!' He pointed to an emaciated young girl.

'I want to speak to you.' Jeannie followed him into the consulting room.

'Look, lass, I've no time for curious ladies who have little to do with their lives except go to a lecture by some bleeding-heart liberal then come to stare at some real poor people.' He turned at the door, ready to close it in her face.

'Then you need my help.' This time, she decided, she was not going to be fobbed off with a cup of tea and polite murmuring about 'delicate situations'. She wrapped her fingers around the edge of the door. She was almost as tall as Jim and stared at him resolutely.

'I always need donations.' He stopped. 'I'm Smillie. Jim Smillie.' He turned to the young girl. 'Go behind the curtain and get ready.' He walked over to his wooden cabinet, got out two bottles, poured powder and liquid into a pestle, then mixed them. 'You don't mind, but I've four hours' work outside.' He pulled on a pair of gloves.

Jeannie fought to hide her disgust at the room where Dr Smillie saw his patients. Her childhood pony had been stabled in better circumstances. It was plain, with faded distemper over the brickwork, a stark contrast to her room at Gordon MacLeod's. Instead of the mahogany desk, there was a simple wooden table. The only other pieces of furniture were a worm-ridden old chair and a small cabinet for linen and instruments. Jeannie hesitated. She still had the sight and scent of the patients about her. Were these really the people she wanted to treat? Was this where she would get her life experience?

'I'm a doctor. Dr Martin at the hospital suggested I ask you for an opening.' Her hand was on his arm, to stop him turning away from her. She had been dismissed already that day.

Jim looked down at it and laughed drily. 'Spent all your training looking down a microscope I'll bet,' he said slowly. 'Or did you study something more ladylike?'

'I have a degree in medicine from Edinburgh,' she replied. 'Although the majority of my training was in a laboratory or watching dissections, I am well read in my subject.'

'All right, then,' he said. He gestured for her to come behind the screen. The girl lay on a table, covered with a piece of paper. 'Twelve years old and has stage-one syphilis, Dr Macdonald.' He reached out for the pestle and mortar that lay on the desk. 'What am I treating her with?'

Jeannie stifled a horrified gasp and looked at the girl.

'Hello, I'm Dr Macdonald.' She cleared her throat. 'What's your name?'

The child smiled uncertainly. 'Nettie,' she whispered, as Jim held up a buff file with her name on it.

'This will help you feel better. It's a mercury compound.' Out of the corner of her eye, Jeannie saw Jim nod. Now he handed her a pair of gloves.

'I'll leave everything on the desk,' he said, and stood back.

When the treatment was over, Jeannie helped the girl get down from the table and handed her her clothes. 'Be sure to come back at the end of the week. You'll not feel very well while the treatment runs its course, but it's for the best.'

'Thank you, Doctor,' the girl said.

'She called me "Doctor",' Jeannie said, almost to herself. 'No one's ever done that before.'

'And no one's ever treated her like a lady before,' Jim said. 'Anyone with a history will have a file. If they don't have a file, you'll have to make one up for them. Sit down and make yourself at home.' He walked out of the room.

Ten minutes later, she was seeing her next patient, an elderly woman with a persistent, hacking cough. Then there was a young girl, nursing a baby who wouldn't feed because of a hare-lip. The morning disappeared under a sea of medical complaints, but gradually, as the afternoon wore on, the stream of patients lessened to a trickle, until finally there was no one left to see. Jeannie was exhausted but exhilarated. She had helped every person who had walked in. No one had questioned her competence: she was the doctor. She'd been accepted at last.

Jim came in.

'Come on, it's dinnertime,' he said, and smirked. 'Although you'd probably be calling it high tea.'

She followed him out into the maze of alleyways and he disappeared through a doorway. Jeannie followed curiously. It was a pub!

'I can't go in there!' she hissed, shocked to the core.

'It's an illegal pub so you won't be turfed out.' He strode over to the bar and called to the barman.

'But it's still a bar! There's no air in here!' She coughed to emphasise the point.

'Drink this.' Jim pushed a whisky over the two railway sleepers that served as a bar.

'Isn't it a bit early?' Her glass was chipped and not particularly clean. 'It's hardly evening.'

'A hundred a year.' Jim held his glass up to her. 'Can't afford to pay you any more. Five days and three nights each week. But you'll doubtless have your own funds.'

Jeannie hesitated. The money was substantially less than she had been getting in the other practice. 'Yes, I do,' she replied, 'but if I was seeking my fortune, Dr Smillie, I wouldn't be coming to you anyway. I accept.' She raised the glass to her lips, hoping that the alcohol would have killed off any germs in it, took a swallow and choked as it slid down her throat.

Jim's beady eyes fixed themselves on her. 'What's a lady doing in a place like this?'

'I want to help people.'

'You'll catch fleas regularly – and use your mask or you'll end up with consumption.' He called for a refill.

'Are you trying to put me off, Dr Smillie?' What was the point? she wondered. She had accepted the position.

'I'm trying to tell you the truth, Dr Macdonald.' He threw another whisky into his mouth.

Jeannie sipped her drink. What could she tell him that wouldn't sound like a slap in the face?

'I wanted the challenge of working with the underprivileged,' she said primly.

'Want to make the world a better place, eh?' Jim Smillie put his chin on her shoulder. 'Or were the good burghers of whatever posh town you live in mortally offended that a mere woman should presume to know enough about medicine to try to doctor them?'

Jeannie turned her head to his. So he knew, did he?

'No one else would come to me. In my last practice I saw four patients in a week.'

Jim looked at her and laughed. 'That's what I need,' he said and slapped her shoulder. 'Someone who tells the truth.' He nodded decisively. 'You just remember that feeling, lassie, when you couldnae get a hearing, 'cause that's what it's like for your patients. Every day of their lives.' He studied her for a moment. 'But you don't talk like some of the idealistic young students I've had before. You look as if you'll cope with the disappointment.'

'The disappointment of being a doctor, or of being one that no one wants?' She took another sip.

'Well, you've not got the religion that makes good men and women want to save the poor from themselves. Whether they want to be saved or not.'

Jeannie felt the burn of the alcohol turn into an almost amiable warmth. Jim wasn't so bad, she thought. 'I've watched most of my family die from one thing or another. And I always remembered everyone waiting for the doctor to come, then rushing about doing whatever he wanted. And I decided I wanted to be in charge of everyone's life. I wanted to be the one who decided if someone lived or died.' She glanced down almost shamefacedly. 'I thought that doctors were held in that kind of awe by everyone, but it wasn't till I came here that anyone called me "Doctor".'

Jim smiled down at his glass. 'I've met lady doctors before, but they were always from the university and in research of some kind or other. Never met one before you who wanted to get her hands dirty.'

'But I'm not the kind of person who gives up because someone tells me I can't do it,' she said. 'My father always told me you have to work to make your mark.'

Jim looked at her shrewdly. 'Remember, there's a difference between helping someone and being taken for a fool.'

'I've never been taken for a fool,' she announced.

'Then you're the only one on this good earth who hasn't.' He drained his glass, then hers. 'Well, I've not got all day to sit and talk like a fishwife. I'll see you tomorrow at six.'

'That's a bit early, isn't it?'

'Six o'clock at night. Evening surgery.' He stood up and walked out, leaving Jeannie alone in the pub. She glanced around her. Although no one was looking directly at her, she sensed sidelong glances. Keeping her eyes firmly on the door, she walked out.

As she made the journey back to the expensive part of town, Jeannie's mind was filled with what she could do in her new position: she'd be able to make a real difference to people. She would be accepted, welcomed even. She could prove to the world that she was the doctor she knew she was. She looked at her watch. It was almost four o'clock. She'd be able to tell Innes immediately.

'It's out of the question!' Innes was sitting at the tea-table eating drop scones dripping with butter and jam.

'But, Innes, it's a job. I can use the skills I've spent six years learning.' Jeannie stood opposite him, holding on to the fire-place for moral support.

'It's not proper, a woman like yourself mixing with people like that.'

'But surely you do, Innes.' She poured herself a cup of tea.

'You even smell of the place!' He wrinkled his nose in distaste. 'And there is a difference, you know, between the honest poor and low-class people who have no desire to better their circumstances. Drinking, gambling and fornication, that's how those people spend their time.'

'Innes.' She sat down next to him. 'Today I saw a twelve-year-old girl. She'd had syphilis for six months. How could I turn a blind eye to such suffering?'

'Listen to yourself, Jeannie.' Innes wiped butter off his chin. 'What lady would talk about such things?'

'Listen to yourself, Innes. You're supposed to be a minister.' She put her hands on his arm. 'We both have something to give these people.'

'I forbid it, Jeannie.'

'I'll do it anyway.' She stood up. 'With or without your blessing.'

'I'll not have you bringing our family name into disrepute by mixing with thieves and women of the night!' he shouted.

'Why not?' Her voice matched his. 'What about Jesus in the temple? Mary Magdalene sold her body. As far as I'm aware, Jesus Christ didn't conduct his ministry on golf courses and tennis courts.'

'I'll not sacrifice my calling to your ambition, Jeannie,' he said bitterly. 'It's about time you realised you're a woman, for all your book learning and naïve ideals, and behaved like a lady.'

'Like Fiona, you mean? Sitting at home getting drunk at lunchtime, then abandoning my husband at every available opportunity?'

'Talking like a lady, behaving like one socially. That's what I mean, Jeannie. If you need something to do I've already told you I need an extra body on the fund-raising committee for the kirk boilers. Now I have work to do, and I suggest you go and rid yourself of the smell you brought in with you.' He strode past her and out of the room.

Jeannie stared after him. What on earth did he mean? Why would her being a charity doctor make the slightest difference to him?

It was almost six o'clock on the following evening when Jeannie parked her car outside the window of the surgery.

'Oh, so you decided to turn up?' Jim said, as she walked in.

'Of course. I said I would,' she told him. 'I've brought my nameplate from Gordon MacLeod's.' She handed it to him.

'I don't think you'll want it put up round here,' he said, as if the very idea tickled him.

'You said they wouldn't care that I was a woman,' she retorted. 'Now, is there someone to do it, or will I do it myself?'

Jim handed it back to her. 'It wouldn't last five minutes on a wall round here.' He chuckled. 'You'd be fixing the bottom in while someone else is taking out the screws at the top.'

'I'm not having some awful wooden sign,' she said resolutely.

'Fine.' He shrugged. 'It's your money you're wasting.' He looked keenly at her. 'And I'll need your registration certificate.'

'Of course.' Jeannie fished in her bag and handed it to him. 'But you let me practise the other day.'

'Oh, I've heard about you, lass,' he said, with a grin. 'But doctors who end up practising here tend to be the ones that have something wrong with them.'

'So what's wrong with you?' she said imperiously.

'My principles got in the way of my ambition,' he returned casually. 'Just like your sex got in the way of your ability.'

40

'You have no knowledge of my ability,' she replied.

'I'm so busy I'd take anyone on.' He ushered her to the door that led to the waiting room. 'Look at them. I've had opium addicts, errant sons and men who had committed the kind of mistake that can only be covered up by a burial. If you last three months I'll be surprised, but no one else will have you so I might just get a dedicated doctor to work with me.' He coughed heartily, clearing his throat. 'Better out than in,' he said, as he examined the contents of his handkerchief. 'Well, no rest for the wicked. First!'

Jeannie stood behind him as he nudged a patient towards his room.

'Next!' she cried, albeit uncertainly. A small boy walked towards her, holding a rag to his mouth, an elderly woman behind him.

'Come into my office.' She put down the name plate. 'And what's wrong with you, my man?'

The small boy removed the rag. It was stained with dark purple blood from deep in his lungs. 'Got the cold, Doctor.'

They went into her room and she tied her mask over her face. She sat him down and went through the motions of listening to his chest. 'How long have you had the cough?' she said briskly.

'Since before the summer.' He looked up at her. 'Will you be sending me away?'

'And where would I be sending you?' she asked softly.

'To the poorhouse where they go to die.' He opened his mouth and she took a sputum sample.

'You've far too much life in you for that,' she said, and scraped the spoon over the neck of the little collection jar.

'But I've got the consumption, haven't I?' He looked up at her with eyes far older than his years.

'It would appear so.' She glanced down at him and saw he had no idea what she meant. 'Yes, you have consumption.'

'Does that mean I don't have to go to school?' He cocked

41

his head and grinned up at her with heart-melting cheekiness.

'No, it means you have to study extra hard.' She touched his head, then moved away. 'I'll put your name down. If it's been this bad since July and it's October already you might need to go to the sanatorium.'

'Will I have to go to school there?'

Jeannie shook her head. 'Come and see me next week.'

She watched him as he walked out. The disease was advanced: he wouldn't see his next birthday.

'No time to stand there dreaming, got a houseful today,' Jim said, as he walked out of his room. 'And don't worry about feeling tired. It's wearing the mask that does it. Next!'

Two elderly women walked forward.

'Are you really a doctor?' one said suspiciously.

'Yes.' Jeannie looked at her – at the faded, patched clothes stretched over a small body with a large sagging stomach that made her appear fat when she wasn't. 'Are you really ill?'

The woman cocked her head to one side. 'You'll do,' she said, laughing. 'Aye, you'll do.'

They went into the examination room and the woman sat down. 'It's ma eyes – you know about them?' she said.

'Let me have a look,' Jeannie replied. She bent over her patient with a match. Straight away she saw what was going on: the lens was turning milky. 'You have a cataract,' she said softly, 'and I'm afraid there's nothing that can be done.'

'So I'll go blind in my eye?' the woman asked fearfully.

'I'm afraid you will, but the other eye seems clear so you should still be able to go about your business.'

'And what if it happens in the other?' she pressed Jeannie.

Jeannie hesitated for a long moment. If the woman developed a cataract in the other eye, she would be blind, and have to go into the poorhouse – she would be unlikely to survive on her own in the mean streets of Pathhead. 'We'll cross that bridge when we come to it,' Jeannie said, inwardly cursing her cowardice. The woman smiled, wiped her bad eye with a handkerchief and got up to leave.

Jeannie sighed. It wasn't supposed to be like this: she was supposed to be more successful. 'Next,' she said. This was a busier evening than she had thought it would be. A man, coughing into a dirty rag, came up to her.

'So, you've survived your first surgery?' Jim said.

'Yes.' Jeannie exhaled loudly. 'I think I've listened to more chests today than I did in all my training.'

'Well, between the mines and the air in the lands, it's enough to choke anyone's lungs,' Jim told her.

'Not to mention the smoking,' she added. 'I had to tell four people to extinguish their cigarettes before they came in.'

'Well, they aren't always the wisest of patients, I'll give you that,' he conceded. 'What are you doing now?'

'I've a blood test to check, and three sputum tests for the infirmary. How about you?'

'Syphilis case for the lock. One of the local mermaids has been spending too much time at the docks.' He raised his eyebrows. 'She's not taking her treatment.'

'Well, the rest of us need protected from her,' Jeannie replied. 'If she won't take any treatment and continues to ply her trade despite the risk, then why shouldn't she be put into a locked ward?'

'Aye, but it's probably not her decision.' Jim picked up each sputum sample and read the name on it. 'Either the man who's making money out of her will be keen to get as much as he can before the syphilis starts to disfigure her, or she's worried about the parish taking her children because without the pennies she earns from selling herself she has no money to feed and house them.'

'But the parish is there to help those in need, and the children lead blameless lives, even if she doesn't. Perhaps they'd be better away from such an influence.' Jeannie took off her gloves and mask.

'Jeannie, as you will undoubtedly learn very soon, going out on the streets to feed your family is not a decision taken lightly. For this girl, it's been fatal.' Jim raised his eyebrows. 'Now, why don't we shut up shop and you let me take you for a turn round the neighbourhood? It's not quite pitch black but there's enough gloom to cover the worst.'

Chapter 5

They walked out of the tenement, and as they closed the door, she looked at the brass sign with her name on it. Jim had screwed it on, and it shone brightly in the dim, damp light of the hallway.

'Good,' said Jim, as he followed her out.

'What?'

'You walk around as if you own the place,' he remarked. 'You'll need that when you go on your calls.' He gestured up the road. 'There are four slum courts, Paton's Court, Seaton's Court, Hill Court and Baxter's Court, that way. And, trust me, you don't want to go there alone. When you go up there, take Charlie and Buster with you. Charlie gets sixpence for it.' Jim took her arm as they went to cross the street. 'And give him a shilling a day for your car.'

'Why?'

'Because if you don't he'll strip it down and sell the parts in the market.'

'But surely I'll be safe in the lands?' Jeannie said.

Jim sucked his teeth noisily. 'I wouldn't want to chance it,' he said eventually. 'But if you're with Charlie, you'll be fine.' He nodded to a skinny boy of about nine. 'That's him.'

'He's supposed to protect me and I pay him to stop him stealing from me?' She looked at the child. 'Shouldn't he be at school instead of working here?'

'Charlie's the bastard son of one of the most prominent

locals around here. And . . .' Jim's eyes twinkled with mirth '. . . Buster is one of the most ferocious dogs I've ever met.'

Jeannie watched as a mangy ruglike dog got up. Buster was obviously part Irish wolfhound. 'Doesn't look scary to me,' she remarked.

'That's because you haven't seen his teeth.' Jim began to guide her down a street. 'We don't usually see much of the people in these tenements,' he continued amiably. 'To live here you need a job, and if you have one you go to a proper doctor, not the charity one.'

'But we are proper doctors!' Jeannie frowned at the tenements, their net curtains and scrubbed steps.

'Aye, but going to us is like being seen in parish shoes.'

'But that's ridiculous!'

'Aye, but the good folk here will go without to afford another doctor rather than visit us and take their chances in the waiting room.' Jim chuckled to himself. 'Nice to know that someone who lives here thinks they're too good for someone with your background?'

Jeannie laughed aloud. 'Wonderful,' she said. 'Just when I thought people were finally beginning to accept me.' She looked over at him. 'Still, we get the ones from the tenement blocks.'

'About them,' Jim said carefully. 'They're called the lands and are dangerous. To be honest, they're so unhealthy you want to avoid them. Usually you'll only need to go there to sign a death certificate, but occasionally we get the chance to make a bit extra from some academic at Edinburgh University, taking samples from them. They seem to think we have a surgery full of a hundred laboratory rats for them to practise on.' He exhaled loudly. 'Still, it's good money.'

'I was offered the chance to go into medical research in Edinburgh,' Jeannie offered.

'Aye, well, that's what they usually have lady doctors do,' Jim replied, and looked at her shrewdly. 'What made you come back here to such a poor welcome?'

'My cousin Hamish.' She smiled tightly. 'He has shell-shock, and there's nothing more the sanatorium can do so he's with us.'

'Some of them have claimed to get results,' Jim said. 'Only last month the *Lancet* carried an—'

'He ran out of money for his bed.' She looked up. 'So, you see, Dr Smillie, I'm a charity doctor to more than those round here.'

'Well, the war's been over almost three years,' Jim said thoughtfully. 'Perhaps there was nothing that could be done for him.'

'But it wasn't as if he was a coward!' she burst out. 'It wasn't as if he was nervous, sensitive, fond of playacting. He was a man, a real hunting, shooting, fishing type.' She stopped and leant against the wall.

'Too much of a man to realise what was happening around him?' Jim said. 'Too much of a man to bear the burden of his guilt, his complicity in the war that has, thankfully, ended all other wars?'

'I'm sorry, Dr Smillie,' she said. 'I got rather carried away.'

'I have the feeling you do that on a regular basis, Dr Macdonald. Come on, the market's up here.' He patted her arm in an avuncular manner.

The market was two long lines of stalls that led from one end of the tenements to the other. Assorted smells, some pleasant, some not so, fought for supremacy in the trapped air of the street. There was the scent of vegetables, and the odour from the meat hanging up on the butcher's stalls. Next to them, Jeannie saw hough and dripping for sale, and fish. All the waste went into one overflowing drain, which lay beneath a pool of dirty water.

'Sometimes you wish the rain would come and give them all a decent wash!' Jim said softly. 'Then you remember what happens when it rains.'

'Which is what?'

'They have to move out of their basements, if they can.' He shrugged. 'If not they get wet.' He raised his eyebrows. 'And give us more work.'

'How can you be so flippant?' she said indignantly.

Jim shook his head slowly. 'Did they never tell you the secret to success as a doctor?' He exhaled noisily. 'I swear the training's not what it was.'

'Then why don't you throw that particular pearl of wisdom in front of me?' she asked.

'Don't take your work home with you.' He put his hand on her arm. 'And don't be too angry or you'll end up with an ulcerated bowel. Or a fondness for alcohol. Don't forget to laugh at life occasionally.'

'And do you take your own advice?'

'Do you live your life the way you tell others to? Because if you do, you're an unusual doctor.' Jim took out his watch and looked at it. 'Time for a quick one?'

'No,' she said decisively. 'I want to get home and face the wrath of the veritable Innes.'

'Tell the good Reverend Macdonald that you're doing God's work,' Jim replied. 'He'll find it much more difficult to stop you.'

When she arrived home, it was quiet. Innes was attending a dinner at a parishioner's home. Jeannie yawned and headed for the bathroom. She'd have a soak and forget her troubles.

'Did you enjoy your first evening at the charity clinic?' Hamish said, coming out of the conservatory.

'Not really,' Jeannie replied. 'I know I helped people, and they were far more thankful for my assistance than Gordon MacLeod's patients were, but I feel a bit overwhelmed, as if I can't make a difference.' She shrugged. 'Sounds silly, I know . . .'

'It doesn't,' Hamish said. 'I remember those nights when we were under bombardment or waiting to go over the top. We felt excited and powerless at the same time.'

48

Jeannie looked at him. Was this what it was like for Hamish? To feel that, no matter what he did, he was like Canute trying to hold back the tide? 'It'll get better.' She squeezed his shoulder as she walked past. 'Just got to hit my stride.'

The next day she drove Hamish's old car away from the pleasant hills and parks of her home to the damp, foul air of her work place. There had been an outbreak of a nameless fever, and as she sat in a filthy basement to put a small thin body into a bag, Jeannie felt her fear turn to anger. How could Innes, a man of God, close his eyes to the suffering of these people because they didn't attend his church and put money in his collecting plate? How could he be worried that she wanted to help them?

'Are you sure she isn't just having a wee sleep, Doctor? She was feeling fine at the weekend and it's only Thursday.' The girl's sister, a filthy fourteen-year-old in charge of the meagre family, had spoken, her rough accent almost turning the words into a threat.

'I'm sorry.' Jeannie tightened the string round the top of the bag. 'There was nothing I could do. Nothing anyone could do.'

'But I promised my mammy.' The girl grabbed her arm. 'I promised her.'

'I'm sorry,' she repeated, ashamed of the paucity of the words. 'The fever was too far advanced.'

'But she was six. It wasnae like she was a wee bairn.' The girl pushed a mop of greasy hair off her face.

'She was malnourished. Didn't have enough strength to fight it.'

'Will we all get it too?'

Jeannie saw the fear in her face. 'Have you been feeling ill?' she asked carefully.

The girl nodded. 'Had a dose of it, but I'm fine, and I eat the same as her.'

Jeannie sat still for a moment. The people who had to live in the building had no clean water, no fresh air, and little money to buy food. The fever could have been caused any of the thousand of germs that flourished in the filth. But whatever it was, it killed quickly and violently.

'Try to drink clean water, not from where you've been getting it,' she began. 'Boil it first. And eat some fresh fruit. There's a market not far from here and you can get bruised apples for little or nothing. Stay away from green potatoes.'

The girl looked at her, then handed her the two-shilling fee. As Jeannie was about to take it her hand froze.

'You'll need that for food for you and the others,' she said awkwardly.

'All right, then.' The girl put it back into her pocket.

'The parish can see about the funeral.'

'Aye, we got them round for Mammy last year. Tried to put us all in the orphanage.'

'You might have been better off there.'

'Does it really matter where you live?' The girl walked away.

But Jeannie knew she was wrong. She suspected that where the family lived would make the difference between life and death.

Charlie, her guide and protector, was waiting outside for her. 'What are you thinking, Doctor?'

'Do you know where they get their water from?'

'Standpipe like everyone else here. Over in the courtyard.' He laughed. 'Usually, though, someone rigs up a little something.'

She stopped. 'What do you mean?' They were wading through muddy drainwater that appeared to have seeped out of the walls.

'Well, someone usually sorts out someplace a bit closer like, to save on your feet.' He smiled winningly.

'Come on.' She turned on her heels, the hem of her smart grey coat splashing in the dirty puddle. 'Let's find out where they got their water from.'

The girl showed them the standpipe at the foot of the

passageway. Even Jeannie could tell that it had been put up hastily by someone who knew only the rudiments of plumbing. And where the pipe met the wall there was a pool of filth.

'Does anyone else drink out of this?' she said thoughtfully.

'People on this landing,' the girl replied. 'It's too far to walk to the proper standpipe, specially first thing in the morning.'

Jeannie fished in her bag and pulled out a jar. She unscrewed the top and carefully turned on the tap, then watched the dank water – water that the dead child and the girl standing next to her had drunk – run into the jar. She had to be wrong. She told herself it was her inexperience – it could be a hundred other diseases: it was just that she didn't know their names. But when she noticed particles of matter floating in the water, her stomach lurched.

'Let's have a talk with the others who use this,' she said, as she screwed the lid onto the jar. And the shiver she felt down her neck had nothing to do with the cold.

'Jim, it's obviously waterborne,' Jeannie said, as she stood in the consulting room holding the jar of brackish water from the pipe. 'And everyone has had a stomach upset. I had to get the ambulance to take two of them to hospital.'

'How long did it take for the wee lass to die?' Jim asked, as he wrapped his hands in paper and took the jar from her. 'You'll need to burn those gloves, you know.'

'Just a few days.' Jeannie looked fearfully at the water. 'I know I'm not experienced in these matters, Jim, but . . .'

'Aye, if that standpipe's been in contact with sewage . . .' He peered at it. 'Even for the courts, this water's filthy.'

'I'll send Charlie with a note to the public-health people,' she said. 'But it can't be, can it?'

'I hope not,' he said. 'For all our sakes.' He looked at her. 'Take all your clothes and burn them, anything that might have been in contact with the water. And let's hope we've caught it in time.'

They looked at the water in the jar.

'It could mean death to everyone in the court,' Jim murmured. 'Hundreds of men, women and wee bairns might die a horrible, painful death, and we can do nothing to stop it.'

'Please, God, make me wrong,' Jeannie prayed. 'Please let us have caught it in time.' She closed her eyes and saw the child, the agony she had suffered etched on her body. She would not be the last. 'Who could let people live like that?' She wondered aloud. 'What kind of a man owns a place like that?'

Jim snorted. 'Ross Macintosh,' he said sharply. 'Made his money during the war. When everyone else was fighting he was here, keeping the wives and widows occupied. They were grateful for his company.'

'That was how he made his money?' Jeannie said, shocked.

'Aye, he's as common as they come, but you'll be coming across him now. He's got the right friends – friends like yours.'

'While he makes his money from the people in these lands?'

Jim nodded.

'That's appalling.'

'Aye,' Jim agreed, 'but, if he wasn't making his money there, someone else would have been.' He raised his eyebrows. 'There are few people in this world with clean hands, you know.' He stopped. 'What are you thinking now?'

'Nothing,' she replied quickly.

'You've a face on you that I wouldn't want to come home to,' he remarked. 'And you'd be wasting your time. He won't change the way he works.'

'He'll have to,' she said. 'Because I'm going to tell him to.'

Jim laughed again.

'What's so funny?' she demanded.

'You remind me of myself,' he said, 'before I got a dose of real life.' He took up a pen and a piece of paper. 'This is his address. It's not far from here.'

Jeannie looked at it. Hardly the address of a successful businessman.

'Off you go, then, Jeannie, go and tell him, and I'll see you back here in an hour or so with your tail between your legs.'

'So you think it's a waste of time?'

Jim shook his head. 'It's not a waste because you'll have a chance to have your say. But I don't think it will change his mind. Macintosh isn't a man with a conscience.'

Jeannie tightened her lips as she got a sack and put her coat and gloves into it. 'He'll not be able to ignore me.' She picked up Jim's overcoat and threw it over her shoulders. 'I'll not let him.'

Unusually for the early winter, the air was crisp and dry with the promise of frost. She took deep breaths, the tang of the sea fighting with the stench from the linoleum works as she walked down the hill towards Ross Macintosh's office. She tried to work out what she would say, an emotive yet logical argument that would convince him.

'I would like to see Mr Macintosh,' she said, to the middle-aged man in the front room, which was furnished only with an ancient sofa, a battered desk and chair.

'Who are you?' He looked her up and down and unconsciously wiped large, work-reddened hands on his thick corduroy trousers.

'Dr Macdonald. My practice covers Seaton's Court.'

The man grinned, his face creasing like an apple left out in the sun. He went to the door behind him. 'Ross, there's a doctor to see you.' He grinned widely as he said it.

Jeannie felt the air cloy around her. Ross Macintosh, the man who had made his money on the backs of the poorest folk in the town, was in the next room.

The man jerked his head in the direction of the main office. She smiled politely and went in to be faced by a surprisingly young man in a sober black suit. He was sitting behind a desk and counting cash from a solid wooden box. Three heavy-set henchmen sat on a sofa against the wall. He seemed to be at home with the others, but not in the way that Kyle had been friendly with the groom or the ghillie, more in the way that Hamish had been with Angus when they had come home from university.

'What?' Macintosh's eyes opened in shock. 'He said it was a doctor.'

'Mr Macintosh, I *am* a doctor. Dr Jeannie Macdonald.' She stopped and took in the almost threateningly broad shoulders, the strong face with jet black hair, the startlingly blue eyes that seemed to look deep inside her. He was a handsome man, and evidently knew it. She cleared her throat. 'In the last two weeks I have attended a number of seriously ill people in Seaton's Court. A six-year-old girl and a four-year-old boy have died already and four of their neighbours are critically ill in the infirmary.' She looked at the three men. 'I don't mind standing but it does make me feel as if I'm lecturing you.'

'Of course.' Ross gestured for the men to leave. 'Can you ask Tam to rustle up some tea for the lady?'

'Please, this isn't a social call. I just want you to understand what's going on in Seaton's Court, a slum dwelling that you own.' Jeannie put down her bag on the desk.

'I know what's going on in my places.' Macintosh stared at the woman in front of him.

'So you know that since the rain the sewers have been overflowing and getting into the water supply? You know you have whole families living in one tiny room with no natural light, walls running with damp, and breathing air full of disease and germs?' She took a step towards him.

'It's got rats too, don't forget them,' he muttered, like a recalcitrant schoolboy in front of the headmaster.

'Disease is rampant, and I've spoken to the public-health people. They'll be testing for dysentery and cholera. Just think, man, you've managed to drag Kirkcaldy's public health back fifty years!'

'And you're an expert on this?' His voice was defensive.

'I've been there, seen the problem. Which you, as the landlord, should have sorted out.'

'Don't tell me how to run my business,' he snapped. 'I can't afford to fix it up on what they pay in rent.'

'You could if you wanted to, Mr Macintosh. You can afford a bespoke suit, but you can't afford to ensure your tenants have clean water for their children?' She stared at him disbelievingly.

'Have you quite finished, Miss?' His eyes bored into her and Jeannie was suddenly reminded of Jim's words. And the gratitude of the women left behind.

'I can't believe you'll just sit there and let people die.' She looked at her hands, which had clenched into fists. 'Yes, Mr Macintosh, I am finished. And for future reference I am *Dr* Macdonald.'

'Get out!' he shouted, then slumped back in his chair.

'There ye go, lass.' Tam walked in holding a mug. 'Oh – she left already?'

Ross nodded. 'We've got a problem with Seaton's Court.' He rubbed his face, then took a bottle out of the drawer and poured a hefty slug of whisky into the mug. 'I'd better inform Carmichael.'

'Like that lazy bastard gives a damn.' Tam held his hand out for the bottle.

'Makes it easier for me to buy.' Ross held up his mug. 'He'll not want the world to know he has that place. Perhaps time to renegotiate.' He looked at the mug. 'This is my chance, Tam, to get into the big league.'

The next morning when she arrived at work, Jim was standing in the consulting room as the cleaners washed down the damp walls and floor. An elderly, distinguished-looking man was with him, studying the appointment book.

'Oh, Jeannie.' Jim looked up from the book. 'This is Dr Martin, Public Health.'

'Hello again Dr Martin, what have you found?' Jeannie said apprehensively.

'Cholera. We've already moved the patients into the cottage hospital. It's become an isolation ward until further notice.'

Jim nodded grimly. 'Anyone who comes in from the courts needs to be tested. Any suspicions, you must refer them to the hospital. Dr Martin will be here for a few days till he's gauged the size of the problem. We've had six people so far, haven't we?'

Jeannie's throat constricted. Cholera was a quick, merciless killer, and spread like wildfire.

'Six deaths, all from the same place – but surely the water must be used by hundreds of people.'

'No, the people affected are in the basement. Looks like it was that standpipe. It happens – can you imagine the trek for water in the winter?'

'To be honest, Jim, I can't imagine what it would be like to live there. Not in my worst nightmares,' Jeannie said.

'Well, the water supply to the entire area has been cut off so we can isolate the outbreak. We must take steps quickly, but they have to be effective. Luckily we've made rapid advances in the treatment of these diseases in recent years.'

'You take the ones waiting to be seen,' Jim told Jeannie. 'Then it's a case of going through the records one by one to see if anyone has come in with this kind of thing before.'

Jeannie looked at the waiting crowd. It was going to be a long day. 'At least it's cleaner now,' she remarked, as she walked into the waiting room, which had been washed down and disinfected with bleach.

'Aye,' Jim agreed. 'Sometimes these disasters have unforeseen benefits. Two more people have been diagnosed, but it looks as if it was isolated to a few houses.' He looked at his watch. 'Luckily there was more than one water supply. We might have caught it in time.'

'Can we get started, please?' She got out her instruments and put them into the boiler, but something was nagging at her. Then she realised what it was. Sighing, she went out of the door and stared at the wall. Her shiny brass plaque had gone. She was simply the charity doctor now.

She stayed late each night with Jim, going over the records, but it soon became clear that there hadn't been any signs in previous patients. Twelve more people had been admitted to hospital, and nine had died, but Jeannie knew that it might have become an epidemic that would have decimated the court.

At last the weekend came and, despite her desire for an early night, she knew she had to go out. It was the prize-giving for the tennis tournament and if she was not there she would be seen as a bad loser. Resignedly she went upstairs to her room and looked out the dress she had worn each week so far. Her feet ached as she forced them into high-heeled shoes. She'd had nothing to eat and she wanted to collapse into her bed.

As she drove to the club, exhaustion hardened into resentment. Ross Macintosh was bound to be there, and she was in the mood to give him a piece of her mind. She'd show him exactly what she thought of him.

Chapter 6

'I've no idea where she is, Margaret.' Innes gazed at his drink as he made awkward conversation with the ever-gracious Margaret; the trophy had been given and triumphantly received. 'Jeannie is usually so reliable.'

'It's one of those things,' Margaret murmured understandingly. 'I believe she has been fighting some awful diseases in the slums. They live in appalling circumstances there. But here she is now!' She brightened and waved.

As Jeannie walked through the busy ballroom, all eyes were on her. She hadn't been in time to congratulate the winners. And that spoke volumes.

'Hello, Jeannie,' snapped Fiona, as Jeannie reached the table where she and Hamish were sitting. 'Glad to see that for once you weren't too busy saving the poor from themselves to bother with civilised people.'

Jeannie stared at her. Fiona was wearing a silk dress that had cost as much as the medicine for a whole tenement of people, with red lipstick and a heavy scent that seemed to sum her up. 'I've been trying to save them from Ross Macintosh,' she said, with an evenness that surprised her. 'Do you know where he is?'

But Innes had spotted her and was on his way over from his usual position at the edge of the heavy Fleming table, his pinched features dark with anger. 'Jeannie, where on earth have you been? You were supposed to be here for the prize-giving. You missed the award,' he snapped.

'It was only second place. I'll just go and circulate.' She rubbed her face and tried to push her mind away from the problems in Pathhead and towards polite conversation.

Fiona giggled loudly to draw attention to herself. 'She's here to see Ross Macintosh, not you, Innes,' she said. 'You're doing it wrong again.' She raised pencil-thin eyebrows. 'And you don't need to talk to Ross, just shake your trust fund at him. That's what someone like him finds attractive.'

'For heaven's sake, Fiona, I'm not interested in him as a suitor,' Jeannie said. 'I only want to talk to him to see if he has done anything.'

'What about?' Fiona twirled the olive in her martini.

'He's a slum landlord and makes his money from the poorest people in the town. If you knew about his business, Fiona, you'd want nothing to do with him.'

'Jeannie, Ross is one of those men who get into the club by escorting elderly widows. And while one might not object to having them here, it doesn't mean one would want to be friendly with them. And you know it's bad form to talk business here.'

Jeannie fled in the direction of Margaret's table and sanctuary.

'I hear you've left your position with Dr MacLeod,' Sir Justin said casually, as Angus ushered her into a seat.

'He no longer required my services,' Jeannie told him, 'so he dismissed me.'

'What did you do?' Sir Justin said cheerfully. 'Kill off all his patients?'

'Quite the reverse.' Jeannie grimaced. 'No one wanted me to treat them.'

'Are you such a bad doctor?' He picked up the bottle of champagne but Jeannie waved away the offer of a glass.

'I don't know,' she said. 'No one will give me a chance.'

'So, once again you find yourself without gainful employ?' Sir Justin asked.

'No, I'm working for a charity clinic based in Pathhead,' she said, as loudly as she could. 'For Jim Smillie.'

'The man's a drunk,' Angus said.

'Then he needs me more than ever,' Jeannie returned cheerfully.

'Working among the poor is admirable,' Margaret murmured.

Jeannie nodded. 'They're too poor to care that I'm a woman.'

'Is it safe?' Margaret continued.

'It isn't safe for a lady to walk about in a place like that,' Angus said.

'No,' Sir Justin said thoughtfully. 'A doctor, like a clergyman, enjoys a certain amount of respect from thieves and ruffians.' He smiled encouragingly. 'I'm sure you'll be able to go about your business with impunity.'

Jeannie returned his smile. 'At last! Someone who can see past the surroundings. And understands why I'm doing it.' She felt her exhaustion drop away. She had an ally in someone now who mattered. Almost immediately she felt stronger. She gazed at the money dancing past. These people could make a difference, and if she could only think of a way to bring up the vulgar subject of money she was sure donations would flood into the surgery. But suddenly she saw a man at the fringes, chatting to a group of older women, women who were defiantly wearing lipstick and the latest fashions when they should have been more soberly dressed.

'It's terrible, isn't it,' Angus spoke softly, 'how a woman can be turned by a set of broad shoulders? I wish someone would talk to Mrs Baker about her behaviour. Her late husband was a magistrate after all.'

'Angus,' Margaret chided, 'it isn't for us to speculate.' She put a hand on his immaculate onyx-studded cuff.

'Brings the place into disrepute,' he went on, as both women looked down, unable to voice their opinions as forthrightly as he had. That kind of gossip was not for a public arena: it was for a lazy afternoon, drinking coffee in a sunny conservatory, where confidences could be shared, or over tea and cucumber sandwiches in the Salutation Hotel before a visit to McEwen's for some new dress lengths. But Jeannie reddened with embarrassment for the ridicule Enid Baker was suffering, and with indignation that he was enjoying himself when there were so many problems in his world. He should be at home working out a solution – or, at least, worrying about it.

As she glared at his back, he turned and looked her straight in the eye, as if he had heard her thoughts. She nodded, in a cool acknowledgement, and he began to make his way towards her.

'Mr Macintosh? How are you?' Much to her shame she stammered over the words.

Ross raised his eyebrows. 'Had a rather troublesome week.' He looked past Jeannie to Angus. 'Mr Carmichael.'

'Jeannie?' Angus tapped her arm. 'What kept you late today?' He was ignoring Ross.

'My day is never suitable fodder for polite conversation.' She raised her eyebrows. 'I was banned from talking about it at home. I always put Fiona off her martini.' She was trying desperately to work out what to say to Ross Macintosh.

'Tell me anyway,' Angus prompted.

'You don't want to know. Nobody does.'

'I do.' Angus looked closely at her and was rewarded with a nervous smile.

'Well, we've still got the people from Seaton's Court coming in for tests.' She eyed Ross accusingly. 'Have you been to see your sewers yet, Mr Macintosh?'

Ross shook his head.

'Why not?'

Ross raised his eyebrows and shrugged.

'Why not?' She smiled at him, but her eyes were hardening.

'Because I don't own the properties that will need to reroute most of their drainage. It's Paton's Court that has the problem,' Ross replied smoothly. 'Since you are such an expert on these things, I'm surprised you didn't know that.'

Jeannie felt the ground open up under her. She could see Angus and Margaret, friends for years back, people she respected, people who had made sharp comments about her studies, staring at her: she had publicly upbraided a blameless man. Now she was a stupid, interfering woman.

'I didn't realise,' she said quickly. 'But I have the name and address of the other owner at the practice if you send someone . . .'

'You don't need to.' Ross shook his head with magnanimity. 'They are owned by . . .' he looked pointedly at Angus. '. . . a local businessman. And I've told him by letter.'

'Angus,' Sir Justin broke in – he had returned to the table from dancing and stood at the side listening to the exchange. 'Don't you have an interest in those terrible places?'

'I believe they're owned by my investment company,' Angus said quietly. 'And you must tell me about my sewage problem sometime, Jeannie.'

'Of course.' She looked around for someone to save her from her gaffe. 'Oh, I think I see Gordon MacLeod. One moment.' She smiled and scurried off.

'Women!' Ross said, and the men laughed. 'They should stick to what they're good at.'

'I think Jeannie needs to temper her interest in the lower classes,' Angus began. 'She seems to have developed the fascination respectable women have always had for a bit of rough trade.' Everyone laughed, except Margaret, who laid a hand warningly on her husband's cuff.

'Actually, she has a point, Angus,' Sir Justin said, over the laughter. 'Perhaps you should take more of an interest in the people who enrich you. Killing them off won't do you any good. Rats don't pay rent.'

There was silence.

'You said you had sent a letter to me?' Angus said tightly to Ross, who nodded. 'Why don't we meet tomorrow and discuss it?'

Ross considered for a moment. 'Of course. I can have my men start work whenever you want them to.'

'You have engineers?'

'I can get you whatever you need.'

'Ten o'clock at Paton's Court?' Angus was talking to Ross but watching Sir Justin out of the corner of his eye.

'Fine.'

'How could you?' Innes said, as they drove back to the house later that evening. 'The whole club is talking about you. How could you embarrass Carmichael like that?'

'I was trying to make that awful Macintosh man do something about his building,' Jeannie said. 'The conditions his tenants live in – well, I've seen dogs in better circumstances.'

'Instead you shamed the son-in-law of Sir Justin Fleming,' Innes snapped. 'The Flemings are generous benefactors to my church and you've put that in jeopardy because you didn't think before you spoke.'

'I'm sorry,' Innes,' she said. 'You know I wouldn't hurt Angus and Margaret for the world.'

'Well, you did, Jeannie,' he replied. 'I really don't know what I'm going to do with you. You're getting far too carried away with all this.'

'I'm not playing doctors, Innes,' she insisted. 'This is my calling, as much as the kirk is yours.'

'Try talking about more ladylike activities, Jeannie. No one wants to listen to a woman talking about business, and certainly not about those patients of yours and their disgusting complaints.'

'People are even wary of talking to me,' Fiona whined, from the back seat. 'Now that Jeannie is queen of the slums, everyone thinks we spend all our time there.'

'Do people really think that of me?' Jeannie said to Innes, her voice higher than it should have been.

'Don't pay any attention to idle gossip, Jeannie,' he replied. 'We know you're a responsible adult.' He sighed. 'It might help if you provided some evidence of it for the club, though.' He parked the car at the front of the house and went in. 'Nightcap, anyone?' he called, as he walked towards the drawing room.

The others followed him but Jeannie headed up the stairs. In her bedroom she stood and stared at herself in the mirror, then stood side on. Did she look different from other women? 'I may not cover myself in paint and powder, Fiona,' she said tearfully, 'and I smell of carbolic soap, but that doesn't mean I'm any different from the rest of you.' Then she tore off her dress and threw herself onto her bed. 'Stupid dress.' She crossed her arms over her chest and bit her lip. 'And I *don't* listen to gossip.'

'Can you get yourself over to Paton's Court?' Jim said, as he walked in one wintry December afternoon. 'Woman bleeding.'

'Not another abortion.' Jeannie sighed. In six weeks, she had become remarkably accustomed to life in the slums.

'Nah, the other end. Charlie's outside.' He gave a grim smile.

Jeannie collected her bag and coat, then hurried up to the court with Charlie and Buster at her side. It was the cleanest one: it was south-facing and sunshine dried out the damp walls and floors, while a brisk sea wind blew some fresh air into the high passageways. When she got to the second-floor room, she found a young woman coughing large amounts of blood. It was obvious she wouldn't survive – and she had three children.

'Go and get an ambulance, Charlie,' Jeannie said. 'Tell them it's urgent.'

Jeannie sat with the woman as they waited for the ambulance to arrive, then got into the cramped space inside the wagon. She sat on the bare floor as the woman was tied to the ledge and they set off for the hospital.

'What's going to happen to me?' The woman struggled to get the words out.

'You must go to hospital.' Jeannie put her hand over the woman's clammy forehead. 'I can't stop the bleeding, but the hospital will.'

But her patient was already losing consciousness. By the time they had reached the hospital, her body had given up the fight.

A few hours later Jeannie arrived back at Paton's Court. Her shoulders bowed, she walked to the door on the second floor.

'Mam!' As a girl opened the door Jeannie's heart sank. 'Oh, it's yourself, Doctor. Is she comin' back the night?'

'Your mother died in the ambulance.' Jeannie hated being the bearer of such news. She put an arm round the girl and held her close. 'She'd lost too much blood.'

'I want my mammy!' The girl began to cry, big racking sobs that shook her skinny frame. Jeannie continued to hold her. She had failed the woman, failed a family destined to be sent to orphanages. What was the point of studying for all those years, if she couldn't help the poorest people, the ones who needed it most? What was the point in any of it? Eventually she walked away, tears in her eyes. She had become used to death as a student, had seen bodies as cadavers to be dissected, but today she remembered that each one had been a person, a wife, a mother, a husband, a son. *I'm a fraud.* The words echoed in her head. I pretend to help these people but I don't. I just take their temperature then walk away, back to my big house.

For once when she got back to the surgery Jim didn't interrogate her. 'They don't all die, Jeannie,' he said gently. 'You'll have times when it all seems as if it's for nothing, and others when you know you're doing well. When you know you're making a difference.'

'But I never make a difference!' she said bleakly. 'Never.'

'You make a difference every day.' He patted her shoulder. 'You're a gentlewoman, and you try to help these people. Don't think for a moment that they don't respect you for it. But I think you've had enough for one day. Why not go home?'

Jeannie nodded and picked up her bag. 'All those years at medical school, Jim,' she began, 'all those years, and it's only now that I've finally realised how cheap life is.' She gripped her bag in her reddened hand and walked out of the door. Immediately she saw a young woman slumped in the doorway. Cautiously she went over to her. 'Can I help you?'

The young woman coughed into her chest and wrapped her dark blue woollen overcoat around her. A coat that was good, but stained and torn. She had obviously been sleeping on the streets. 'No one can help me, just give me something, please, Doctor, till I can get to my family.' She covered her mouth.

'Where are your family?' Jeannie said, as she put a hand on the woman's brow. There was no fever, but the cough rattled in her chest.

'They got the cholera – you took them away in an ambulance. Now I've got it too.'

Jeannie had taken a step back before she thought. 'You don't have cholera. If you did, you would have died by now, my dear,' she said.

'But I've nowhere to go. They closed up the house, and when I came home from where I'm in service,' she coughed again, 'they told me what had happened. The mistress wouldn't have me back in case I brought it with me.'

'But that was almost a month ago!' Jeannie exclaimed.

'And now I'm on the streets, and I'll never get another position. Not looking like this.'

Jeannie took a deep breath. The woman needed a bed to fight off the illness, and there was only one place that might take her. But would the hospital admit her? She wasn't the most seriously ill person on the streets. I can't let another die, she told herself. Not today. They made their way slowly to the hospital, and walked through the heavy front door that, although it was in almost constant use, scraped along the groove it had ground out of the battered wooden floor. She could feel the reluctance of the girl beside her. 'Come on,' Jeannie said, and hurried her along. As they walked along the corridor, their shoes stuck in the dirt brought in by the hordes of people who struggled in every day in search of assistance. Eventually they came to a set of double doors. Jeannie held them open as the girl went through, slowly and rather fearfully.

'They'll look after you here,' Jeannie murmured. Legions of people were standing, sitting or lying on the floor and a sign read 'Communicable Diseases'. There was a chance that the woman's cough might be enough for her to be admitted while the doctors did some tests. But Jeannie would have to fight for it.

'We've no room for her,' a doctor informed Jeannie, as she stood next to the examination bed in the bare ward.

'She has a severe chest infection and has lost her employment.' Jeannie's voice was clipped, like Fiona's when she complained to a waiter. 'She needs rest to recover. Without it she will die on the streets.'

The doctor stared at the young woman. 'We have others more in need of a bed. I'm sorry.'

'Just till she recovers, and I won't ask you again.' Jeannie took a deep breath. 'I suspect that her chest complaint may be more serious than it seems.'

The doctor looked down at the woman. 'She needs some rest, but we're not a house for unfortunates, Dr Macdonald,' he reminded her, none too gently.

'Yes, but if you care for her now, while she is treatable, she will survive. If you wait until she is desperately ill, nothing will save her, Dr Balliol.'

He stood in front of Jeannie, summoning every inch of his dignity to ignore her, she could see. But he was a bursary boy, and she was from a higher social class. The son of the clerk capitulated to the daughter of the owner.

'She can have a bed for two days.'

'Two days.' Jeannie nodded and, smiling with relief, left the hospital.

She drove out of the slums towards the green gentility of Kinross. She could see the sun setting over the hills, the lush green slopes bathed in warm tangerine light. At home, she got out of the car and stared at the natural beauty before her. 'Why do you let this happen, God?' she said to the sunset. 'Why make this – and cholera? Why make this and the slums?' She watched as the sun set behind the hills in a stream of peach and pink light. So soft, so gentle. Almost as if someone cared.

'No, Fiona, if you want to go out, go,' Jeannie said, as she watched her linger in the doorway of the conservatory late that weekend. 'I'm exhausted so I'll stay with Hamish. He wants to finish his jigsaw and needs some help.'

'Please yourself.' Fiona glanced at her husband, who was hunched over a puzzle of a war scene. 'Maybe you don't need adult company but I do, and now I'll be stuck with Innes all night, talking to his friends because he disapproves of mine.' She walked over to her husband. 'Don't wait up, darling.' She kissed his cheek.

'Just us,' Jeannie said happily, 'like it used to be.'

Hamish raised his dull eyes to her. 'I'd never have passed up a dance in favour of a jigsaw, and you would never have wanted to spend so much time indoors.' He gave a tight little smile and turned his attention back to the Jacobite rebellion that was being fought in a thousand pieces.

The exchange stayed in Fiona's mind, ticking away as the band played jaunty tunes such as 'If You Were The Only Girl In The World'. She drank quickly, listening with only half an ear as

Marjorie and George brayed about nothing in particular and amused themselves at the cost of other, more staid members of the club.

Ross Macintosh stood on the fringes, as always, and watched. He could tell that Fiona was upset about something, dangerously so. The other men there were chinless wonders who wanted nothing more than to take their fun, then boast about it afterwards, which was why they never got to know women the way he did. He glanced at Heather Bunting, who had adopted the flapper look after a visit to London. With her short crop and her simple dress belted about her hips, she was in the height of fashion. She preened herself, puffing at a long ivory cigarette-holder as she played with her string of pearls. She crossed her legs then smoothed her skirt – and the cigarette touched the fabric. Before she knew it, it had burned a hole in her dress. Heather screamed.

Once the commotion had died down, Heather dashed past their table.

'Heather, darling,' an obviously drunken Fiona Macdonald drawled, 'at last you've found a way to make everyone look at you.' She laughed unkindly. Heather turned, her painted lips wobbled and a tear fell down her face.

Fiona seemed to hesitate. She had only said what everyone had been thinking, Ross knew, but now the whole club was staring at her. Even the band was playing quieter. Her face was red, and no one spoke.

'Why don't you and I take a turn round the floor, Mrs Macdonald?' Smart in his new dinner jacket, Ross had taken the initiative from the braying young men who had stopped to watch the sport.

'Of course,' Fiona said, and took his hand. Ross escorted her to the centre of the dance-floor: he knew she would want to be far enough away from the tables to overhear any remarks about her, and he wanted to be in the middle where he would be seen. It was the first chance he'd had to dance with the lovely Fiona and he intended to make the most of it.

'Not here with the family?' he said to her, as he pulled her to an appropriate distance from him and they began to waltz. 'Have you worked out how to escape from the house without a chaperone?'

'Jeannie's looking after Hamish. She's content to sit at home and play happy families.' She snorted. 'She delights in showing the world what a martyr she is and what a terrible wife I am.'

'What do you mean?' Ross said, as he looked around discreetly to check that his dancing with the club beauty had been noted.

'She's spending so much time at her charity surgery that she's never at home for anything. No time for drinks, or dinner, or even a game of tennis or golf.'

'Perhaps she has a vocation?' Ross was careful in his choice of words.

'Not really, she just likes being in charge of things,' Fiona said bitterly. 'Every time we have friends over, she insists on asking them for money to buy bits and bobs for her surgery. Poor Innes is dreadfully embarrassed. He has a position to keep up and she has compromised him. He hasn't spoken to her for ages.'

'It is a charity surgery, and the people who go to it are in pretty desperate circumstances,' Ross reminded her.

'Then why don't they spend some of that relief money they're given, or get themselves a job?' Fiona continued. 'You managed it.'

'I'm different,' he said, as they returned to her table.

'I know.' She smiled bewitchingly. 'George, have you drunk all the champagne?'

Ross smiled as he beckoned to the waiter. He had his purposes, and pleasing Fiona was one he was happy to undertake. He was on his way in.

Chapter 7

Jeannie watched Innes as he stood in his pulpit and talked about God in a flat monotone. Why couldn't he make it more interesting? she wondered, as her fingers played with the Bible her mother had given her all those years ago when they were a family. Innes's church was patronised mainly by the local gentry, and most of the pews had been in each family for generations. The kirk itself was obviously wealthy, with ornate pillars and a beautifully carved wooden lectern. Jeannie glanced down at her kneeler: she had embroidered it while she was at school; Margaret had one the same. It didn't seem particularly cold, even with the existing boilers, and warm light streamed in through the jewel-bright stained-glass windows, which seemed at odds with the stern, dry atmosphere.

Jeannie lowered her eyelashes demurely as she gazed around the congregation. There was Gordon MacLeod, and the high-rolling slightly disreputable MacLarens, including the foxy *femme fatale* Jenny, and, of course, the Flemings. Then she caught her breath: sitting in the pew behind the MacLarens, and the object of Jenny's less-than-subtle hair-tossing, was Ross Macintosh. What was he doing there? As she stared at him, his gaze met hers before he lowered his eyes piously. Now that he knew she was there she would have to speak to him after the service. And apologise. At last they stood and left the church, filing out after Innes's interminably slow walk up the aisle. She nodded to the others she knew. If only she could sneak away through the crowd, but the slow movement of people meeting friends made it impossible.

'Dr Macdonald.'

She knew it was him. His voice had a rough, manly quality that tugged at her to turn and speak to him. It was unnerving, the way he could ruin her composure simply by being there. And he was the only person, apart from her patients, who called her 'Doctor'.

'Mr Macintosh,' she murmured, and nodded in an unusually coy greeting. 'I didn't know you were one of Innes's parishioners.' She saw his face tighten, and felt a momentary childish glee.

'I think he's the right one for me,' Macintosh returned quietly, as he touched her elbow to guide her out of the church.

'He's a priest, not a dance partner.' Finally she met his eyes and stifled an unseemly smile. 'You make it sound so intimate,' she ended clumsily.

'Isn't your religion intimate?'

She could feel his breath against her hair, and suddenly felt uncomfortable. 'Let me show you the grounds.' She smiled brightly.

'Why?' His grip on her arm tightened.

Jeannie took a deep breath. She might as well get it over with, she thought, and steeled herself against the shameful excitement that was gathering inside her. 'I wanted to talk to you alone. I owe you an apology. And an explanation.'

Ross tapped his forefinger against his lips. 'There's no need, Dr Macdonald,' he replied in a low tone. 'Why don't we just pretend that meeting never happened?' He raised his eyebrows cynically.

Jeannie felt her cheeks flame. She could tell that he wasn't dismissing it as unimportant. Taking the moral high ground, somewhere she preferred to inhabit.

'Please.' She put her gloved hand over his.

There was minimal resistance as she drew him away from

the crowds and walked in a businesslike way towards the little cemetery that lay on a hill overlooking the beautiful rolling valley.

'So this is where the rich and famous have their peaceful rest.' He snorted. 'If you look over that hill, there's a slagheap that my father's buried under. Not quite as scenic, but who would waste good money on digging out men already half dead from black lung?' He looked at her evenly. 'And that's something they don't know about me at the club.'

'Then why tell me?' she asked. He was planning something, she could tell. He drew his hand over one of the elaborate headstones that competed against each other for the ultimate in understated, pious elegance.

'Because of your position, you'll find out a lot worse about me.' He raised his eyes briefly.

'Where?'

He gave a short dry laugh. 'You're the only person who works where I work and goes to the club. I'm not stupid, Dr Macdonald. I know you'll be running to them with every tale that comes to your ears.'

'No, I won't,' she returned. 'But why shouldn't I, if I were to discover something unseemly . . . ?' She tailed off at the expression of triumph on his handsome face and walked away from him to a well-tended corner of the pretty graveyard.

'Like the fact that I own a building where the tenants live in the worst poverty in the town? Oh, no, that was one of your friends, wasn't it?' He shook his head mockingly.

Jeannie gripped a pale granite headstone for support. There was something about Ross Macintosh – it was almost as if he could look inside her and see all the things she wanted to hide, all the parts of her nature that she wasn't proud of. But he could unearth them. Unconsciously her long fingers traced the name of her grandfather; she would have had to reach down to touch her father's and brother's names. But they were there, giving her strength and resolution. 'I wanted to say that I'm deeply sorry for the embarrassment I caused you,' she said, in rather stilted tones.

'No, you aren't, you're sorry for the embarrassment you caused yourself,' Ross said calmly.

'Will you just listen to me?' Her voice was sharp, and she saw uncertainty cross his face. 'I'm sorry I jumped to the conclusion that you owned the place because you were the person who collected the rent and who was responsible for the upkeep of the building. And as such, you were remiss in your duty. But that is by the by. I shouldn't have brought it up at the club, and I promise I will not put either of us in that awkward position again. I let myself down and I embarrassed you. And I would like to thank you for your discretion in not mentioning it to anyone.' She swallowed and awaited his reply.

'So, is that an apology? Or is it a reprimand because I work for Angus Carmichael, and a warning that if I ever want to show my face in the club I should never mention it again?' He looked puzzled. 'You know, Dr Macdonald, I was happy to do that. You don't need to tell me what to do. I had already decided it was the best course of action.'

Jeannie stared at him, almost six feet of strong, ambitious man, yet he seemed to be acknowledging that she was more powerful than he. 'You think I would prevent you under-taking certain social activities? Why?' She stared at him uncom-prehendingly.

Ross shrugged. 'It's what you people do.'

She saw the bitterness in his expression. 'It's just that we are used to our own set.' She didn't know why but she felt a compulsion to defend her position. 'New entrants can come in, but you can't expect everyone to admit you into their con-fidence immediately.' She was trying to ignore what she knew: that to most people in the club, Ross Macintosh was a shameless carpet-bagger, who was willing to humiliate formerly respectable matrons by escorting them; that they would point out his background at every opportunity; and that every woman, while despising the ones he courted, was secretly wondering what they had that she lacked.

'I have to go.' She went to move past him.

'Is this your family?'

While she had been considering his words, he had been reading the headstone. 'Yes, they're all there. My grandfather, uncle, father, and lastly . . .' She stopped and put a hand to her mouth.

'Your brother, 1917. One of the twenty-minuters.' He stared at the stone.

'He didn't even last twenty minutes,' Jeannie said sadly. 'He had just taken off on his first flight when he was shot down by a German ace. It was somewhere in France so we never had his body to bury.'

'But you have a stone to remember him by.' His voice was softer, kinder. 'It says that your father was married to the late Kirstin. Why isn't he buried with your mother?'

'Only the men of the family have been buried here. The women are in the corner.' She pointed to a shady spot, with a considerably smaller stone.

'Why?'

'I don't know. It's just the way it is.' She nodded to him as she walked away, leaving him with the dead of her family.

When she returned to the church, Gordon MacLeod was chatting to Innes. As usual, he attempted to avoid her, but Jeannie, still stinging from what Ross had told her, was galvanised into action. Gordon had let her down, and just as she would try to make amends with Ross, perhaps she could persuade Gordon to make up for sacking her.

'Ah, Jeannie.' He was obviously discomfited by her arrival and his fingers went to his cufflinks.

'Gordon,' she returned, and took a deep breath.

He gestured that he was about to leave. 'What do you want from me this time?'

75

'Why would you think I want something from you?' she asked, surprised.

'You've a look on your face that gives me a wee hint.' He patted her hand and began to walk down the gravel pathway that led to the road. 'And I'm not the enemy, despite what you think. What is it? Old linen? Equipment? We can send you a little.'

'It's a bit more than that,' she replied. 'I need to find a live-in position for a young woman who was the victim of the cholera outbreak. Her family died, then her employer panicked and dismissed her.'

Gordon shook his head. 'An all too common occurrence, I'm afraid.'

'She was a kitchenmaid, and I wondered . . .' Her nerve failed her.

He was silent as his fingers played with his moustache. Jeannie felt ashamed that she had even mentioned it to him. 'My housekeeper has been complaining about the amount of time she spends on our linens, now that the surgery is growing,' he said contemplatively. 'Perhaps a laundrymaid, but she would need to see the housekeeper first.'

'Thank you.' Jeannie's smile almost split her face.

'I haven't said she could have a position,' he cautioned.

'But you'll give her a chance,' Jeannie countered, 'and that's the most anyone could do for her.'

Early the next morning, Jeannie went back to the hospital, carrying a large parcel. The young woman looked better already.

'Bronchitis, but she'll recover well, with a few good meals inside her,' the doctor said quietly, as they went over to the narrow bed where she lay. 'Miss Strachan, you have a visitor,' he said, and left them alone, putting a torn screen round the bed.

'Doctor, thank you,' the woman said shyly. 'I don't know what I would have done without you.'

'These are for you,' Jeannie said. 'Probably a bit big, but they'll suffice till you get back on your feet.'

'Are you telling me I have to leave?' she said fearfully.

Jeannie nodded. 'But don't worry,' she continued. 'You have to see the housekeeper in Dr MacLeod's household. About a position as laundrymaid.'

'A job? And somewhere to live?' The woman caught her breath and coughed.

'Not if you make that noise,' Jeannie replied. 'Tomorrow. Here is the address. They need someone who is clean, honest and respectable.'

'I'll be the best laundrymaid they've ever had! Bless you, Doctor. God bless you.'

'Just don't let me down,' she warned. 'It's up to you now.'

'Why are you doing this?' the woman asked. 'You don't even know my name.'

'What is your name?' Jeannie said curiously.

'Margaret,' the woman replied. 'Margaret Strachan.'

'Well, Margaret,' she said, 'I'm doing it because it's my job. To help people get better. And now I'd better get to work.'

'Thank you, Doctor.'

As Jeannie walked down the corridor, her heels clicking on the floor, a smile spread over her face. There were more ways to heal than by giving medicines, she thought.

'Happy New Year!'

As the piper struck up 'Auld Lang Syne', Ross watched the others as they toasted the New Year, and thought back a few years to when he'd wanted to be one of those people. And now he was. Almost. He smiled as Fiona whirled past. For some reason, she had recently become more amenable. She had noticed him. Perhaps what he had heard about her was true – perhaps she took lovers now that her husband was no more than a shell.

Fiona. A woman at his beck and call. A rich, beautiful

society mistress, who would do anything for him. His New Year resolution.

But as he watched the dancers, Ross felt a pang of home-sickness. He wanted to be here, but he wanted to be at home.

He wandered out on to the balcony, where Jeannie, oblivious to the cold, was looking up at the stars.

'It's a lovely night,' he said, as he walked over to her, 'but you ought to be inside, dancing.'

'I used to enjoy New Year. I'd make my resolutions and couldn't wait for the next day so I could start working on them.' The night was lit by the crisp white snow that lay in thick sweeps over the smooth expanse of green.

'But you don't now?'

'Now I just feel like I've proved everyone right and me wrong.' She traced a pattern in the snow. 'A situation I imagine you've never found yourself in.'

Ross shrugged. 'Everyone has their ups and downs.'

'I can't make a difference,' she said sadly. 'I want to but I can't.'

'You've made a difference already.'

'I haven't. I just keep people alive till another bout of illness kills them. In those awful courts you make your money from.'

'That doesn't sound like the woman who took me to task over my drains,' he said, in an amused voice.

'I've learned a lot in two months.' She slumped against the wall.

'So, you're giving up?'

'It had crossed my mind.' She chewed her lip. 'It would delight Innes. He hates me working there.'

'Well, I wouldn't want my wife working there.'

'Are you married?'

Ross shook his head. 'Haven't had time to find myself an appropriate woman.' He paused. 'Thought you had more in you than that. But maybe you're right. Maybe you *are* just like all the rest of the women here. Not really suited to work.'

'How dare you?'

'I dare to do a lot, Dr Macdonald.' He looked her up and down. 'It's why I'm successful. And I happen to know that the people of Pathhead think a lot of you and Jim Smillie. For what it's worth, you have their respect. And mine. You've got guts.'

'Really?' A curious expression crossed her face, then a tiny smile.

Ross nodded. 'They know you don't have to be there, you could be working for any other practice or at the hospital, but you choose to go where they need you. You aren't afraid to get your hands dirty.'

'I didn't know.' A resolute look came over her face. 'But I'm going to do something, not just bring out the dead.' She walked over to him. 'If only I could think of some way to help them. They live in such dire circumstances . . . but, of course, you would know that.'

'I can only presume you've taken Angus Carmichael to task on that score,' he murmured, 'since I work for him.' He saw her face fall and laughed. 'But no. You wouldn't do that, now, would you, Dr Macdonald?' He put a finger under her chin and forced her face up till he could look into her eyes. 'It would be such bad manners to do that to a friend.'

'Is it true what they say about you, Mr Macintosh?' she asked. 'About how you made your money?'

He nodded casually. 'I never pretended to be an innocent, Dr Macdonald. My hands are as dirty as everyone else's in this place.' He led her to the door into the club. 'Would you like me to point out everyone I've had business dealings with here so that you can rebuke them for their actions?'

'They don't all own slums,' she snapped.

'How do you know? And what about the linoleum factories, the potteries, the coal mines, and the other places where people slave for a pittance? How did your family make their money?'

'I have to go.' 'Her voice had thickened. 'Happy New Year, Mr Macintosh.'

'Don't forget your resolution, Dr Macdonald,' he called after her.

As Jeannie walked away through the carefree throng of people, she wondered if he was right. Were these people, who were laughing and enjoying themselves, doing it on the backs of her patients and their like?

'You're pale, Jeannie,' Innes said, as he came up beside her. 'Times like this, you remember those who are no longer here to share it with us.'

Jeannie smiled wanly. Let Innes think she was missing her family. It was easier than explaining the truth.

Chapter 8

The next day she stood in a shabby set of rooms at the top of Seaton's Court, having climbed a narrow flight of stairs, festooned with damp washing on lines that hung from the slimy, mossy walls. The only furniture was a double bed, with linen that was almost worn through, and a tea chest that served as a table. She looked at a new born baby, who was dead.

'It came out like that.' A haggard woman of barely thirty, but prematurely aged, eyed her warily. 'I know. Thirteen weans I've birthed, and only seven lasted the week.'

'Can I see the mother?' Jeannie said, as she slipped on her gloves.

'Iris!'

A small sullen girl walked in with the rolling gait of a seaman. Her legs were bowed with rickets. 'Do all your children have it?' Jeannie asked the woman.

'Two. As for the others, well, life was a bit easier for them.'

'How old are you, Iris?' Jeannie looked the child up and down. She couldn't be more than ten. Far too young to be fertile.

'Fourteen, Miss. Have you come to take the babby away?'

Jeannie gazed searchingly at her. She was totally divorced from responsibility for what she had done – and she wasn't much more than a child herself. Except in the eyes of the law. 'What happened?' she asked.

Iris clutched her breasts, which were swollen with milk. 'When it came out it wisnae breathing. Mam tried but . . .'

Jeannie nodded. Mam had tried, all right. There were malnourished fingermarks on the baby's neck where it had been strangled.

'Who is the father of your child, Iris?'

Iris looked at her mother. The mother looked at her daughter. 'Just someone.'

'You can't keep having intercourse, Iris,' Jeannie warned, 'or you'll end up with another baby.'

'Yes, Miss.' Iris stared at the floor as Jeannie packed the dead child into a large wooden box she had brought with her.

'Thank you, Doctor.' The woman looked at the box, then dug into her pocket and held out a few pennies.

Jeannie hesitated, then took them. 'Come to the surgery tomorrow.' She looked at Iris. 'Now I'll just examine you, if I may.'

As Jeannie walked down the stairs with the body in the box she was quiet.

'Imagine wanting to get your end away with her?' Charlie remarked, as they headed out of the court.

'Charlie!'

'Well, she's a cripple. You'd have to be really sick.'

'She's just a child.'

Charlie looked at Jeannie, with eyes far older than hers. 'I forgot.' He yawned. 'You got anything else tonight?'

'No, Charlie, off you go.' She paused. 'Do you ever go to school?'

Charlie laughed. 'Too busy working. What could school teach me?'

'Reading, writing, history, geography . . . morals.'

'I can read a bit and write my name. I know that we won the war and that America's over there.' He pointed into the distance. 'I'm going to go there one day, make my fortune.'

'If anyone can, then it's you,' she said. 'Let's get back, the drizzle's setting in.'

'Jeannie, come in.' Angus was obviously surprised to see her at his door, but she was no less welcome for it.

'I'm sorry about this, Angus, but I've a problem and I need your advice.'

'Come in. The library'll be fine – Margaret's in there reading.' He stopped. 'If you prefer . . .'

'No, I don't mind. Perhaps she can be of some help too.'

Jeannie followed him into the library, sat down in the heavy leather armchair next to the fire and spilled out the sorry tale. 'I'm sorry to be indelicate but . . .' She stared at the military stripe on the wallpaper.

'Not at all, Jeannie.' Margaret's handsome features softened. 'There's no way you could have told it without the full horror.'

'So what should I do?' She accepted a glass of Madeira from Angus.

'What do you want to do?'

'A child has been murdered,' she said. 'A child who deserved the chance of life. But if I report it the mother could be sent to prison.'

'But you cannot simply kill a child because you don't want it, Jeannie,' burst out Margaret. 'What I would give to have . . .'

Angus sat back against the green studded leather and considered. 'Do you want justice or vengeance, Jeannie?' he asked quietly.

'I want justice, Angus, but the way the law stands, she won't be given a hearing. They'll just see a murderer.'

'Oh, what a harsh view you have of the legal profession, my dear.'

'She's fourteen years old, malnourished, disfigured, and her life means so little to her that she cannot comprehend how precious it is.' She looked at her friends, who were sitting there,

83

quietly intent. 'She doesn't seem to realise that the baby was a person too.'

'So, are you saying that she is as much of a victim as the infant?'

'What I'm saying is that she did the wrong thing, I know she did.'

'A wrong thing done for the right reason is still wrong,' Margaret said passionately.

'That's what I think, too. And I don't believe she really thought about her options.' Jeannie spread her hands wide.

'Are you sure that the child was strangled at birth?'

'There are fingermarks on the baby's neck.' She shuddered. 'But the mother needs help from the likes of us, not condemnation.'

'The law is blind,' Angus said softly. He looked at Margaret, who nodded, then left the room. 'And you'll never get another chance to help these people if you report the mother.' He stopped. 'Was she alone when she had the child?'

Jeannie nodded. 'Mother's a casual at the market.'

'And you're certain the girl strangled the child, or are you certain that she put her hands around the baby's neck?'

'What other reason could there be for the marks?'

'You're the doctor, Jeannie, you know far more about birthing children than I ever will.' He raised his eyebrows. 'But if there was another reason why she might have put her hands round the neck then you would have a certain amount of doubt.'

'To weigh against the certainty that she didn't want the child, that she didn't want it to live?' Jeannie let out a large sigh. 'I don't know.'

'Then weigh up what you don't know for certain against what you do know. One child is dead, a victim, and your testimony may send another victim to prison for infanticide.'

'I just feel that either way I'm letting myself, God and everyone else down!' she said despairingly.

'In our world, Jeannie,' Angus went over to her and took her hand, 'doing the right thing can have terrible consequences. I went to war and came back, my brother didn't. Hamish went to war and will never be the same again.' He stroked her fingers. 'I can't tell you what to do, but whatever you decide you will have to live with the consequences. And so may that child.' He hesitated. 'There is a defence of insanity but that would send her to an asylum, which is hardly a fit place for a child.' He scratched his head. 'I'm not a criminal-law expert, I deal in business, but I do remember that some women have been declared temporarily insane if they kill their child within thirty days of giving birth.'

'She doesn't have the money for an advocate to defend her,' Jeannie walked to the door, 'but thank you. I've got some food for thought now.'

'What the hell are they, Ross?' Tam had walked into the shabby office and seen the shiny brown boots and tweed jacket in the corner.

'My new riding clothes.' He smiled expansively. 'Very important to look the part.'

'Now you're gentry.' Tam rolled his eyes.

'Aye – yes,' he corrected himself. 'Well, I'm moving up in the world, and that's the kind of thing you worry about when you're one of them.' He grinned.

'Right.' Tam made a face. 'But surely you should say "one of us", not "one of them"?'

'You know what I mean.'

'Your mam would tan your hide if she heard you say someone was better than her, Ross . . .'

'I told you, I don't have a family,' Ross repeated. 'Not yet.'

'But you—'

'Tam, I left Lochgelly behind a long time ago.'

'And your friends. Like forgetting to invite us to your nights out at the club in case you get embarrassed by us.'

'If there was any other way, Tam—' Ross began.

'But there isnae?' Tam glared at the younger man. 'Me and your mam, we're just not good enough for yeh any mair.' He walked to the window. 'Why don't you go and play with your friends now, move your office to some fancy street and forget we ever existed?'

'I will be one of them!' he shouted.

'Aye. Till they find yeh oot. Then where will yeh be?'

'Feck off, Tam.'

'I'm off tae the pub.' Tam looked at him. 'Said I'd meet some folk there. Got some business. He's a load of lead he wants rid of.' He stared pugnaciously at his boss. 'Or are yeh no interested in yer business any mair?'

'Course I am.' Ross grabbed his overcoat and they set off down the road.

The pub was dirty, dark and filled with the warm odour of tobacco and second-hand air. Ross nodded to the man standing at the bar, who joined them at the scarred, battered table. And began to earn his wages.

Jeannie sat with the infant's body, grey and still, on her examination table as a single gas lamp flickered over them both. She gently moved the head, the marks still visible. What else could have caused them? She placed her hands round the infant's neck, willing herself to think of a reason for them to be there.

It was almost midnight when she finally wrote 'stillborn' on the certificate. Then she locked the baby's body in the cold store and went out to her car. What had begun as a cold, drizzly day had aged into a freezing damp night. Somehow any other weather would have seemed disrespectful.

'So, did you make a decision?' Margaret said, as they sat in the Salvation Hotel having tea a few days later. It was busy, with pristine aproned waitresses gliding from table to table, laden with plates of cucumber sandwiches and cream buns, to the accompaniment of quietly clinking teacups.

Jeannie stared at the pristine tablecloth. 'I took Angus's advice . . . But I just feel as if I'm letting her off with something, that perhaps I ought to have gone to the police, but I had no idea what I could tell them.'

'Couldn't they get someone else to examine the body?' Margaret asked.

'She says the marks round the baby's neck could have come about when she was trying to wrench the child from her body,' Jeannie said, 'and I have to give her the benefit of the doubt. But I still think I've let them down.'

'But you will have told her not to do it again.' Margaret picked up her cup. 'I'm sure she's learned her lesson and won't sleep with a man again until she's married.'

'I don't know how much choice she had in the first place. She's so young.' She chewed her lip.

'But, Jeannie,' Margaret said, shocked, 'who would want to sleep with a child like that?'

'I don't know,' she repeated. 'But I just have to hope that whoever it is, he will think twice before he does it again.'

'What about you?' Margaret said. 'Why don't you try to get out a bit more? Meet someone and have your own family to worry about, help take your mind off it.'

'I'd love to.' Jeannie stirred her tea unconsciously. 'I'm twenty-six in two months' time and without even a sniff of a fiancé. I'll be a spinster for the rest of my life if I don't get one soon.'

'You're being silly, Jeannie.' Margaret patted her on the knee. 'You'll find someone. Someone whose family you know. Someone like us.'

'But what if I don't?'

Margaret took a deep breath. 'Then I'll hire out Angus to you.' She laughed. 'Twice a week and alternate weekends!'

*

Winter warmed into spring and still Jeannie was no further forward. She seemed to drift, and there were never enough days in the week for her to think about anything except the next patient.

But one night, as she sat working through the never-ending list of bronchial complaints, a familiar girl walked into the surgery with her distinctive rickety gait. 'Hello, Doctor.' Iris wiped her nose on a ragged sleeve.

'Hello, Iris,' Jeannie replied. 'What can I do for you?'

Iris wandered over to the table. 'You took the baby away, remember?' She looked up for a second. 'And I wondered . . . I wondered if you could do it again.'

'What do you mean?'

'I've another one.' Iris picked at her grimy nose.

'Where is the baby?' Jeannie said carefully.

'In my belly.' Iris looked round the room. 'What's that for?' She pointed to a microscope.

'Looking at things very closely.' Jeannie tried to collect herself. 'Do you know when the child is due?'

Iris shrugged.

'Get on the table so I can examine you.' Jeannie went over and helped her up. 'I'm just going to feel your tummy.' She put her hand on Iris's stomach and could feel that the womb was distended. 'When did you last menstruate?'

'What?'

'When did you last bleed?'

Iris shook her head.

'You didn't? When did you start having intercourse after the baby?'

Iris looked away.

'You can tell me, Iris, I can help you.' Jeannie took her hand.

'I just want you to take it away. I don't want Ma to know.' Iris screwed up her face as if she had been rebuked for pinching a piece of cake.

'Don't want her to know what?'

'That I've another one,' Iris explained patiently. 'She won't like it that I've fallen again.'

'Iris,' Jeannie said softly, 'you can't keep having intercourse. You're too young and it's wrong.'

Iris turned her head to the wall.

Jeannie looked at her: she seemed unconcerned abut the moral implications. Suddenly a thought struck her. 'Are you having intercourse with just one man or with different men?' She didn't want to know the answer, but she had to ask.

'What do you think I am?' Iris replied indignantly.

'So you have a special friend?'

Iris snorted.

'Who is the father of your child, Iris?'

'I don't know,' she said sullenly.

'Liar.' Jeannie put her hands on her hips.

'What difference does it make?'

'I need to know.'

Iris sighed. 'Ma's new man.' She studied her knees.

Jeannie walked back to her table and put on her coat. 'I want to speak to your mother,' she said, through gritted teeth.

Together they walked through the dirty wet streets to the little market. Iris led her to a stall with great grey vats that stank of fat and entrails.

'Ma!' Iris shouted to her mother, who was potting the mixtures. 'The doctor.'

'Kate.' The man next to her nudged her. 'That's your bairn, isn't it?'

Wiping greasy hands on her apron, the child's mother came over to them. 'What do you want now?' she demanded. 'Can you no see I'm working?'

'I wanted to talk to you, Mrs McKee,' Jeannie said coldly, 'and I would add that it's not the kind of business you want to discuss in public.'

'Yes, Doctor.' Kate looked at the man. 'Come round the back.'

They walked to where some large vats of a lardy substance were cooling, giving off a pungent smell of rancid fat.

'Your daughter is pregnant again, Mrs McKee,' Jeannie began.

'What did you go tae the doctor for, Iris?' Kate said angrily, shaking a reddened fist at her child.

'So she would take it away,' Iris squealed.

'There is nothing I can do for Iris, except to help her with her pregnancy and ensure that she does not lose the baby.' She looked straight at the woman.

'You silly wee besom,' Kate snarled at her daughter.

'It wasnae my fault, Ma,' Iris protested.

'She alleges that the father is your gentleman friend.' Jeannie clasped her hands together. 'You must tell the police about him – because if you don't, I shall.'

Kate looked down for a moment. 'It's a good room, better than I could afford,' she said slowly.

'Are you saying you knew this was going on?' Jeannie said incredulously.

Kate looked away. 'If you've nothing more to say, Doctor, I'd better be getting back to work.'

'So you'll do nothing about this man?' Jeannie could hardly believe what she was hearing.

'What is there to do?'

'You can't just close your eyes to what is happening to your daughter!' Jeannie hissed. 'As a mother.'

'As a mother,' Kate replied, 'I have to keep a roof over their heads and put food in their bellies. And I can't. So we all have to do our bit.'

'How would you feel if your mother had let some old man sleep with you in return for the rent?'

'It's not like that,' Kate replied. She turned her head away. 'He's not a bad man, earns decent money when he can get work. He's good to us, doesn't have to be, none of the bairns are his.' She swallowed hard. 'You won't tell anyone, will you?'

'You've ruined her chance of marriage.' Jeannie looked at the mother with disgust.

'Look at her!' Kate pointed to Iris, who was dipping a finger into the grey sludgy mess. 'No one's going to want her. She'll be lucky to find work. At least this way she's earning her keep.'

'You're not fit to be a mother, Mrs McKee,' Jeannie said, 'and I will be informing the parish that she is with child.' With that she walked away, her face scarlet with anger and frustration. She ignored the market folk as she walked back through the damp, rubbish-strewn streets, the cobbles slick with muddy water, but in the heavy crowds, it was impossible to hurry.

'Hello, Doctor,' a heavy-set man said cheerfully. 'Doing a wee bit of shopping?'

'What?' She shook herself out of her reverie. In front of her stood a working man, vaguely familiar. He was small and wiry, but with a grimy, flat look about his face. His clothes were worn but clean and he certainly didn't look as if he would have used her services. He looked as if he could afford a doctor.

'Just passing the time of day,' he replied. 'I'm Tam, I work for Ross Macintosh. He goes to the club with you and your family every week. What are you looking for?'

'Someone who understands the difference between right and wrong,' Jeannie returned.

'That's a bit pricy for round here,' Tam remarked cheerfully. 'You look a wee bit upset.'

'I am.' She pressed her lips together to stop herself saying any more. 'And Mr Macintosh doesn't go to the club with us. He's just there when we go.'

'That's not the way he tells it,' Tam said. 'You know, if someone has upset you, you should tell Ross. He'll sort them out.' He ushered her out of the way of a passing handcart, groaning with dirty green vegetables.

'This is a matter for the police,' she said firmly, as she stepped over a muddy pool of greenish water and rotten leaves.

'Folk round here don't take kindly to the polis,' Tam said. 'Why don't you and I go for a cup of tea back at the office and you can talk it over with Ross?' He smiled. 'You've got a right face on you at the moment and mebbe it would be better if you spoke to him.'

Jeannie stopped in her tracks. He might be able to help. He might give her a perspective on how Kate thought, how she could be persuaded to care better for her daughter, and protect her from the man she was living with.

They walked back round the market, Tam conscientiously pointing out where she could get the best vegetables. 'You'll find a lovely ham shank from over there. Makes good soup,' he said conversationally.

'I don't know where we get our food from,' she replied, distracted. 'It just arrives on the table.'

'You don't do the cooking for your family?' he said incredulously.

'Too busy with my work to bother with all that,' she muttered.

'One of them old maids, eh?' Tam ushered her down a sidestreet. 'It's just over there.'

They walked up some steps to a heavy oak door, opened it and went inside. Another door led off the hall, which Tam opened. Ross was standing behind his desk, remonstrating with a shabbily dressed man who seemingly hadn't done as he was told. 'What did yeh expect he would do?' Ross opened his arms wide.

'I didnae ken he wid . . .'

'Just get out of here!' Ross hissed, and glared at Jeannie.

She watched the other man leave, then said, 'You might have introduced me to your friends.' Her curiosity was roused and she felt she had to point out Ross's *faux pas*.

'You really have no idea, do you? Would you want your

friends to meet Jim Smillie, with his stained clothes and stinking of ale at ten in the morning?' As he spoke, he straightened his clothing; the dark grey wool was immaculate, well cut and obviously new.

Tam walked in, carrying a tea-tray with three mugs on it. 'There you go, Doctor,' he said cheerfully, and handed her a mug. 'And I made one for you too.' He passed it to Ross and took the last for himself.

'Dr Macdonald, what do you want?' Ross sat back on his desk.

'It's really a matter for the police, but Tam here thought for some reason that you might be able to help.'

'Who's broken in now?' He sighed.

'I need to find a man,' she said.

'Don't we all know it?' Ross mocked.

'One of my patients, a young girl, is being bothered by her mother's man friend. He has made her pregnant twice and I want to go to the police, but Tam persuaded me that I should seek your advice before I do anything.'

'Where do they live?' Ross said grimly.

'Paton's Court. Do you think I should speak to him myself? The mother is aware of the situation, but won't do anything as he is the family's main provider.'

'Who are they?' Ross said.

'I can't tell you that,' she said. 'I cannot give out confidential details about my patients.'

'You want him to stop, then talking to him will probably just get you a broken rib,' Tam interjected. 'But if me and a few of the lads go and see him . . .'

'You will talk to him in his own language?' Jeannie said. 'Make him realise that his behaviour is unacceptable and that he should stop?'

'Something like that,' Tam said.

'It ought to be me,' Jeannie insisted.

'This is more of a job for Tam,' Ross said. 'Who is he?'

'I can't.' She looked down.

'You won't be able to stop him,' Ross said quietly. 'You don't think you'd get a hearing, do you?'

'Then I'll go to the police,' she said resolutely.

Ross and Tam looked at each other.

'They won't do anything because he'd only deny it.' Ross stood up. 'This kind of thing happens all over the place. The only thing these men respect is a stronger man.'

'So you'll tell him that unless he stops bothering Iris we'll report him to the police?' Jeannie looked from one man to the other.

'Yes,' Ross said. 'It needs to come from someone like Tam. A man. Not a woman.'

Jeannie sipped the strong tea. She knew she shouldn't tell them who it was, it was breaking a confidence, but if the police wouldn't help she had a responsibility to poor little Iris. 'I would have to have your word that you will keep it confidential,' she said slowly.

Both men nodded.

'The man lives with Kate McKee and her children.' She looked from one man to the other. 'He has been forcing himself on her daughter Iris.'

'We'll have a word with him, hen.' Tam patted her arm. 'Isn't right, someone like you having to know aboot things like that.'

'You'd be amazed at what I've seen,' she said. 'Being here is certainly an eye-opener. But you learn quickly.'

'You can go now.' Ross took the mug from her hands. 'And I trust you won't tell anyone that you came to us with your problem either.'

'Of course not.' She smiled, puzzled, and walked out.

Ross and Tam stared at each other.

'You get a couple of the lads, and give him a talking-to,' Ross said.

'It'll be a pleasure.' Tam glowered. 'I'll make sure he never troubles that wee lass again. Or the doctor.'

'Tam,' Ross said, 'if she asks, we just talked to him.'

Tam nodded. 'She really has no idea how we do things, does she?' he said.

'And she isn't going to learn,' Ross replied. 'Ever.'

Chapter 9

Almost a week went by, and Jeannie smiled and even passed the time of day with Ross when she met him in the back-streets that housed both their workplaces. But although he was polite, he was also distant, and she noticed that he avoided eye-contact. Jeannie was only too aware that she was hardly the height of fashion, but nevertheless she felt the slight. Just when she was finding a grudging liking for him he had obviously decided that he had none for her. How could I have thought we might be friends? she chided herself, as she watched him out of the window. But even as greasy raindrops obscured the sight of him, she knew the answer. And it was tinged with desperation.

On Monday morning, as she walked into the surgery, the waiting room was buzzing with the news.

'They say they found the body at the bottom of the stairwell,' one said.

'I heard that it was in the lavvy, the head down the pan!' a young boy butted in.

'Have a bit more respect – they were only young.' An old woman cuffed him round the ear.

'What's going on?' Jeannie said, as she shook the drops of rain off her hat.

'There's a right stramash,' Jim said, as he put his instruments into the boiler. 'A woman and her daughter have been found dead in Paton's Court and, unusually for that place, not of natural causes.' He poked at a long pair of scissors. 'The police are looking for a man, but he's disappeared.'

Jeannie shook her head. 'Sometimes I wonder if there's any good left in the world.' She raised her eyes to the mouldy ceiling. 'Well, I might as well get started.'

That afternoon she was getting ready for evening surgery when a policeman came in. 'Miss Macdonald?' He nodded to her. 'I am Inspector Pettigrew.'

'And I'm Dr Macdonald,' she returned. She put out her hand and he shook it automatically.

'Dr Macdonald,' the inspector began, 'I'm investigating the murders of Kate and Iris McKee, patients of yours, I believe.'

Jeannie froze. 'I had heard someone had died,' she said slowly, 'but I didn't know who.'

'We're looking for the man she was living with,' Inspector Pettigrew said. 'Likely that he killed them both.'

She nodded, but her mind was whirling dizzily. And with it the suspicion that she was somehow tied up with it. Along with a vague, bitter sensation she recognised as guilt. 'What makes you think that?' Her voice was quiet and studied.

'It's usually the husband or bidey-in who kills them,' he said, 'and he's run off.'

'What do you want me for?' She looked at his immaculately clean yet worn clothing.

'Wondering if you knew anything,' the inspector said. 'You talked to mother and daughter in the market a few days before they died.' He cleared his throat. 'You had a bit of a go at her, if reports are to be believed.'

'I was asking her how she planned to take care of her child.' Jeannie looked down again. Her hands were shaking. 'And her grandchild.'

'Aye, the lass was expecting,' Pettigrew acknowledged. 'And, just for the record, what was the outcome of the conversation?'

'That she felt she was doing the best she could for Iris.' A thought struck her. 'What about the other children?'

'They've been sent to a parish orphanage.' The inspector stood up. 'So, there was no other man who could have been involved? A man who would have wanted them dead?'

'You mean Iris's father?' she said, horrified. 'I have no idea who would want to kill her.' She stared at the lapel of Inspector Pettigrew's jacket. It was easier than looking him in the eye.

Inspector Pettigrew made his excuses and went out. Jeannie realised she needed to talk to Ross. Now.

'Have you heard?' she said, as she reached the door of the office.

'Heard what?' Ross looked up from the ledger he was writing in. 'You know, Dr Macdonald, my life doesn't revolve round you. I have a business to run.'

'But this is important.' She went over to the desk and took the ledger from his hands. 'Iris and her mother are dead.'

'I know.' Ross looked up at her. 'They're looking for Ernie Tummel, but from what I heard he's nowhere to be found. On a ship bound for somewhere else.'

'What else do you know?' she demanded.

'What do you think?' He looked at her incredulously. 'That I killed her?'

'No, but I think you know where he is. What did you say to him?'

'Just told him to stop.'

Jeannie backed away until she came to the unyielding wall. She wrapped her arms round herself protectively. 'Was he angry?' she asked quietly.

Ross gazed out of the window. 'No, he was delighted that someone had found him out.' He walked over to her. 'If you must know, he was scared to death.'

'So he went back and took it out on Iris and her mother,' she said.

98

'It happens,' Ross said. 'More often than you would imagine.'

'Thank you, Mr Macintosh.' Jeannie nodded resolutely. 'For attempting to prevent me meddling.' She pushed past him and stumbled out of the door.

'Hullo, Doctor,' Tam said cheerfully, as she pushed past him. 'You want some tea?' As she disappeared out the door he looked at his boss. 'You two had a fight?'

'You know the bloke we sorted out, the one who murdered the girl and her mother?'

'She isn't going to tell the police we had a word with him, is she?' Tam scratched his head.

'Shite!' Ross rushed after her, slamming the heavy door then heading into the wide, sodden street.

'Dr Macdonald!' he shouted, as he scanned the road for her. 'Jeannie!' He saw a plum cloche hat turn, and Jeannie's pale face framed by the hat and her beautiful rich hair.

'Please don't shout at me in the street,' she said, as he caught up with her.

'Not here.' He took her by the arm and hustled her round the corner to a small alley. 'Get lost, you,' he ordered a couple of small boys, who were hanging round beside them.

'What do you want?'

'You aren't going to the police, are you?'

She closed her eyes. 'Do you really think I have anything to tell them?' She sighed in defeat. 'I gave him a motive but nothing else. And I'm not so brave that I'll throw myself on my sword. Did you think I'd go to the police and tell them I'd persuaded you to talk to him?'

'It had crossed my mind.'

'It'll just be our secret.' She began to walk away.

Ross grabbed her arm. 'It wasn't your fault,' he said.

'Yes, it was.' She pulled away her arm. 'I didn't protect her, and I blamed her mother. I came here to help people, I didn't want to at the beginning, but then I realised that they need me in a way they don't in Kinross. And look what I've done.' She opened her hands. 'I've caused the death of two people who led possibly the most miserable lives I've ever come across.'

Ross reached for her but she shook him away. 'So gloat, Mr Macintosh!' She backed away from him. 'I imagine you're delighted that I've got my comeuppance.'

Jeannie kept her guilt to herself, but after a few days it was still eating away at her. And there was only one person in the world to whom she could talk about it. Who truly understood her.

'You don't seem yourself,' Margaret said, as she sat down next to Jeannie on the elegant cream brocade *chaise-longue* in her silk-lined drawing room. 'Are you sure you'd like tea? You wouldn't prefer something stronger?'

'No, tea will be fine.' Jeannie smiled at Margaret's concern. 'Your cook makes the best scones I've ever tasted.' She sank against the thick lavender cushion at her back. 'I had a patient, the girl I asked you about.' The words spilled out. 'The one whose baby died.'

Margaret sat down next to her, brushing the thick black and beige plaid of her hobble skirt. She laced her fingers together; her gentle face showed that she was steeling herself for bad news. 'You can tell me anything, Jeannie,' she murmured. 'You know me.'

'She's dead. She was murdered by the man who had fathered her child.' Jeannie waited as the maid brought in the silver tea-tray and left the room. 'I failed to protect her. I told her not to have intercourse, but I couldn't stop her.'

"What are you going to do?' Margaret asked.

'In order to help people like Iris, I have to give them . . .' Jeannie searched for the word '. . . a choice.'

'What kind of choice?'

'There was no point in telling Iris not to sleep with the man because she had no choice in the matter.' She chewed her lip pensively.

'She was a lady of the night?' Margaret put a hand to her mouth.

'No, but the man was her mother's friend.' Jeannie cleared her throat. 'Iris was her means of keeping him with the family. They needed the money.'

'Oh, my goodness!'

Jeannie nodded. 'And I've been thinking. I can't stop girls like her being abused by men but I can stop them becoming pregnant.'

'How?' A light dawned in Margaret's eyes. 'You mean like that doctor who's been in all the papers? Marie Stopes? I've read her book, you know.'

'She's in London, and there's a clinic in Edinburgh,' Jeannie told her. 'But it isn't a charity clinic so my women wouldn't be able to afford it. They need a guardian angel. Actually, we need an army of them.'

Margaret sat back in the *chaise-longue*, and brushed her hand over its padded arm. 'It's not right,' she said slowly. 'Little girls and unmarried women shouldn't be doing it anyway.'

'They don't always have the choice,' Jeannie said. 'And I can't give it to them. But I can give them the choice as to whether they end up bringing another helpless child into the world to be starved and hurt as they have.'

Margaret tapped her lips with her fingers. 'You sound like my mother, when she used to harangue my grandfather about the workhouses.' She put her hand on the silver teapot, then pulled it back. 'She used to say that until women and children were seen as people and not as possessions slavery would exist.'

Jeannie looked up. Even now Margaret could surprise her.

'Go and see Marie Stopes and ask her advice. My mother left me a small allowance. I never told Angus about it as he has so much pride.' She took Jeannie's hand. 'I'll pay for the things you need.'

'I can't ask you to fund a whole clinic!'

'You don't have to. I'm offering to do it,' Margaret said. 'After all, I'll only spend it on crockery and curtains.'

'Then I'll do it,' Jeannie said resolutely. 'I'll do it this week.'

'Now will you relax and have some tea with me?' Margaret smiled.

'Drinking to success with Earl Grey.' Jeannie groaned in mock-despair. 'What kind of Scots are we?'

'Sensible ones,' Margaret replied. She turned as a harassed-looking Angus walked in. 'How was Daddy?'

'In lively spirits,' Angus replied tightly. 'Hello, Jeannie.' He bent and kissed both women. 'Having a lazy afternoon chatting? I wish I had the time.'

Margaret rushed to her friend's defence. 'Jeannie and I have been putting together a plan for the poor of Kirkcaldy,' she replied, a trifle sharply.

'You ladies and your good works.' He wagged a finger at them like a schoolmaster. 'But let's not sully our home with the poor. I've just had an afternoon with a client of mine, a horse breeder, who might have a mount available for Hamish to purchase.'

As he began to tell them about the horse, Jeannie lowered her head. It was no fun listening when there were no funds to purchase it. And no way she could tell Angus without embarrassing everyone.

Less than two months later, as spring was stretching into summer, Margaret's legacy was paid to the clinic. And Jeannie went shopping at Dr Stopes's Edinburgh clinic where a forthright nurse showed her exactly what to do. Jeannie filled her suitcase with dutch caps and tubes of fruit acid spermicide. Now she was certain she was doing right by the women of Kirkcaldy.

It was late when she got back, but Margaret was there to collect her and together they went back to Jeannie's house.

They went upstairs to her bedroom and, under the buxom shepherdesses of her Toile de Jouy wallpaper, they sat cross-legged on her bed. Jeannie got out one item after another.

'Come on, then, show me everything.' Margaret giggled.

It was just like being back at boarding-school, Jeannie thought, only this time it wasn't contraband sweets they were exclaiming over.

'This is a diaphragm.' She handed the thick rubber cap to Margaret, who made to put it on her head. 'They call them dutch caps. The nurse showed me how to fit them.'

'What do you do with it?' Margaret said, tilting her head.

'Well,' Jeannie wrinkled her brow, 'you wear it inside.'

Margaret blanched.

'And it acts as a barrier for you so that no babies will result.'

'Really!' Margaret looked at it in a new light, poking at it with her finger. 'It feels horrible.'

'When you put it in, you can't feel it.'

Margaret giggled. 'You know something, Jeannie,' she said airily, 'I think it's about time I had one of my ladies' luncheons.'

'Any chance your cook will produce those scones?' Jeannie twinkled. 'No, it isn't fair that you would be expected to invite people who are . . .'

'Not close friends?' Margaret said, with dry humour. 'That's something you don't need to tell me about.'

'Surely after four years your father must have accepted Angus,' Jeannie said.

Margaret shook her head. 'My husband will always be less of a man than he wanted for me. My only hope is that one day, when we have a family, he can accept our child.'

Jeannie grasped her friend's hand and held it tightly. 'We'll have it in the club,' she said, wishing she had the words to talk about what they both wanted to. Margaret's inability to produce an heir.

*

'So, have you heard what happened between Cathy MacLaren and Jeremy Campbell?' Fiona said, as the ladies withdrew to the club's airy conservatory after a light meal of salmon in a white wine sauce and apple tart paid for by Margaret. 'Apparently they aren't getting married any more. And she wants to sue for breach of promise.'

'Hardly surprising. The Campbells are all the same,' Mrs Lassiter said spitefully. 'Can't see why she took up with him in the first place.'

'Because there are no decent men left,' Fiona said. 'Have you seen the advertisements in the *Lady*? Women are advertising for handicapped ex-servicemen from good families. They'll look after them as long as they can marry them first.'

'Ladies!' Margaret stood up. 'As many of you know, Jeannie Macdonald is now working as a physician in Kirkcaldy. She has kindly agreed to give us all a talk on some recent scientific discoveries.'

Jeannie smiled. 'I'm sure, ladies, you'll have seen the reports about the scandalous Dr Marie Stopes.'

There was a hush as the ladies turned to look at her.

'I have met with Dr Stopes, and talked to her about what she's doing. Work that involves all of us.' She opened the box she had with her. 'Today, ladies, I'm going to tell you about the science of planning your family, ensuring that you have children when you want them, enabling you to enjoy a full married life.' Suddenly even the sound of genteel breathing stopped.

'You will not!' Evangeline Macintyre stood up, anger bristling from her salt-and-pepper hair and impressively corseted bosom. 'I will not stay here and listen to such – such—' Her pince-nez glasses quivered.

'Biology?' Jeannie suggested.

'Filth.' She pushed her way past the others, dragging her stocky daughter with her. 'I'm not staying here to listen to you talk about the act of procreation as if it was a bit of fun.'

'But it can be,' Jeannie replied. 'This way—'

'I'm not listening to this filthy biology of yours.' She pushed her daughter towards the door. 'And I'm disgusted that you ladies are choosing to stay.' She glared slowly, malevolently, at each in turn. A few more got up, and headed for the ornate door.

'If they're shocked now, wait till I bring out my bits and pieces.' Jeannie laughed and, thankfully, the rest did too, albeit rather cautiously.

'Any questions?' Jeannie was holding up a diaphragm.

'What's going on in here?' Mr Macintyre, one of the committee, rushed in, followed by his wife. He was a small, scrawny man with a surprisingly artistic wave to his white pomaded hair, and a silk handkerchief that a theatrical actor might have hesitated to wear in his breast pocket.

'I'm taking questions at the moment.'

'Oh, my goodness!' Mrs Macintyre pointed to the table. 'Look at what she's been doing.'

'Right, that's enough,' he said, ripping off his jacket and throwing it over the table. 'There's been enough filth for one night. Ladies, please accept our apologies for this – and you, young lady, will have to answer to the committee.'

'But I'm not doing anything indecent,' Jeannie insisted.

'What is the world coming to when respectable ladies can discuss such matters?' Mr Macintyre turned and stared at each woman in turn. 'You disgust me, Miss Macdonald.'

'I'm Dr Macdonald, and if the thought that married people might enjoy the closeness of intimacy disgusts you I suggest you join a monastery.' She stifled a grin as she picked up the jacket he had thrown over her supplies.

'What is on it?' He looked at a jelly-like stain.

'Something that you would undoubtedly find repellent,' she retorted. 'Same time next week?'

'The committee will be writing to you,' he replied, as he stalked out. 'You're skating on thin ice, Miss Macdonald, and I for one will be happy to see you fall through it.'

Jeannie looked at Margaret, who stuck out her tongue.

'So, you're to be hauled up in front of the committee to explain yourself.' Margaret raised an eyebrow.

'What can they do to me?'

'Give you lines. "I must not corrupt the ladies of Perthshire." Write it out a thousand times, Dr Macdonald.' Margaret grinned.

'No, really,' Jeannie pressed.

'I suppose you could be suspended for a while,' Margaret said. 'Give the rest of us a chance to win a tennis match.' She squeezed Jeannie's arm. 'But don't worry, Daddy's on the committee, remember. He'll sort it all out.'

Jeannie smiled gratefully at her friend. She suspected that Margaret had thrown herself into helping with the cause because it was connected with babies. Margaret and Angus had been married almost as long as Fiona and Hamish and, like them, there had been no issue. But there was nothing wrong with Angus, unlike Hamish. Which left only one person to blame.

Chapter 10

The rest of the week came and went, and it was the weekend, with Innes and his sermon. After his lecture on endurance, Jeannie wandered over to the little graveyard, where her father lay with the other men of his family. 'I'm doing something now, Daddy,' she said, as she touched the stone. 'You'd be proud of me.' She gazed up at the hills, the heather that covered them sprinkling the low green slopes with vibrant violet and slate grey. 'Well, perhaps not. You weren't one for women's matters, were you?' She sighed wistfully, and her reverie was broken as she heard a footfall on the gravel. She turned, expecting to see Innes, looking for his weekly reassurance that his sermon had been incisive, thought-provoking and, above all, interesting. But instead she saw Ross Macintosh a few graves away. He had deliberately made a sound to alert her to his presence. He was holding his black felt hat as he returned her gaze. They stood, framed against the skyline, as the wind caught at his cashmere overcoat, exposing the charcoal wool suit under it.

'Oh.' The wind whipped away the glove she was holding, and both of them ran to catch it before it flew over the low stone dyke and was lost for ever in the wilds. They knelt, but he found it, on a mossy headstone that was hundreds of years old, the family long since lost.

'Thank you.' For some reason she felt vulnerable with him, his face inches from hers.

'Last time I told you a confidence,' Ross said contemplatively. 'It must be that this place brings the truth out of you.' She could feel his intensity – he was sweating it. And it was frightening.

'I was . . .' Jeannie stopped as his hand stroked away her rebellious windswept hair.

'I know, Dr Macdonald,' he replied. 'You were here to speak to the dead, not the living.' He stood up and walked away, his feet crunching on the neat, raked gravel.

'I didn't mind,' she called after him, but her voice was lost on the wind. And she felt the pull of him, deep in her stomach.

The next day, Jeannie arrived at the surgery, just as Jim came in from his night shift at the infirmary. 'Good to see you, woman,' he said gruffly. 'Now, let's have a look at some of the stuff you got in Edinburgh. I was talking to some of the boys about it at the infirmary, they were all interested.'

'I got so much, Jim,' she replied. 'And it's all practical, easy to use. Look!' She opened the case and extracted a thick rubber cap. 'They recommend use with spermicide, and all you need to do is show the women how to wear them.'

'Hold on a moment, Jeannie.' Jim looked worried. 'If you want to do that, fine, but I don't.'

'Why not, Jim? You know better than I do the damage caused by all those unwanted pregnancies. Deaths from abortion, premature ageing from constant demands on the women's bodies . . .'

'They shouldn't be having the sex and . . .' Jim hesitated. 'Well, it isn't right, is it? These women won't be telling their husbands.'

'Or their brothel keepers, or their fathers, or whoever makes them have sex.' She rounded on him. 'It's all right for you, Jim, you can sleep with whoever you want and nothing will come of it, but for a woman it's different. Every time she has intercourse, whether she wants to or not, the thought of a child must be uppermost in her mind.'

'Then perhaps she ought not to be doing it.'

'Exactly,' Jeannie said. 'I can't see what the attraction is of that kind of thing, but I have a duty to protect my patients. This way I can. I was thinking of holding some public meetings, then starting up a clinic here on a Thursday evening. You don't need to be part of it, but I would like your support.'

'I've seen a damn sight more than you have, young lady, and the idea fills me with dread. You know the trouble it's caused in London, and folk round here don't take kindly to change. But you can use the surgery for consultations.' He looked down for a moment. 'I've seen more than enough women bleeding to death from abortion not to want to help you.'

'Thank you.' She smiled, a trifle too triumphantly, but then Jim smiled back.

'You've certainly got guts, Dr Macdonald,' he said.

Jeannie threw herself into preparing for her clinic with the same amount of energy that she had once devoted to playing tennis, or to any of the activities she had once excelled at and now seemed trivial. Tonight the bills advertising her talk on women's health had gone up in the neighbourhood of the surgery, courtesy of Charlie and a couple of young boys who were pasting them for the princely sum of sixpence. That Thursday night, she would have her first meeting. At last she was achieving her new-years' resolution.

'What is this?' Innes demanded, as he walked into the drawing room after a late dinner with one of his parishioners and thrust a leaflet into her hands.

Jeannie looked up from her copy of the *Lancet*. 'It's a talk I'm giving on women's health.' She sneaked a covert glance at her cousin. He was pale, even more so than normal.

'You're advocating abortion!' His knuckles tightened. 'You

of all people, the cousin of a Church of Scotland minister, are telling people how to rid themselves of the greatest gift God can give!'

'No, I'm not—' she began.

'This talk, is it the same talk you gave to my parishioners at the club a few days ago?'

'Well, I'm going to use more earthy language. These women won't understand big words—'

'Jeannie, I forbid this!' he hissed. 'What you're doing is a sin and you'll burn in hell.'

'No, I won't, but I would be remiss in my duty to women if I let them keep risking their lives having child after child or having abortions,' she replied, as she stood up and walked over to him. 'Innes, Kirsty McLellan is leaving for India today on a boat. She's pregnant and it's probable that she'll lose the child on the crossing. She may lose her own life as well.'

'You don't know that for certain.'

'Is that a risk you would want to take with your own wife?'

'You're going against the teachings of the Bible,' Innes declared, 'and I will not have you do that.'

'Innes, I believe that a child is a gift from God.' She laid a hand on his arm but he brushed it away. 'And I need not tell you that when one of your parishioners is ill and having a minor stomach operation, she is not curing a gastric problem.'

'And that is what you'll be doing?' He said aghast.

'No, but there are ways to stop a child being conceived.'

'It's the same thing. What difference is there between someone who does that and someone who removes a child from its mother too early?'

Jeannie was unsure of the answer.

'If God really means for the child to be, then it will come.' She stared at her cousin's anguished face. 'I'm not more powerful than God, but I've seen the results of too many illegal abortions not to want to help.'

'What you're doing is wrong, and I'll not be in the same

house as you if you intend to carry on. You'll be cut off from the family.' He stared at her.

'Innes, please.' She closed her eyes for a moment. 'What would Hamish do without you?'

Innes looked down. 'Your being here hasn't made as much difference as I'd hoped.'

The words were like a knife twisting in her guts.

'I can't cure everyone, you know.' Her voice was shrill but she was past caring. 'And you give up on people so easily, Reverend Macdonald!'

Innes walked to the window and stared out for what seemed like hours. 'Please, Jeannie,' he said eventually, 'I worry for your moral fibre. That place you work in, it's seeping into your bones.'

'Into my heart?' she said gently. 'I'm like you, Innes. I wouldn't do something if I didn't want to.'

'I don't want you to do it,' he said quietly. 'It's wrong.'

'I will do it for my patients,' she said slowly. 'But I will not embarrass you at the club again, I promise. Even though plenty of the women who were at the meeting have approached me for advice since then.'

'I'm not just doing this for myself, Jeannie,' his tone became sharper again, 'and I will be speaking out against immoral behaviour in my sermons.' He was offering an olive branch, and they both knew it.

'Since your parishioners have no need to be in Pathhead, they will not know what I'm doing.'

'I think you're wrong,' he concluded, and left her alone.

'So do all men,' she replied, to the empty room, 'but their wives and daughters think differently.'

It was almost seven when Jeannie arrived at the hall. It was dark and empty and there were only a few people lingering listlessly standing about inside. She swallowed her disappointment, walked to the front and began to set up a table with some leaflets.

'Not much going on here,' Margaret said, as she came in, the smooth leather soles of her soft shoes catching on the rough wood.

'What are you doing here?' Jeannie said. 'This isn't the kind of place for someone like you, Margaret, but it's lovely to see you.'

'Moral support,' Angus called, as he walked over to the table and kissed her cheek. 'My goodness, is that what I think it is?' He held up a thick french letter.

'Apparently it'll keep your barrel dry if you have to cross any rivers,' Jeannie retorted. 'I'll be talking about ladies' matters so if you want to make a discreet exit I won't be offended.'

'What Jeannie is saying, darling,' Margaret looked at him fondly, 'is that you may find out more than you bargained for.' She nudged Jeannie. 'He didn't know how to say no to me but he really doesn't want to be here.'

'But you know Margaret will be safe with me.'

'It's not really the kind of place I want my wife to be.' He smiled wryly. 'But she wanted to be here for you.'

'Wish I could find a man like you,' Jeannie said. 'Does he have a brother?'

Margaret looked at the floor. 'I do have something to tell you,' she began.

'I know that look!' Jeannie declared. 'You're expecting, aren't you?'

'There's been no announcement yet.' Angus patted his wife's arm.

'Congratulations.' Jeannie hugged her. 'And now, if you'll be patient, you can find out exactly how to avoid the same thing happening again.' She grinned widely.

'Perhaps it would be better if we waited in another room?' Angus said to his wife.

'Nonsense!' Margaret said firmly. 'Jeannie might need help.'

'The kind of help she might need involves the police, or

perhaps the army,' Angus said firmly. 'These kind of people are low-born and violent. Jeannie will undoubtedly cause a riot.'

'Why?' Jeannie asked.

'Because that's what these people do. We have parties, they have riots.' Angus shrugged and, for a moment, Jeannie glimpsed an ugly smugness in him.

'We won't have a riot,' she said quickly. 'We probably won't have anyone here at all.'

'Is this where the women's health talk is?' Three women walked in nervously.

'Yes,' Jeannie answered, with a smile. 'Are any of your friends coming?'

'A few. What are you going to talk about?'

'Family planning. Do you know what it is?'

'I know how to have bairns,' the woman said wryly. 'Had seven. Lost three.'

'Well, I'm going to tell you how to avoid them.'

'Pour enough drink down his throat, or let him talk to that Jessie Harris, that'll keep him busy!' the woman shrieked, loud enough for everyone to burst out laughing and nod to their friends that Jessie Harris was, indeed, an accommodating woman.

'I think perhaps we ought to adjourn to a back room, my dear.' Angus led a fascinated Margaret away.

'No.' Jeannie rolled her eyes at the woman. 'I'm talking about ways in which you can enjoy a normal married life, and avoid pregnancy.'

'Really!' They moved a little closer and Jeannie recognised a few. Wrapped in dark shawls or wearing mud-spattered coats that had seen many winters, the harshness of their lives was etched on their pinched, windburnt faces, cracked lips and prematurely greyed hair. The women were worn down by their lives, and many were simply skeletons covered with sallow skin. The stench of old damp rose from most of them, like filthy rotting carpets. But, like the smell of the outside area, Jeannie was getting used to it. So much so that she was beginning to worry she smelt like that too.

'Yes.' She went on the stage, where a ripped banner proclaimed the need to save the last of the town's potteries. 'Ladies, I'm Dr Eugenia Macdonald, and I'm here to talk about women's health . . .'

. . . Jeannie held up the thick brown rubber diaphragm as she explained to the little group of women what they did with it. 'You can't feel it. All you have to do is put a little of this jelly on it.' She demonstrated. 'And then you put it inside yourself, as high as you can. It will help prevent pregnancy, but not disease. To do that you must use a sheath, or french letter.' She held up the long rubber item. 'And you must wash it after every time.'

'Can't see my man using that!' a woman shouted.

'Then you must be careful in your choice,' Jeannie told her. 'Have intercourse with only one man.' She looked at each woman. 'And marry him first.'

'That's the easy part,' another woman yelled. 'It's getting him to keep his willy to himself that's difficult.'

'I have a leaflet for each of you to take home, and please tell all your friends,' she said to the twenty women before her. 'I will be here at the same time next week.' She gave each woman a handbill. 'Remember to tell your friends!' she called as the last one left. Then she sighed. Only twenty. But it was a start.

'So, how was your meeting?' Ross Macintosh's voice echoed across the empty hall.

'Fine.' For some reason she was glad he was there. 'But what are you doing here?'

'I was curious as to what you were telling them.' As he walked towards her, she could hear the sound of his leather soles on the wooden floor.

'Or was it the sight of Angus Carmichael's car outside?' She watched as he reached the table and picked up the diaphragm.

'Actually, yes.' He looked around. 'Is he still here?'

Jeannie laughed. If nothing else, Ross was honest.

'Well, Jeannie,' Angus walked back into the hall, 'how did it go?'

'Slowly.'

'Mr Macintosh, hello,' Angus said. 'What brings you here?'

'Same as you.' Jeannie patted Ross's arm. 'Moral support.'

'Margaret and I will be heading off now. I was going to invite Jeannie for a late supper.' He looked meaningfully at Ross.

'Why not come with us?' Margaret walked over to the group.

'Not at all,' Ross replied. 'I don't mind sharing Jeannie with you.'

They handed the key to the caretaker and went to Angus and Margaret's elegant home.

'Your grin is spread all over your face,' Jeannie remarked, as they went inside. 'Can't you be a little less pleased with yourself?' But she smiled despite herself. It was nice to be part of a couple, even if it was simply for appearances. 'Good God, Ross Macintosh, you're possibly the only man that could make me seem subtle.' But something about Ross made her smile. He was so transparent, black and white. You knew where you stood with him.

After an evening of pleasant conversation, Ross drove Jeannie home, then went back to Pathhead and the pub where he knew Tam would be.

'Where have you been?' he said, as Ross walked in.

'Some friends invited me for supper.' He walked over to the bar and called for a pint.

'Bloody hell.' Tam laughed. 'You'll be having tea in a cup with a saucer next and sandwiches with the crusts cut off.'

But Ross was too happy to take offence.

Chapter 11

The next week a few more women came, and the week after even more. And each went home with a contraceptive, courtesy of Margaret.

'You seem to be getting through to them,' Jim remarked, as he packed his bags for the evening.

'Well, I'm beginning the women's surgery soon, and that's the acid test.' Jeannie rubbed her gritty eyes as she got out the microscope. 'I might as well have a look at these samples, see what the locals have caught now.' She shook her head. 'If they would only try to keep themselves cleaner and eat more vegetables. They've got no money but they seem to live on dripping and whatever you can buy from the chip shop. Fresh produce from the market is cheaper and healthier.'

'Well, they can't afford a cook, or even a kitchen.' Jim attempted to lock his case, and put string round the large box he was carrying. 'Remember that they're out all day trying to earn some money, or just getting away from their miserable existences.'

'No, that doesn't wash,' said Jeannie. 'They're all on relief so they can't work and they've plenty of time to buy good food.'

'You still don't understand what it's like for these people.' Jim picked up his load. 'You can't force people to change, Jeannie, and you aren't always as right as you think you are.'

Jeannie glared at Jim. 'I'm not giving up on these women,

Jim,' she said. 'I'm going to make them change the way they live.'

'Whether they like it or not?'

'Sometimes people don't know what's good for them.' She stuck her chin out pugnaciously. 'And they need people like me to tell them.' She folded her arms. 'I suppose that makes me what you would call a do-gooder.'

Jim looked at her warily. 'You missed your calling, Jeannie,' he said, with a grin. 'You should have been a nanny.'

Jeannie stood outside the committee room. She wanted to laugh but she couldn't. Despite everything she was nervous. They had to understand that what she was teaching wasn't disgusting or revolutionary. But she had upset their sensibilities, told their wives and daughters secrets that only male doctors were allowed to know. And she had the uneasy feeling that, no matter what she said, the committee had already decided their verdict and were looking for a reason to find her guilty of bringing the club into disrepute. She set her lips as the door opened and a man nodded for her to come in. She was not going to make it easy for them.

'Good evening,' she said brightly, as she faced the seven men sitting behind a desk. 'Is this one for me?' She pointed to a thin-backed chair that faced them.

'Yes.' Mr Macintyre pursed his lips and peered over his glasses at the piece of paper. 'Miss Macdonald,' he intoned, 'you have been charged under section four, clause three paragraph one, of bringing the club into disrepute. How do you plead?'

'Plead?' Jeannie said innocently, stifling a smile. Mr Macintyre looked more than usually like an off-duty pantomime dame. 'I thought you were interested in what I was doing, not having some kind of mock trial.'

'How do you plead to the charge of bringing the club's good name into disrepute?' he repeated, his watery eyes narrowing.

'Well, I haven't.'

'That is for us to decide,' Mr Macintyre informed her.

'You seem to have come to your conclusion already,' she returned tartly. 'All I did was hold a talk on women's health. For women only. It didn't concern men and I had to be frank about matters that might embarrass ladies if they were discussed in front of their husbands.'

'Ridiculous!' Mr Macintyre blustered. 'Wives should have no secrets from their husbands.'

'Would you really like to listen to me talking about menstruation, Mr Macintyre,' she asked. 'About what happens during the cycle? And have your wife and daughter there with other men when I discuss in detail the most intimate workings of the female body?'

Mr Macintyre blushed.

'So, what were you talking about, Dr Macdonald?' Sir Justin Fleming asked, with a grin.

'About women's bodies, what happens when they are with child, and advances to enable women to determine when their children are conceived so that they arrive at the right time to fit in with their husbands' busy lives.' She looked innocently at each committee member. 'The right time for the school term, so that they are able to get the best schooling. The right time for the hunting season, or so no one has to go to India in the aforementioned state . . .'

'You are encouraging fornication,' Mr Macintyre accused her. 'With this knowledge you will lead these poor women astray.'

'There isn't anyone to stray with!' she burst out. 'There's hardly a spare man left in the country.' As she said it she saw Macintyre's face redden, but this time with anger. 'What I'm telling them won't cancel out years of teaching from the Church or their families.'

'Some women have already put such sensibilities behind them,' he replied nastily.

'If someone has decided to live that way then surely it is better that I show them a way to avoid becoming pregnant out of wedlock?' she said, in a puzzled voice. 'After all, a woman has to sleep with someone and no one wants a bastard in the family.'

The committee looked around worriedly. Was Macintyre the only one who would speak? she wondered.

'Is there any chance you could tell me the names of the fallen women in the club?' Sir Justin sounded amused.

'If it makes it any easier I could promise not to hold another lecture here,' Jeannie said quietly. 'I have no intention of offending anyone.'

Mr Macintyre nodded. 'I think that will be all, Miss Macdonald,' he said sternly. 'You will be hearing from us within the week.'

Jeannie walked from the room. Why couldn't she just have kept her mouth shut a little longer? Why couldn't she have apologised and then it could all have been forgotten? Why couldn't she have let those silly men have their say, then gone away? She strode grimly along the hallway, went out to her car and drove home.

A few days later she received the letter informing her of the committee's decision. She opened it at breakfast and giggled.

'What's funny?' Innes asked, between spoonfuls of porridge.

'I've been banned from the club for a month and forbidden to give any other talks there.' She laughed. 'Have you ever heard the like?'

'What on earth have you been doing?' Innes went over and took the letter from her.

'I gave a talk on women's health.' She raised her hands in mock-innocence. 'Hardly radical stuff.'

'Have you any idea what this means?' Innes thrust the letter in front of her face. 'Have you any idea what you're doing to our good name?'

'Innes, your father gambled away every penny you had.'

'Don't you dare criticise him!' He stormed away to the window.

'I'm not criticising him,' she said. 'But can't you see how silly and snobbish they're being?'

'It doesn't matter if they are being silly.' Innes stared out of the window. 'It's a matter of being able to hold up your head in public.'

'I can hold up my head in public,' she replied. 'And the ban is only for a month. Four weeks. I spent longer away from the club when I was at university.'

'You've been cut. It will affect you in other ways,' Innes said tightly.

Jeannie laughed. 'Look, Innes, I've lost Kyle and Daddy. I spent years at university on sufferance simply because I was female and there were no men to take up the places. No one in my chosen profession will employ me and I have to work in the slums to make ends meet. Compared to that, what Macintyre and his bunch at the club have done pales into insignificance, doesn't it?'

'You've made this family into a laughing-stock! And you've usurped me as the head of it!' With that Innes left the room.

'Do you really want to be head of a family like ours?' Jeannie called after him.

'Wearing the trousers again?' Fiona drawled, as she walked into the dining room.

'I've been banned from the club for a few weeks.' Jeannie rolled her eyes heavenwards.

'You really have no idea how to play the game, do you?' Fiona trilled, as she helped herself to some scrambled eggs from the row of silver salvers.

'How should I play it?' Jeannie stared at her cousin.

'Couldn't you try to make yourself a bit less hearty and bit more feminine? More like me?'

'I plucked my eyebrows till there's hardly anything left of them and I got some dresses.'

'Yes, but you stride about in them as if you're climbing a mountain.' Fiona raised an eyebrow. 'And you ought to have known that they wouldn't stand for a talk on sexual intercourse.'

'And which of your friends would want six children?' Jeannie said.

'You could have just let it be known that you were able to help women.' She looked up. 'I'd like one of those french caps,' she murmured casually.

'It's a dutch cap or french letter,' she remonstrated. 'But why? You and Hamish . . .'

Fiona looked at her pityingly. 'For what it's for,' she said.

Jeannie got up. 'Perhaps it's about time you started a family with Hamish. A child might help him.'

'I already have a child!' Fiona sniped. 'How else would you describe my husband?'

'Hamish is ill.' Jeannie flew to his defence as always.

'And his illness means he cannot hold a conversation for more than five minutes because he forgets what he's saying, avoids socialising because he gets nervous in company, can't make simple decisions about what tie to wear and can't be a proper husband because at night he urinates during a nightmare.' Fiona's glittering eyes were cold. 'Have you any understanding of what it's like for me to suffer the indignity of being married to a man like that?'

'But he's your husband, he loves you,' Jeannie persisted. 'It shouldn't matter.'

'But it does matter,' Fiona snapped. 'It matters more than anything.' She stalked out of the room, her back poker straight.

Jeannie finished her breakfast and drove over to Pathhead. A crowd of people were waiting at the surgery. She collected her instruments, put on her mask and waited for the first patient, a young girl.

'I saw your notice,' she began nervously.

'My women's-health one?' Jeannie said. 'It's really just for married women, you know.'

'I got told it was how to stop babies. They said you knew how to get rid of them.'

Jeannie stiffened. 'It is illegal to do that operation.'

The girl swallowed. 'I'm desperate, Doctor, he'll kill me if he finds out.'

'I am not an abortionist,' Jeannie told her, 'but if you're pregnant, I can help you. The parish . . .'

'The parish will send me to an unmarried mothers' home and make me work my fingers to the bone!' the girl cried. 'They treat you like dog muck in there.'

'The parish is for people like you who need help.'

'I want you to get rid of my baby.' She threw down a collection of coins. 'I can pay for it. See?'

Jeannie took a deep breath. 'I will not abort your child, and if you value your life you'll not go to one of those women either.'

'I have no choice.' The girl began to weep. 'I'm not married, I'm a housemaid over by Raith Park. It's the master's. If they find out I'll be on the streets.'

'I'm sorry.' Jeannie stood up and put her hand on the girl's shoulder. 'I can't give you an abortion.' She squeezed the shoulder and felt the unaccustomed warmth of good fabric.

'I can come again, when it's late.' The girl looked up. 'I can pay good money.'

Jeannie crouched down. 'It isn't a matter of money. It's a matter of what I can do in law. And my duty is to care for people.'

'Having this baby will kill me.' The girl burst into heartrending sobs as Jeannie patted her shoulder again. Little puffs of dust rose up from the coat. But why would a coat be dusty? It made it look older and more used. And her shoes were good, if a trifle worn. And soft kid gloves.

'I'm sorry, but the parish will be the only ones to help you now.' Jeannie's uneasiness about the girl was growing by the moment.

'Please!' She grabbed Jeannie's arm. 'You're a woman. What would having a baby do to you?'

'I sympathise, but there's nothing I can do except advise you on ways to care for yourself until you deliver the child.'

The girl grabbed her bag and stormed out.

'I have addresses of charities,' Jeannie called after her, but the girl had gone. Jeannie rushed out of the door after her and stopped.

'I tried, Mr Birse, but she wasn't having any of it,' the girl was saying, to a young man in a dark grey suit and bowler hat.

'Did you offer to pay for it?' he asked earnestly, as he stroked the neatly trimmed black moustache that highlighted his thin, almost sharp features.

'Aye, but she just kept saying she didn't do abortions. Sorry, but she just refused.'

Mr Birse sighed. 'It would have been a better story if she hadn't.'

'A better story?' Jeannie asked, as she walked over to them. Two young boys ran past with a wooden hoop. 'What are you talking about?'

The girl and the man exchanged glances.

'I'm from the *Courier*,' he said eventually. 'We heard reports that you were offering abortions.'

'I'm a doctor. I have morals and there are laws to which I adhere.' She stared at each in turn. 'And far too much work to be talking with someone who has so little to fill his life that he indulges in mischief-making.'

'It was a proper investigation,' Mr Birse insisted.

'If you wanted to know what I did,' she hissed, 'why not ask me?'

'If you were an abortionist, Dr Macdonald,' he said calmly,

'would you have told me?' He smiled. 'Now I can tell my readers that it isn't true.'

'You will write nothing about me, Mr Birse,' she said furiously. 'Now, go and find a story in some of these streets, with some of the people who have no choice but to live here, with no work and nothing to look forward to until they die a horrible death from an illness they had no way of avoiding. Surely that's enough scandal even for you.' She turned and marched back to the surgery.

'If you need me, the name's Robert Birse,' he called to her retreating figure.

'I'll never need you,' she muttered, as she walked back inside and was surrounded by people. 'Next!'

'So, the girl was working for a reporter?' Jim said, after surgery that morning.

'It would appear so.' Jeannie busied herself with writing up the never-ending stream of patients' notes.

'Well,' Jim said thoughtfully, 'it was bound to happen.'

'It's happened and it's over with, so maybe I'll be able to go about my business now.' She sighed in exasperation. 'Perhaps I'll even get a chance to do some work.'

'First night of the clinic tonight,' Jim said. 'At least you'll have a chance to look your critics in the eye now. And show them how wrong they are?'

'Yes,' Jeannie smiled with satisfaction. 'They'll soon realise I'm right.'

'As usual?' Jim ventured. 'Has it ever occurred to you that you need to consider what other people think?'

'But I'm right, Jim,' Jeannie said, with utter conviction. 'And they'll see that eventually.'

'If you say so,' he muttered.

But when she arrived at the surgery that evening, Jeannie was in for a shock. A group of women was standing outside, sheltering from the drizzle that seeped into every crevice. And across the road, standing at the open door of an unlicensed public house, was a band of men.

'Ladies.' Jeannie nodded to them as she went to open the surgery door.

'Harlots!' one man shouted.

'Whores!' another called.

'Got the pox, the lot of you!'

She ushered the women into the surgery, but as she did so, she saw that the number had dwindled. 'Don't let them upset you, ladies,' she said, but she could see they were frightened. 'Now, who was first?' She could smell the damp arising from the women and they were a pathetic sight. Carefully she lit the lamp, but the dim, amber light only highlighted the guilty, suspicious air that had pervaded them. She went into her consulting room and lit her own lamp. Now she felt as if she was doing something wrong, and her throat constricted. It was nothing more than a band of ruffians, she told herself sternly. But her shaking hands betrayed her.

One at a time the women made their way in. Jeannie gave them a cursory examination – she couldn't afford to test them for syphilis unless they showed symptoms. Then she demonstrated putting in the cap by poking it inside a pot that had once contained heather honey, Hamish's favourite.

As the evening wore on, Jeannie's enthusiasm waned. She didn't feel much like a crusader, and the women didn't seem grateful. They didn't want to talk about what they were doing, or why they had chosen to do it. It was almost as if they were trying to pretend that they weren't really practising family planning. Was this how it felt to visit an abortionist? she wondered, as she washed her hands in the bowl.

The next patient came in and tried to compose herself in the dusty half-light. 'There's more of them out there now,' she said fearfully.

'Well, they'll just have to wait their turn, like you did,'

Jeannie said, as she reached over to the boiler to take out some scissors.

'No, I mean men,' she muttered. 'Those men outside, shouting in the street.'

'Just letting off a bit of steam,' Jeannie replied, as she opened the package that contained the contraceptive. 'Lie down so I can examine you.'

A flaming rock hurtled through the window, narrowly missing both women. The patient screamed but Jeannie, with a presence of mind that was more instinct than sense, threw the bowl of water in which she had washed on to it and tipped the woman under the table.

'What on earth—' The woman pulled her clothes round her as they heard the roar of the small mob, which was pressing against the window now. Someone must have had the sense to lock the front door.

'Now,' Jeannie said, as the flaming rock was followed by a hail of stones, some alight, but most just heavy and sharp, 'you should leave.' She sent the woman in to the pharmacy, where there was a door that led out to the back of the building, then went back to see the others. 'I think we should stop for tonight, ladies,' she said, above the mêlée of cursing, breaking windows and screaming. There was a crash as a stone smashed the barred reception window. 'Out now, ladies!' She pushed and hustled the women through the narrow corridor to the pharmacy from where they could escape.

In the pharmacy, the air was heavy with the smell of burning sugar: the paper wrapped round the rock was coated with it to make it flame better. The windows were mostly broken now, and Jeannie could see that it was only a matter of minutes before the mob broke the wooden frames and were in the surgery. She rushed to the windows. The faces outside were dirty and unfocused, as if they were drunk – on liquor or power, she didn't know which.

'Listen to me, you'll destroy this place!' she shouted, but to no avail. The wooden frames cracked, and she felt a smack on the side of her head as another burning rock hit her. She reeled, then saw a hand reach through the broken glass and cracked wood.

'No!' She grabbed the hand and pushed the forearm down hard on a jagged shard. She heard the scream, like that of an animal, and felt the arm rip as it was pulled back. The smell of blood was in the air, and Jeannie knew she was in trouble.

She dashed to the main surgery and had time only to bar the door as she heard a man throw himself heavily against it. Then the other window was smashed, showering her with glass. Blood ran down her face, as if she had been stabbed with a thousand pokers.

'No!' she screamed, but it was too late. She grabbed the poker from the old fireplace and brought it down heavily on an arm reaching through the window. She heard a scream and the arm was snatched back. Jeannie ran towards the pharmacy, and opened the precious drug store. She had to stop the mob getting the small supply of medicines.

'Ah!' The final window smashed, and a hail of glass caught her left side, slicing into her skin and shredding her clothing. Jeannie felt the pain hit her, and it seemed to sedate her.

Suddenly Ross Macintosh was beside her. And the mêlée seemed louder.

'Now, Jeannie.' He was at the back door. 'Now!'

'But the opium.' It was difficult to concentrate on what was happening. She could see a man climbing through the broken window and stumbling into the room.

'Leave it.' He rushed past her and punched the thug, who reeled back, clutching his nose. 'Go.' He grabbed the man and threw him outside, in a rush of splintering wood and shouting men.

'But—'

'Have you any idea what they will do if they catch you?' He turned and put his arm round her waist, forcing her to the door.

'I will not let myself be bullied.' But he almost threw her into the back alley. 'What are you doing here?'

'I was worried about you,' Ross said, as he helped her up. 'You're bleeding.'

'I know.' Her hands went to her head and she felt the glass sharp in her scalp. Then she saw that her blouse was ripped.

'Come on.' He took her hand and together, with four other men carrying iron bars, they made their way to Ross's car.

'Why aren't the police here?' she asked, as they climbed in.

'No one's called them.' He started the engine.

'But surely someone must have seen what happened?'

Ross laughed as he drove away. 'Round here no one sees anything.' He glanced at her quickly. 'I'll take you home. You're bleeding like a stuck pig.'

'Not home.' Jeannie met his gaze. 'I ought to go to Jim's.'

Ross looked at her. 'He'll be fou. Isn't there another doctor?'

'What?'

'He'll be drunk.'

'Please.' She put a hand on Ross's arm.

Chapter 12

When they arrived at Jim's house in a quiet end of the town, Jeannie realised that Ross knew her partner better than she did. Jim was quietly drunk, sitting in front of the fire toying with his glass.

'You have to help me,' she began, in a shaky voice. 'The surgery was attacked.'

'Good job I moved everything out.' He opened a door and she saw, in his bare, functional kitchen, the contents of the pharmacy.

'You knew?' she said incredulously. 'You knew this would happen and you let me go there on my own?'

'Nothing I could do to stop you. Let's get that glass out of you. You're covered with it. Get that shirt off, woman.'

'But I had patients. That mob terrified them.' They continued their argument as he took off her ruined high-necked blouse and shook it. Glass fell to the wooden floor like snowflakes.

'Nasty.' Jim looked at the shards protruding from her bloodstained hair and chest. 'Give me those scissors, Macintosh.'

Ross had been determinedly staring at the ground. Wordlessly, he did as he was asked.

'Brace yourself,' said Jim, and she put her hands on the table behind her. Ross cocked his head.

'That's the first out.' Jim eased out a splinter of glass and put it on the table next to her. Then he looked up at Ross. 'You'll get a crick in your neck doing that.'

Ross turned away.

'For God sake's man,' Jim said, 'give the girl something to hold on to.'

Silently Ross put his hand next to hers, felt her fingers curl round it and squeeze tightly. She was in a lot more pain than she was letting on. Despite himself, he felt a stab of admiration. He wouldn't look at her, but when Jim eased the liberty bodice off her shoulders he glimpsed her generous breasts, running with blood.

'There.' Jim poured some iodine on to a cloth and gave it to her. 'You'll sweat out the rest.'

'Thank you.' Jeannie held it to her head as Jim took off his cardigan and gave it to her. She slipped it on over her liberty bodice. 'But what will we do about our other problem?'

Jim shrugged and looked at Ross. 'You can come forward now. There's nothing to see that you haven't already.'

Jeannie turned her head to look at him, iodine high in her hairline, staining her blood-spattered hair brown. She took in his expression, and shakily pulled the cardigan round her, suddenly aware that both Ross and she had noticed her body's response to his gaze.

'Jeannie, Mr Macintosh is a man, and all men, with the exception of doctors and undertakers who know just how mundane the human body can be, will peek when a woman takes off her shirt.' Jim gathered up the instruments and wiped them down with alcohol.

'Who started the riot?' Jeannie wanted to make sense of the events.

Ross leaned back against the kitchen cabinet. 'There's a lot of opposition to you, Dr Macdonald,' he said. 'From all quarters.'

Jim opened a bottle of whisky and poured three measures. 'Just takes a few words to some hotheads when the pubs come out. Wasn't anyone in particular.'

'But why?' Jeannie said, as she took the glass. 'Why would a man be angry that I was showing his wife how to avoid falling with child every time they come together?'

'What is the mark of a man, Jeannie?' Jim drained his glass and poured himself another.

'Good manners, social responsibility.' She looked directly at Ross. 'Kind, successful, solvent.'

'Ross?'

'Strong, in charge of his life . . .'

'His life?' Jim persisted.

'His family. His sons,' Ross said.

'What about daughters?' Jeannie took a slug of the whisky.

'No one cares about daughters,' Ross told her. 'It's how many sons you father that makes you a man.'

'But that's ridiculous.' Jeannie coughed as the cheap whisky burned her throat.

'Is it?' Jim offered the bottle to the others. 'Look at our royal families. Victoria's children ruled Europe. She had nine children. If the mark of a successful royal family is how many sons you have, why should it be different for any other man?'

'Do you really believe that?' She stared hard at Ross.

He hesitated, then nodded. 'It's all right when you're mucking about with a woman, you don't want her to fall then, but when I get married I don't want my wife to decide such things.'

'Because?' Jeannie said, her hackles rising.

'Because I'd end up with only one or two children, and what if they were girls?'

'What indeed!'

'Now, Jeannie.' Jim put a hand on her shoulder. 'Mr Macintosh has told us his views. You may not agree with them, but at least think about what he has said. Opposition to your work stems from the more respectable of our patients, not the lowest.'

'But they're wrong!' Jeannie stamped her foot. 'You have no idea what you're talking about, Mr Macintosh.' She walked over to him. 'You talk as if your wife is your property, like a horse whose only function is to serve you and breed.'

'Fine! Tell me I'm wrong!' Ross's temper had frayed till he couldn't control it any longer. 'Then you go and tell that mob back there that they're all wrong too. Think about the kind of hearing you'll get.' He picked up his coat. 'And while you're at it, did you know that you're an abortionist? That's what they all think.' He stormed out of the house and got back in his car.

'Ross!' Jeannie ran after him, clutching the cardigan about her. 'Don't go, please.'

Ross stared ahead. 'Why not?' He spoke precisely, as the elocution teacher had taught him.

'Because I've no other way to get home.'

'Left your broomstick at the clinic, did you?' He leaned over and opened the door. 'Get in.'

They drove to Jeannie's home.

'Park at the back,' she said quietly, as she rifled through Jim's cardigan for a handkerchief, found one and, after a cursory examination, discarded it. She felt run down and miserable. She just wanted to go and hide where there was no one to tell her she was wrong, or she was stupid, or that she was acting like a fool.

'For crying out loud,' Ross snapped, 'I saved you from a mob who would have beaten you into a pulp and I can't use the front door?'

'I don't want my family to see me like this.' She tucked her top lip behind the lower one in a curiously childlike gesture. 'Give them another excuse to harangue me.' She touched his shoulder. 'Not everyone knows me the way you do. They think I'm playing, doing a little something for charity. They don't understand like you do.'

'Has it ever occurred to you that you might not always be right?' Ross said, as he parked at the back of the house and came round to open her door.

'What I'm doing is the right thing,' Jeannie replied, with utter conviction. 'Thank you for what you did tonight.' She thought for a moment. 'But how did you know there would be trouble?'

'As you said, Jeannie, you don't become as successful as I have without getting your hands dirty. And if you tell me when you're doing your clinic I'll have a man watching to make sure it doesn't happen again.'

'It *won't* happen again!' Jeannie retorted hotly, then felt herself blush. 'What I mean is—'

'What you meant to say is, "Thank you for your kind offer of help for my clinic,"' Ross replied smoothly. 'We both know that as long as you have it, you will have the problem.'

'Thank you, Mr Macintosh,' she said, as she looked into his eyes. 'For whatever reason you were there, thank you. And thank you for helping me. So many people don't want to. But I can't pay you back.'

'There is something you could do,' Ross said softly. 'I'd like you to allow me to escort you to the club. I'm not asking to court you. It's just that you don't have a partner and neither do I.' He kept his eyes lowered as he said it, as if he was ashamed.

'There are no expectations of romance on your part?' she said nervously, unsure how she wanted him to answer.

'I know my place, Dr Macdonald,' he replied.

Jeannie's stomach lurched.

'Then yes, I agree. That would be an acceptable trade for your man to be at my women's clinic,' she said, too brightly. 'Once I can return there of course.'

She waited for him to answer, but he merely nodded, got back into his car and drove off.

The next day, Jeannie and Jim tried to run their surgery while two cleaners cleared up the mess and two glaziers put in new windows, but it was well nigh impossible. As people walked in, she examined their faces closely: if she found a single one of the mob, she would send him straight to prison.

'See the lads were round,' Charlie remarked, as he walked into the surgery to have a look, his boots crunching on the glass.

'Any idea whose they were?' Jim asked, as he shook the single chair they had left and blew thin needles of glass off it.

'I'll have a word. Shite!' Charlie pulled his hand away from the shattered cabinet, two fingers bleeding.

'Come in, let's get that cleaned up,' Jeannie said wearily. 'If we've got anything left.'

'It's only a cut,' Charlie said patronisingly. 'Just a wee rag or something will do.'

'Hold this.' Jeannie handed him a bandage, and went to fetch disinfectant.

'I'll have a word to a few people,' Charlie said cheerily, as Jeannie cleaned and bandaged his cut hand. 'It'll be worth my while, won't it?'

'Of course, Charlie,' she answered, through gritted teeth. 'Wouldn't expect anyone to do anything round here out of kindness, would we?'

The day stretched on, as the little band determinedly cleaned the place. Jeannie kept on her mask: the smell of vinegar disinfectant was stifling and her hands were red and wrinkled from constant immersion in water.

'My goodness,' Margaret's voice was as out of place in the little surgery as she herself was, 'what on earth happened?'

'Some local men object to my telling women how to be in charge of their own bodies.' Jeannie put her hands on her hips and blew a stray hair away from her nose. 'But what brings you here?'

'I wanted to . . . I was looking for something to take my mind off things,' Margaret said. Her hands, small in their kid gloves, played with the grey chiffon scarf she had arranged artfully at the neck of her slate and pastel yellow suit.

'It's not usually this bad,' Jeannie replied defensively, as she whipped off her apron. 'And how are you?' She made as if to examine her friend. 'A bit peaky, but that's normal for a woman in your condition. No sickness, cravings to eat coal?' She smiled.

Margaret shook her head, and put her hand to her mouth, evidently shaken by the reality of life in the slums. 'What kind of women do you get here?' she asked quietly.

'Poor ones. Sick ones.' Jeannie waited for Margaret to stumble out an excuse that she wouldn't be able to help the clinic. Because Macintyre or one of his cronies had got to her.

'What diseases?' She glanced about her, as if the building housed them, in the damp walls, the rotten wooden skirting-boards, the broken windows.

'All kinds, but mainly chest infections, diseases they get from their surroundings.' Jeannie cocked her head to one side. Suddenly she was seeing her workplace as she had on that first fateful visit. 'And, trust me, I wouldn't know what to do without your donations. I haven't told Angus, don't worry.'

'Do you have to deal with women of the night?' Margaret asked.

Jeannie looked at her curiously. 'Well, they don't tell me that that's what they are and I don't ask. It might seem odd, but if you know for certain it colours the way you look at them, and I mustn't let that happen.'

Now Margaret was tugging at a loose thread in her chiffon scarf. 'They have diseases?'

'Please don't say you won't allow your money to be spent on helping them,' Jeannie begged, 'because I want to treat anyone who comes to see me, not just those whom someone like Innes would deem worthy.'

'I didn't mean that. I meant what kind of diseases and how do you treat them?' Margaret persisted, with a certain elegant urgency in her questioning.

'Margaret, do you really want to know those details? They're rather salacious.'

'I've heard about syphilis.' Margaret shivered as she said the word.

'Syphilis?' Jeannie beckoned her into the treatment room. 'It's a death sentence, and you die in the worst possible way.'

'I thought it could be cured.'

'There is a cure but it doesn't always work, and it's expensive. It takes over two years sometimes. For my patients, there's no cure. The symptoms can be treated, but it attacks the internal organs, eats away at what we call soft tissue until it attacks the brain. Then you go insane and die.'

'How can you tell if they have it?'

'Lesions, like burns or ulcers. They start on women inside the body, but by the end you have them on your face. In the final stages people become reclusive.' She looked sympathetically at Margaret. 'If you want to help people with syphilis, I'm afraid there isn't much you can do.'

'But you can catch it anywhere,' Margaret said, horrified. Her chiffon scarf was unravelling at the end.

Jeannie laughed. 'Don't worry yourself, Margaret,' she said comfortingly. 'You can only catch syphilis from having sexual intercourse with someone who has it. So you and I are safe.'

Margaret's eyes widened.

'Have you been to one of those public-health lectures and got all worried about it?' Jeannie enquired.

'Foolish, I know.' Margaret turned away. 'Jeannie, because of my current condition, I have to change my will. I want you to have enough money to continue your work, whatever happens.'

'Thank you.' Jeannie smiled. 'Now, I was thinking about a trip into town for lunch. Do you want to come too?'

Margaret shook her head. 'There's something I have to do.' She walked over to Jeannie and embraced her. 'You keep yourself safe from everything, Jeannie.'

Jeannie tapped the mask round her neck. 'I always wear this.' She grinned. 'And I've got my own protection.' She hesitated for a moment. 'I'll come and see you at the weekend. We can go for a walk, since you'll not be riding any more.'

'You always did it better than me anyway,' Margaret said. 'Like everything else.'

It had been a hard afternoon ride over the low hills, and Jeannie's face was windblown but exultant. Hamish, too, was smiling, with some colour in his skeletal face.

'It's good news, isn't it?' Jeannie said, as she trotted back into the stableyard. 'About Margaret and Angus?'

'Yes,' Hamish replied pensively. 'Fiona's green with envy.' He dismounted and handed the reins of his horse to the waiting stable lad.

'What's wrong, Hamish?' she asked, as she jumped down, brushing the dust from her jodhpurs.

Hamish waited, then took her arm as they walked away from the stables, their high boots sliding on the mud and crunching over the small stones as they made their way towards the track that wound round the dyke-lined fields to their home.

'It's just . . .' he hesitated. 'I want to have a family, and Fiona does too, but since I've been ill . . .' He turned away.

'It's very common, Hamish, that problem,' Jeannie said gently, slightly shocked that Hamish could allude to something so personal. 'Have you spoken to Gordon MacLeod about it?'

'What can I say?' He turned to her, an agonised expression on his face. 'That I'm not man enough for work or for my marital duties?'

'Something like that would suffice.' She glanced around to ensure that no one was bearing witness to the conversation.

'Is there anything he could do?' He bit his lip. 'Fiona's an attractive woman, and she's not going to waste her time with someone like me if she can find a man who can satisfy her. It's shameful enough for her to have me here, like this.'

'There is nothing to be ashamed of, Hamish.' She looked him straight in the eye. 'You are ill, and don't ever let anyone tell you otherwise. What you have is like a chronic illness. It debilitates you in different ways. In time—'

' "In time!" Everyone says that – in time it will change!' he exploded pushing himself away from her. 'Well, it's 1922 and nothing has changed. I wasn't injured, I've got all my limbs. Look at me!' He stood before her, arms outstretched. 'Not a thing wrong with me.'

'Your injuries aren't physical. They're in your mind.'

'You know what happens at night. I have nightmares – only children have those.'

'These things happen.'

'But I don't want them happening to me!' he shouted. 'I don't care if they're happening to other people, *I* don't want them! And I have to live off your charity, Jeannie! A woman who goes out to work with the lowest people on earth, who sees real suffering every day of her life. I have to live off you!'

'I don't grudge you a single penny, Hamish,' she said. 'You know that.'

'But I begrudge you giving it to me, Jeannie!' He grabbed hold of a bare twig and pulled it down, but the sodden wood didn't snap: it simply stripped the wet bark off the larger branch from which it grew. 'Look at me. I can't even snap a twig any more.'

Jeannie took a deep breath. 'I don't have any patients with shell-shock, Hamish, so I don't know if there are new treatments. But I can look, write to a few places and enquire if they would be willing to have any men to try the remedies. Would you like me to see if there is anywhere you can have some treatment?' She looked up at the grey sky.

'I don't want to be an invalid, Jeannie,' he said desperately. 'All I want to do is hide in my room until I die. I don't want to see the world, not one full of people.'

'What do you want, Hamish?'

'Peace and quiet, Jeannie. Peace, quiet and my dictionaries.'

That night, as she waited in vain for women to turn up at her clinic, Jeannie had a chance to think about what Hamish had said. Was there any treatment he hadn't already attempted? Listlessly, she looked at the pile of old medical magazines lying in the corner – shell-shock was still a big talking-point. She leafed through them, but no one seemed able to show more than anecdotal evidence that anything had worked. But Hamish had said that, more than a cure, he wanted peace and quiet. Was that the problem? That Hamish wasn't the man-about-town he had been and Fiona still expected him to be?

Perhaps if she spoke to Fiona, tried to persuade her to take more of an interest. They always needed help in the clinic, and that might mean she would spend less time at the club, and less money they didn't have, mixing with people who made Hamish feel inadequate. Yes, she decided, as she gestured for the shabby middle-aged woman who had just entered the room to sit down, she would speak to Fiona. Make her see sense.

Chapter 13

Her mind playing over scenarios with her cousin, Jeannie slept ill that night. Before she knew it, morning had broken, she was putting on her clothes and heading back towards the mean streets of the town.

'Next!' she called, as she ushered out a coughing woman. 'Can you get the mop and bucket, please, Charlie?'

'Aye, Doctor.'

'Hasn't your hand healed yet?' She took hold of it.

Charlie just looked at her.

Gently Jeannie took off the bandage. The flesh under it was dark, the wound open and weeping. And there it was: the unmistakable sweet stench of gangrene. 'Charlie, you let it get infected,' she said. 'You, of all people, should know how important it is to keep a wound clean and dry.'

'Sorry, Doctor.'

'Come.'

They went back into her surgery and she cleaned it as best she could. 'Why didn't you show it to me before?' she asked.

'It's only a cut.'

She went next door and got Jim. Together they studied Charlie's rotting hand.

'The little finger will have to come off,' he said eventually.

'But I need my fingers, all of them,' protested Charlie.

'This way we'll be able to save the rest of the hand before it becomes infected. If it isn't too late.' Jeannie put her hand on the child's arm.

'But I can't go to America with only one hand!'

Jeannie felt a stab of guilt. 'Get your coat,' she said. 'I'll take you over to the infirmary now.'

'How is he?' Jim said, as she arrived back at the clinic later that day.

'Two fingers have to come off,' she said regretfully. 'We should have spotted it, Jim.'

'He's his own person.' Jim looked at his watch. 'I'll need to get someone for tonight.'

'He's a child,' Jeannie said, exasperated. 'And we have conveniently ignored that because it suited our own ends.'

'Jeannie, for the first and last time, take a look around you. The people round here don't have a chance to be children. By the time they're six, they've experienced more life than you will probably ever have to.'

'That doesn't make it right.'

'Aye, but it's life. Get used to it.' He looked around. 'At least we've still got Buster. I'm not going up those lanes without a bit of help.' He caught her expression. 'What? It wasn't your fault he let his hand get infected.'

Jeannie stood still, gazing at her own fingers. 'I could have done more.' Because she knew that she could.

That night, as she sat in her surgery, she thought of the people who were coming in. There was no one with shell-shock. After the last had left, she went into the notes store to look it up.

'What are you doing?' Jim said, as he saw her opening drawer after drawer.

'My cousin has shell-shock, and nothing I've read mentions the ordinary soldier, just the officers.'

'Shell-shock is too expensive an ailment for someone round here to suffer from,' he said. 'If a man comes back from the war with the likes of that, they're left in a back room to die of some lung complaint. Doesn't take long, as you can imagine.'

'That isn't fair,' Jeannie said. 'It isn't right.'

'But it's the way of the world, Jeannie,' Jim replied patiently. 'How is someone going to afford expensive medical care? We can't give electric-shock treatment.'

'I don't know,' she said slowly. 'Why can't the government pay for some of it? They sent those poor men off to war.'

'And the rest of us pay more tax?'

'I never said that.'

Jim took the last of the files from her hands. 'Accept it, Jeannie,' he said firmly. 'There are the rich who can afford to be ill, and the poor who rely on us. And no way for one to pay for the other.' He cleared his throat. 'And I see that your clinic isn't proving much of a draw.'

'The women can't come,' she replied defensively, 'not with all those men out there. And they say the priest is taking notes of all those who do come.'

'Well, now everyone knows you're a women's doctor,' Jim said thoughtfully, 'perhaps you could let them come at any time. A lot of the women ask for you anyway.'

'Just treat them as any other patient?' Jeannie said cautiously.

'Until it's sorted out and they feel happy coming at night, I think we have no other choice. Just be a little more circumspect about it, eh?'

'They'll never know,' Jeannie said. 'No one will realise.' She smiled. 'More than one way to skin a cat, Jim.'

'And more than one way to kill yourself.'

Jeannie looked at the clock. It was seven and Ross Macintosh was due: tonight was his first as her escort at a formal dance.

'What on earth are you doing here?' Fiona said, as Ross walked in through the door.

'Is Jeannie ready?' He appraised Fiona, who was always worth a second look.

'What? Isn't she a bit young for your tastes?' Fiona laughed aloud.

'She's a very pleasant young lady,' Ross said stiffly.

'She's an heiress.' Fiona smoothed her hands over her dress. 'Oops, here she comes. Still, someone like you isn't that choosy, are you, darling?'

Ross watched Jeannie walk down the stairs. She was wearing a dress that disguised a bosom he had admired on a number of occasions. Why on earth was she wearing something that made her look like a farmer's wife? She could buy herself dresses to emphasise her figure, which he considered womanly – many women were little more than skin and bone nowadays.

'Here at last?' She smiled tightly.

'Hamish isn't coming. He's unwell.' Fiona's face fell. 'We'll be an odd number.'

'You never complain when I'm the spare woman,' Jeannie added.

'You're used to it.'

'What about Innes?' Ross suggested.

'He telephoned. There's some disaster he must deal with. Someone has probably decided to die.' Fiona was singularly unamused by the timing.

'Can't imagine why the victim would want Innes there.' Jeannie grimaced. 'If I was about to shake off my mortal coil, I'd rather have someone slightly closer to God than him.'

As they arrived at the club, Ross could feel a self-satisfied smile on his face. There he was, walking in with Fiona Macdonald, the acknowledged beauty of the tennis club. How often had he watched her flit about? How often had he hung about on the edges of the fringes with whoever he had persuaded to sign him in as a guest, hoping that Fiona would make some remark to him, utter some amusing comment that showed she knew who he was? And he had been glad to fill their bellies with champagne, in return for the occasional dance. Because now he had officially become the women's escort. This was his chance.

'Would you be able to find me a clinic?' Jeannie said as they sat at one of the tables.

'Why don't you stay where you are?' Ross acknowledged a passer-by whose shocked expression proved he had mistaken Ross for someone else.

'Jim gets donations from charities and others,' she raised her eyebrows, 'and they're concerned that I'm corrupting my patients' morals by playing God so I have to stop treating the women here although I'll still work with Jim on everything else.'

'Do we have to talk about your boring little life, Jeannie?' Fiona drawled.

'I was answering a question, but I know my work isn't to everyone's taste.' Jeannie put her hand on her brow. 'What did you do today, Fiona?'

Fiona's lips tightened and Jeannie had the unerring feeling she had upset her. She's worried about Hamish, she thought. That's why she's behaving like this.

'I'll just go and say a few hellos.' Jeannie excused herself and got up.

'Aren't you going after her, Ross?' Fiona said pointedly. 'You're her new lap-dog.'

'No.' He smiled into her eyes.

'I want to dance,' Fiona said, and looked around her. 'Ross, take me to dance so I can see if anyone interesting is in tonight.'

Jeannie saw Fiona and Ross get up to dance. So he had made another conquest. As she walked through the archway to the part of the hall the older members preferred, she kept the cheerful look on her face, only too aware that Ross was delighted to be with Fiona and that he was using her. At least she herself was safe with him, Jeannie consoled herself. Ross was here as her escort and he was dancing with Fiona out of duty, a charitable act that Hamish would approve of. Perhaps it was the ideal solution.

But where were the Flemings? She strode confidently towards the quieter alcoves where they usually sat.

'Have you seen Sir Justin?' she asked an elderly solicitor friend of her father's.

'Have you not heard?' his wife said. 'It's Margaret.'

'The baby?' Jeannie said in alarm.

'Was she expecting a baby?' the solicitor, Mr Farnham, said. 'Apparently it was a riding accident. They did everything they could but . . .'

'She's dead?' Jeannie asked, as the room spun round her. 'But I spoke to her only a few days ago.'

'Terrible tragedy.' Mrs Farnham nodded. 'That poor woman. She had her life ahead of her.'

'Yes, thank you.' Jeannie went out to the patio, where she always fled when she couldn't face the crowd. Margaret had been her closest female friend since they had played together in the garden at Hilltop House. They had shared secrets at boarding-school and Jeannie had been a bridesmaid at Margaret's society wedding. Now she was dead. There were tears in her eyes and she rummaged through her embroidered evening bag for her handkerchief.

'Jeannie?' Ross walked over to her. 'Fiona has found another partner, so we can . . . You're crying.'

'Margaret's dead.' Her voice came out in a high-pitched squeal.

'Margaret?' Ross said. 'Margaret Carmichael?'

Jeannie nodded. 'Oh, Ross, she was the loveliest, sweetest person in the world. My best friend. She gave me the money to start my women's clinic because she wanted to help.' She put her head in her hands, barely aware that his arm was moving round her shoulders and that he was pulling her to him.

'Come on, Dr Macdonald,' he said gently. 'Fiona will be fine with her friends.'

When they arrived, the house was in darkness.

'You have a lovely home,' he remarked.

'It's only a house.' Jeannie opened the door and walked along the tiled hallway. 'An enormous, empty, unhappy house.' She opened the doorway that led into the drawing room. 'And the fire's gone out.'

'I'll light it if you pour the drinks.'

He took some kindling and soon the room was bathed in warm, amber half-light. He sat down and patted the sofa next to him. 'Tell me about her.'

Jeannie sat down and Ross put his hand on her arm. 'She was like the sister I never had.' She accepted Ross's monogrammed handkerchief. 'I grew up with my brother and my father – my mother died when we were babies. My father was a countryman, and there was his brother, too, and Hamish and Innes. We used to climb trees and go riding, and I was just another boy. But then I met Margaret and I had someone I didn't have to be strong or brave with. We went to school together and had our Season together. That's when she met Angus, Hamish's friend.' She laughed sadly. 'She used to say we should have had a joint wedding, but I was her bridesmaid.' She looked up. 'I'm sorry, you must think I'm so weak, getting upset like this.'

'You're a woman, Jeannie, and women cry over loss, especially of someone who meant as much to them as Margaret did to you.' He brushed away a stray hair that had fallen into her eye. 'Would you like me to accompany you to the funeral?'

'That would be very kind of you,' Jeannie murmured, shakily.

Ross put his hand on hers. 'You'd do it for me,' he said simply.

*

The funeral took place in Innes's church. As Ross took his place in the third pew next to Jeannie and Fiona, he could see people looking at him. And knew that his appearance would pay dividends. A society funeral was not as important as a society wedding but he was there. And it had been noted.

After the interment, Ross ignored the curious stares of the other mourners as he accompanied Fiona, Jeannie and Hamish to Sir Justin's country home for the traditional meal. And, being the man he was, he felt his heart quicken as he saw Aberleith Castle rise up from the wood that surrounded it. Although it was more of a thin, high lodge than a grand castle, he was there as an invited guest. His palms were sweating at the thought of shaking hands with a knight of the realm. Then he looked at Jeannie, whose numb expression showed that she was still in shock at the death of her friend. He patted her hand. She smiled briefly and Ross was gratified that he had been of some comfort. He had never been formally introduced to Margaret, but his dealings with her husband hadn't endeared him to the family. This poor dead woman had lived off the money her husband made from the slum courts he owned. And he'd bet his last shilling Margaret had never shed a tear over her tenants' misery. Still, he mused, as he approached the reception line, it was an ill wind. He would now be acknowledged by the people here. Inadvertently, Jeannie had ushered him into her circle.

'Why has he come?' Innes asked. He had taken a pale, drawn Jeannie to one side as they enjoyed Sir Justin's hospitality.

'He was there when I found out, and offered to come to support me,' Jeannie murmured. 'It was kind of him.'

'He's an interloper. He sees this as a way to make friends. He's profiting from your grief.' He stopped as he saw Jeannie's shadowed eyes staring at him.

'Without him, there would have been only myself and Fiona,' she said. 'Hamish has retreated into himself and is scarcely able to hold himself together. Mr Macintosh is doing this out of friendship to me.'

'I suggest you find out what this friendship means to him,' Innes warned. 'Because I think it means something different from what it does for you.'

Jeannie could see Ross chatting to Angus, who was obviously isolated from the family. She forced herself to remember that Ross was doing it for her.

She walked over to Angus and took in his pain, evident in his stiff bearing. 'I'm so sorry, Angus.' She held back a sob.

He touched her fingers lightly. 'You've been so dear to us, Jeannie,' he murmured. 'And I know she would have liked you to have a keepsake. Please say you will.'

His face, so strong and yet vulnerable, the cut of his jaw and the softness of his brown eyes, made it impossible for Jeannie to refuse. 'Of course,' she replied, still stifling the tears that she wasn't allowed to shed in public. 'I'd love something to remember her by.'

Ross Macintosh, who was standing next to them, wondered if this was how the rich got richer: by passing it among themselves.

Jeannie pushed her unhappiness down inside her and continued with her work. No matter how wretched she felt, there was always a long queue of patients waiting for her, someone who needed her. Duty came before grief, before worry, before everything. And, much as Jeannie hated to admit it, it was a welcome relief.

The next week there was no mob – a steady drizzle had seen to that. But there were only a few women, either brave or ruined enough not to care what the men thought of them. For Jeannie, hiding in her work, nothing seemed to change. Mealtimes became a thing of the past, and as her clothes grew looser, she hardly noticed. She was too busy even to check her appearance. But as the last of the summer drifted carelessly into autumn, she felt ready to think about Margaret, to remember her without tears clouding her memories of happy times.

She found herself driving towards the house she had loved to visit, the one she had secretly coveted, when she realised she was flouting custom by visiting an unmarried man without a chaperone. But that was ridiculous, she rebuked herself. Angus was like a cousin to her. But he was also a charming, charismatic man. And Jeannie's denials sounded hollow even to her.

'Hello, Angus,' she said, as the housekeeper opened the door to his study where he was working, wearing a rather fetching cardigan over his shirt and tie. He looked pensive, as if life was grinding him down one day at a time. 'I'm sorry, I should have made an appointment but I was passing.'

'No, please.' He removed his thin-rimmed spectacles and jumped up to usher her into a studded leather armchair – an obligatory feature of everyone's study or library. 'I'm glad of the distraction. Business doesn't hold the same fascination it once did.'

'I can imagine.' Jeannie took a deep breath. 'But having a distraction such as work does help to . . .'

'Don't, Jeannie,' he said softly, 'don't look away. People do, when death is at hand. They turn their heads so they can't see it, or so that someone else can't see their reaction to it. I saw it in the trenches, but I never thought I would experience it on a daily basis with people I thought were my friends and family.'

'Oh, Angus,' Jeannie said, and without thinking she pulled him into her arms, trying to comfort him as she wanted someone to comfort her.

'God, Jeannie.' His voice was high and she felt his tears on her cheek. She closed her eyes and they wept together.

After a few minutes, Jeannie opened her eyes. Angus was watching her, the tenderness in his expression more loving than anything she had ever thought she would see for herself from another person.

'I didn't think I could be so honest with another person,' he whispered, 'but you aren't any other person, you're Jeannie.' And he smiled. And somewhere, even in her inexperience, Jeannie could sense that they had a bond that went deeper than grief, deeper than familiarity. A bond that went into her heart.

It was a few weeks before Jeannie consented to return to the club. But she had promised Ross to introduce him and knew that it was a way in which she could thank him for his help. The club was busy, with yet another dance, and as Ross escorted her and Fiona in, they caught sight of Innes talking to an older man and a younger, studious-looking woman.

'That's Innes's intended. Her name is Gail,' Jeannie whispered, 'and her father is very high up in the Kirk, so he won't want to be seen with the likes of Fiona and her fast set.' She gazed over at her cousin who was heading as usual for her friends.

'Oh, I'm well aware that I'm not good enough, Dr Macdonald,' he returned. 'I know what you think of me. It's the same as these people think of your being a doctor.'

Jeannie hesitated. She'd never thought of it like that before. 'It's just that you work at the wrong end of town,' she began.

'Two streets away from you,' he replied, as he scanned the crowd.

'And you don't have a family here,' she continued.

'Neither do you,' he replied.

'And your accent makes you sound like a servant.'

'A servant whose help they all need.' They went to take their places at the table.

'Are you accusing me of being snobbish?' she asked.

'You think you're better than me, don't you?' He held her gaze.

Jeannie blinked and stared at the tablecloth. 'Of course not. We're all God's creatures,' she murmured.

'Liar.' He turned to watch Fiona, who was talking to some friends.

'Hello Jeannie,' Bess Henderson, a friend of Innes's, came over to the table. 'How are you?'

'I'm well,' Jeannie said. The young woman before her was dressed in an A-line dress of puce velvet that drew attention to her stolid build. 'Have you met Ross Macintosh?'

Bess considered him over her glasses. 'No, but I'm pleased to meet you.' She turned her head back to Jeannie. 'I was at your meeting here.'

'Did you hear what happened to me because of it?' She grimaced.

'I thought it was none of their business,' Bess said vehemently. 'And I would like to talk to you,' she continued.

Jeannie saw that Ross was staring at Fiona and her friends. 'Why don't we take a turn round the patio?' she suggested.

'So, Bess,' she said guardedly, as they walked outside, 'how can I help you?'

'I wanted to get married, you know,' Bess said quietly, as she played with a stray hair that had fallen out of her severe, curled style, 'but the war came and I didn't get a Season. Now I'm too old and I just thought that no one . . .'

'Bess, a number of women here tonight feel the same way,' Jeannie said sympathetically. 'I'm not married either. There's no shame, just no husbands.' She laughed feebly.

'I've never been the belle of the ball,' Bess raised her wide shoulders, 'and when I met someone and they took an interest in me . . .'

'Are you with child, Bess?' Jeannie said quietly.

'I love him, Jeannie, with all my heart,' Bess said, 'but he's just a postman.'

'Poor yet respectable,' Jeannie said. 'Your parents object?'

'They won't have him in the house. You have to help me, Jeannie, you must be able to understand, being an expert on women's matters.'

'Well, you're presenting your parents with a *fait accompli* now,' she said. 'Why don't you just explain to them that you've found someone to love who will do his best to keep you? With their help or without.'

'I was wondering if I could have that little operation.'

'Bess, it's wrong!' Jeannie said shocked. 'You can't.'

'He doesn't want to know any more,' Bess said desperately.

'Then you must talk to your parents. You can go away to the country for a while and have the child adopted.'

'I couldn't give birth and send it away.'

'Then talk to your parents,' Jeannie said. 'Together you will work out your options.'

Chapter 14

'Jeannie, when you've a moment,' Jim said, as he pulled the mask from his face after surgery the next day.

'I've just finished. Only the specimens to look at and the others for the hospital,' she returned. 'After this one, of course.' She pointed to a pale woman, holding her stomach.

'You know we were talking about you moving your clinic to somewhere else?' he began.

'I'm looking at a possible clinic next week.'

'No point now.' He picked up a letter and handed it to her. 'Apparently the Ferguson Trust have decided that we aren't a suitable place for their money.' He snorted contemptuously. 'Made all their bloody money from slavery but are the most churchy people I know.' He threw the letter into the bin. 'Now I'll be fighting you for some money.' He pulled a comic face, but Jeannie could see the anger beneath it.

'I have a trust fund,' she said slowly. 'There's no reason why I can't use at least some of it now, is there?' She leaned back against the damp wall. 'After all, why can't I give to charity?' She smiled. 'And now I know how to get hold of some of it.'

'What will you do?'

'I'll ask Innes, he's my trustee. But I'm sure he'll do it. I'm keeping his family, after all.'

But the letter she got by return of post from her trustees wasn't what she had expected.

'I don't understand, Innes,' she said, as she stared at the letter. 'Why won't the trustees let me spend my own money?'

'Because you don't want to spend it, you want to give it away.' Innes poured out two parsimonious glasses of sherry in the chilly drawing room, the pale cream walls cold in the gathering gloom of winter and Innes's miserable fire. 'A small charitable donation would be acceptable but not on the scale you're proposing.'

'I'm not buying dresses, I'm trying to keep my clinic open.'

'Then why not apply for some charitable grants? There are plenty of foundations who give money out.' His hand rested on a dusty, lacquered urn. He removed it, brushed it with the other, and an expression of distaste marred his thin, peaked features.

'They are all church ones and you know what they think of my work. I'm a heretic going against God, remember?'

'I'm not your enemy, Jeannie,' he said evenly. 'I'm just a steadying hand on the tiller.' He stared at the sherry. 'I've no taste for this.' With that, he left the room and the confrontation.

'Do you have to shout?' Fiona came in, disapproval painted on her pretty features.

'My trustees won't give me my own money till I'm thirty or married!' She punched at the wall in front of her. 'It's ridiculous. I'm twenty-seven years old, and every day I make decisions that can affect whether people live or die!' She glared at Fiona.

'Then why don't you get married?' Fiona ran a red-tipped fingernail round the rim of Innes's abandoned glass. 'Surely there must be someone at the club.' She smiled as if she was privy to the secrets of the men in their circle.

'I'm not like you, Fiona,' Jeannie said slowly. 'I've never been the first to be picked for dancing.' She glanced up at the other woman, unwilling to admit the truth that stared her in the face every time she looked in the mirror. 'I can talk to them, but when it comes to romance, they forget I exist.' She sniffed. 'You don't know what it's like. I'm never going to find a husband.'

Fiona's face softened under the powder and paint. 'Perhaps if you let it be known about your money,' she began.

'I couldn't do that!' Jeannie was aghast. 'Have some gold-digger look towards me for what he could get?'

'Why not?' Fiona returned wryly. 'I always made a few enquiries about a gentleman's suitability before I let him court me.'

'But you married Hamish.' Jeannie put her hand to her mouth. 'I mean . . .'

'Hamish swept me off my feet.' Fiona picked up Innes's glass of sherry and drank it. 'When I met him he was wearing his uniform, and there had never been a more handsome man. And he would talk to me about his plans. About how he would come here and set up his own periodical, dedicated to hunting, shooting, all the manly pursuits.'

'Hamish wanted to be a publisher?' Her own problems forgotten, Jeannie stared at Fiona in amazement.

Fiona nodded. 'He was going to work with Angus until it was established. And I knew I wanted to be by his side when he did, going on trips to all the estates, meeting people, making a select circle of friends, perhaps even having my own salon.' Suddenly her face closed in.

'And instead he was injured,' Jeannie put in.

Fiona stared out of the window for what seemed like for ever.

'When it happened I thought he had been shot and had a head injury. I thought he would die. Then, as time went on, I began to wish he had. Sorry, I know that sounds brutal, but all I could think of was how we would live, with little or no money, on the family's charity. Sometimes it's like being in prison.' Her eyes glistened with bitter tears. 'I'll never have a place in society, other than as the wife of someone who isn't quite right. I'll never have children, never be seen as anything other than the girl who made an unlucky choice.' She pulled herself up abruptly. 'But enough of my problems. Let's see what we can do about getting you a husband.'

'You'll help me?' Jeannie felt nervous. Was Fiona playing another of her little games?

'Why not? After all, what else do I have to do all day?' She walked round to where Jeannie was standing. 'Look at your clothes! You dress like a matron.' Her hand swept over the serviceable navy dress that Jeannie was wearing. 'You've lost weight and that dress hangs off you like a sack. Since you're not me, you don't look attractive in it. You'll need to visit a dressmaker, and do something about your hair.'

'But I wear the dresses you recommended and I still look clumsy.'

'Yes, but you stride about in them like a man. And stop trying to join in the men's conversations. When you talk to them, make sure they know you're there and that you're a woman. No talking about business, talk about them, men love that. And smile, and giggle. Men want to be adored. And that is where a clever woman can shine.'

'I don't think I can adore a man,' Jeannie said doubtfully. It didn't sound like her at all.

'Then practise.' She laughed. 'I know. Practise on Ross Macintosh. Once you feel you can do it properly, move on to someone who matters.'

'But won't he feel I'm encouraging him?'

Fiona laughed. 'Ross knows his place. And he knows that it will never be as a respectable husband.'

Jeannie went on with her work. As the winter bit deeply, more of her patients went down with lung disease, lacking the strength to fight it. And she found herself on calls, time and again, which meant the days stretched to the point at which she hardly saw natural light, and her world became an amber dusk.

Still, she found herself popping in to see Angus every week, ostensibly to ask about finance, but usually her visit ended in a long, deep, comfortable silence beside the fire. The way a wife might relax with a husband after a hard day.

Jeannie packed her bag and smiled at the elderly man lying on the low truckle bed.

'So they'll not be seeing the end of me yet?' He smiled weakly, but with real relief in his ruddy, workworn face.

'You'll be with us for some time yet, Mr Campbell.' Jeannie suppressed a smile. 'That heart of yours isn't finished, but you'll have to be careful and try to keep healthy. Is there anyone who could come and help you around the house?'

'My daughter's coming to stay with me for a few weeks till I'm back on my feet.'

'Well, you take it easy.' She put on her coat and hat and left the tiny, one-roomed cottage. The old man had a bad heart and lungs, and the cold and damp he lived in was weakening him. But somehow, and Jeannie wasn't sure why, his heart kept going, through bouts of bronchitis and influenza that should have killed him. He was a survivor.

She walked down the road, her mood lightened by Mr Campbell's recovery, and saw a familiar figure, in tweed jacket and thick corduroy trousers, crossing the road in front of her. He nodded a greeting and stopped as if he wanted to talk to her. Jeannie was taken aback. Why would he bother doing that? But she was secretly pleased. She strode towards him, then remembered what Fiona had told her. Ross was someone she could practise on. She shortened her stride, but the change in rhythm made her stumble and she landed on her hands and knees in a puddle.

'Are you all right, Jeannie?' Ross took her arm and helped her to her feet, proffering a white cotton handkerchief for her to wipe her hands.

'Yes.' But she wasn't. She couldn't even walk like a woman.

'I was thinking about you,' Ross began. 'I've got something back at my office that I'd like you to help with.'

'Me?' she said in surprise. 'Of course.' They crossed the street and headed towards his shabby office in the nearby tenement, Jeannie concentrating on walking in a ladylike fashion rather than with her normal, confident stride.

'Have you hurt your leg?' Ross asked, as she trotted along next to him. 'You're walking strangely.'

Her heart sank.

'They're in here.' Hurriedly Ross moved some boxes off the battered *faux*-leather sofa against the plain distempered wall. 'It's some materials for the curtains in my new house and coverings for the chairs. I thought you would know about these things,' he ended uncertainly.

He's noticed I'm a woman, thought Jeannie triumphantly. But he was asking her advice about something she had no experience of. She ran her fingers over the heavy materials. 'Well, the ivory watered silk would look nice in the dining room,' she said slowly, 'but . . .'

'But what?'

'It's terribly expensive. People are using wallpaper instead of fabric now.'

'What would you use?' he asked.

Jeannie bit her lip. 'A pale wallpaper with a pattern. I wouldn't use the silk.'

'I want my house to look the best.'

'But there's no point throwing money away. Hand me that book of samples.'

They spent the next hour poring over house furnishings and Jeannie was amazed at how much she enjoyed it. She had laughed at women who spent their day considering the décor of their homes, but she had never known how exciting it could be. 'Will I be able to see it when it's finished?' she asked shyly.

Ross laughed. 'Of course. When it's decorated and I begin to entertain, you and your cousins shall be the first guests.'

'My cousins and I would be delighted,' Jeannie said, in a small, disappointed voice.

As the weeks passed, Ross became an accustomed fixture with the Macdonalds, taking the place of Hamish, who was only too happy to retire to the conservatory and watch the birds. Fiona came to the club every Saturday night with Jeannie and Ross, then disappeared to laugh and joke with the fast set. Jeannie watched Ross come and go. She introduced him to the older members, most of whom treated him with polite distance. Then, when he was dancing with Fiona, they made veiled enquiries to Jeannie about possible marriage. He was being accepted, Jeannie knew, but only as her beau. For his part, he was witty, generous company, he knew how to entertain and the mob outside the surgery had all but disappeared. But so had her efforts with the women: she had given the money from Margaret to the surgery to keep it open. Time and time again she felt herself watching Ross and wondering if there was a further step they could take, which would meet the needs of them both.

'He's good, Tam,' Ross said, as they watched the skinny young men sparring in the cold bare gymnasium. 'Really good. Put up a good fight on Tuesday.'

'Chip off the old block,' Tam grunted. 'Don't drop your guard!' he shouted, as the two men threw punches at each other. 'As good as my brother and far better than me.'

'Might put a few shillings on him myself,' Ross smiled. 'Been a while since I've been in a place like this.'

'Aye, you were a good fighter,' Tam said, as they walked away from the sweat, damp and chalk. 'Could have gone all the way.' He looked Ross up and down, from the carefully combed black hair to the expensive leather shoes. 'Till you decided on another path.'

'He proves himself, I'll see if I can put him in touch with a few people I know,' Ross nodded to the wizened trainer.

'Mr Macintosh,' the other man said respectfully.

'Bill.' Ross acknowledged the greeting. 'Your boy's doing well.'

'I know,' Bill said proudly, 'and after Tuesday things won't be the same for him. He'll make his name.'

'Aye.' Ross sighed with satisfaction as he and Tam went out to the car.

'Back to the office, or do you fancy nipping down your ma's for a bite of dinner?' Tam said, as they began to drive through the village.

'I'll drop you off, but I'm to the Macdonalds' this afternoon,' Ross told him. 'She's helping me to decorate the house.'

'But you haven't got your posh clothes,' Tam remarked.

'I'll be going back to get changed. Can't turn up looking like this, can I?' Ross grinned, as he gestured to the rough corduroy trousers and collarless shirt he was wearing.

'Aye,' Tam replied. 'Wouldn't want anyone thinking you worked for a living, now, would yeh?'

Ross bridled. He stopped the car outside a tiny cottage, little more than a room with a roof. 'Jeannie wouldn't want to know you if she saw you looking the way you are at the moment,' Tam continued. 'None of those new friends of yours would.'

'Jeannie's seen me in my working clothes,' Ross said gruffly. 'She's no bothered about things like that. But her family are, and I wouldn't want tae embarrass her.'

Tam stared at him. Then he smiled to himself and shook his head. 'Just drop me off at my ma's house,' he said good-naturedly, 'and run off to play houses with the gentry.'

It was shortly after two that Ross arrived at Jeannie's home. He got out of his car and stared at the ivy-covered walls with the large, elegant windows. This was the home of people who knew their place – at the very top.

'I wondered if I might speak to Dr Macdonald?' he said to the maid, who opened the heavy mahogany door to him.

'Come in,' the housekeeper replied uncertainly. He followed her along the wood-panelled hallway and into the light, airy drawing room, the room he had copied so faithfully in his own house. He was drawn as always to the ornate french windows. Even now, with the spring rain falling in a gentle drizzle, the gardens looked lovely. This was what his home would look like, he resolved. One day.

He heard a noise and looked round. Fiona was hovering at the door. She had just arrived back from a long lunch with friends and he could see the effects of the alcohol upon her.

'Hello, Ross.' She smiled coyly and Ross nodded to her.

'I need to talk to Jeannie,' he said, relishing the sight of Fiona: there was an appealing flush in her face. 'We've something to discuss.'

'Unless you're a poverty-stricken urchin with fleas, I'm afraid Jeannie will have no time for you.' She went over to the drinks table and caressed the tops of the bottles and decanters as if she was too tempted by everything on offer to make a considered choice. 'She has no time or inclination to spend time with less interesting specimens of humanity such as ourselves.' She giggled mirthlessly. 'Can I offer you some refreshment while you consider your next course of action?'

'Well,' Ross felt his mouth suddenly dry, 'what would you suggest?'

Fiona lifted her eyes to his. Ross could feel her gaze filtering into his bloodstream, wrapping itself round him like a silk scarf.

'I think we could find a way to amuse ourselves without her, don't you?' she said eventually.

Ross was silent. He didn't want to betray Jeannie, but Fiona was sidling up to him. 'I want a woman's touch for my home,' he said slowly.

'I was just about to retire.' She drew a finger down the lapel of his jacket. 'Just think, if you'd arrived a few minutes later you'd have caught me undressing. Perhaps even naked.' Her hand reached for his waistcoat. 'And I don't even have a ladies' maid to help me.' She pouted.

'Do you need help undressing?' Ross asked thickly. He wanted to take a step away from her – he could tell that the flush was from alcohol – but his fantasy had come true: Fiona, the beautiful Fiona, was throwing herself at him.

'Of course, you didn't come here to help me take off my clothes, did you, Ross?' she went on blithely. 'You came to talk about furniture with Jeannie. So much more interesting than little me.' She looked up at him coyly.

'Why don't you try to distract me, then?' There he had said it, thought Ross.

She looked meaningfully at him. 'Well, I could give you the not so grand tour?' Fiona grasped his hand and they went up the stairs. She played with his fingers as she showed him Innes's suite, pressed herself against him as she showed him the empty top-floor rooms, and when they got to the dusty attic, she let her fingers drift across his trousers. 'Why don't you show me what you can offer?' Fiona said, as she began to unbutton him.

Ross said nothing as she took hold of him, sharp fingernails running up and down.

'You're pleased to see me.' She looked up at him from under her fringe.

'I haven't seen you yet,' he said.

Slowly Fiona slid her silk dress up her legs, past her lace stocking tops. 'As you can see,' she teased, 'my underwear appears to be falling off.'

He took her roughly, standing behind her as she held on to a low eave for support, his hands on her hips as the soft silk of her dress fell round him.

'Be careful,' she hissed. 'Not on the dress.'

Ross pulled away immediately and wrapped the skirt round

himself. He felt a vicarious stab of pleasure at Fiona's horrified expression.

'Where are you going?' she whispered angrily, as he buttoned his trousers and headed back in the direction he had come.

'To see what's happened to Jeannie.' He closed the door, leaving Fiona to wring her hands in frustration.

'What are you doing here?' Jeannie asked as she walked into the hall.

'I was talking to Fiona.' He winked at her. 'But she can get rather tedious after a while. I was just passing and I wondered . . .'

'What?' There was something wrong about this, thought Jeannie. He was here uninvited. And it was good to see him – but something was wrong.

'I wanted to ask you about the hallway in my house.' He smiled appealingly.

Jeannie's heart sank. She was back on duty in a few hours and had wanted to put her feet up with a nice cup of tea. 'Of course, if you can give me a moment,' she replied, as she looked down at her dowdy black work suit.

They turned as Fiona came down the stairs in a clean dress, her face like thunder. 'Fiona, can you entertain Ross while I freshen up?' Jeannie asked.

'No, Jeannie, I shouldn't have come here unexpectedly,' Ross interjected. 'Perhaps we can have lunch one day and talk then.'

'Well, I've had a busy day,' Jeannie demurred, 'but I will help you, or Fiona might be able to advise you. She has excellent taste in the decorative arts.' Glad to escape, she fled into the drawing room.

Ross smiled down at Fiona's foxy little face. 'I ought to be at work,' he murmured.

'Oh, yes,' Fiona trilled. 'I forgot. You aren't one of us, you have to work for a living.'

'Better than living on charity.' He held her gaze for a long moment, then walked out, his feet struggling to stay on the ground. He drove off at speed, flashily, like a man trying to get himself noticed.

Fiona sauntered into the drawing room and stood elegantly beside the drinks table. 'You ought to be more friendly to him, you know,' she murmured. 'He's a man.' She poured himself a drink. 'I've got such a thirst.'

'It's barely four o'clock,' Jeannie said.

'Some of us have had a busy day,' Fiona drawled. 'Well, are you having one?'

'I have to go back to work,' Jeannie replied.

'Oh, you have to work, Hamish has to do his crossword, and Innes has his parish duty. There's never any one around.'

'Why don't you get yourself a job, then?' Jeannie said. 'There's plenty of charitable societies looking for people.'

'I don't think so,' Fiona replied, with a look that could have etched glass. 'I really don't think so.'

Chapter 15

Jeannie smiled to herself as she walked down the lane with Charlie and Buster.

'Never saw someone do that to an arm before,' Charlie said, as they climbed the hill, past the rows of tiny one-roomed cottages. 'How do you know how to do it?'

'You have a space where your shoulder fits, and what you have to do is put the bone back in,' she replied, 'without trapping the nerve.'

'But what about the ribs? Shouldn't he go to hospital if they're broken?' he persisted.

'Wrapping them up tight is all you can do. Bones have to stretch a bit, like toffee, when they move, like your ribs do. And he'll have to stop fighting, unless he wants one of his broken ribs to puncture his lung and kill him.'

'So he'll be dead by morning,' Charlie said, 'since he owes money to Alec Conner?'

Jeannie looked down at the small boy, who knew so many secrets. Secrets he kept, despite his youth. The unconscious man had received a beating as punishment, had he? 'Tell the woman who lived here to come and see me tomorrow,' she said gently. 'I'll ask Innes if he can—'

'Don't your family get tired of you asking them to give jobs to your patients?' He cocked his head at her. 'It's getting to be three a month.'

Charlie noticed a lot more than he let on, Jeannie thought.

'You know, if you went back to school, I could see my way to paying for you to go to a grammar,' she murmured, none too casually.

'That's very kind of you, but I can make my fortune without school.' For a moment, they stared at each other. Jeannie searched the child's face for a sign that he understood what she was offering, but she knew he saw no future in school and not even her formidable will could change him. She laughed to herself.

'What's funny?' Charlie asked, as they got to the market.

'Just learned something about life. It's happening more and more often.'

But just as Jeannie was becoming more at home in the slums, someone else was doing as much as he could to leave them. Ross was showing Fiona how much of his house he had redecorated. Since he now lived where the richest of the town did, he wanted her to see it. And be impressed.

'I wondered where you lived,' she remarked, as they went inside. 'Oh, my goodness, it's a ruin.'

'I've just bought it, but some of the rooms have been done,' Ross told her.

'It'll do,' she said resignedly, 'but next time you'll have to find somewhere better.' She opened the door to the drawing room, then laughed. 'You've copied ours.'

Ross's stomach turned over. The room was his pride and joy. And she was right. He had copied the Macdonalds' – because he thought theirs was so lovely.

'Well, I'm having his wife,' he said shortly, 'so I thought I might as well have his wallpaper too.'

They had a drink, then went upstairs and made love, but it lacked the magic it had held before. Ross was almost glad when Fiona dressed and informed him she was ready to return home.

Later he went back to his house and sat by the fire. Fiona was everything a man could want in a woman, but he felt irritated, used and discarded. Most of all, he wanted to talk to Jeannie. He wanted her to know what he was like, to tell her the truth about his life, his hopes, his dreams. He wanted her to understand him.

'Have you seen anything of Bess Henderson recently?' Jeannie asked, as she and Innes had breakfast the next day. 'I haven't been to the club for a while.' She glanced at Hamish but, as always, he was immersed in his own thoughts.

Innes took a deep breath. 'What do you know?' he asked warily.

'She had a lot on her mind.'

'You know?'

Jeannie nodded.

'She's been committed. Her father came to me in the most terrible state. She refused to go away to have the child, and he had no option.'

'She wasn't mad, Innes, she was pregnant.'

'And what was her father supposed to do? She left him with no choice.'

'No choice but to have her declared a threat to moral standards and locked up in an asylum?' Jeannie looked at him incredulously.

'What else could he do? Bring up the child as part of his family?' He looked at her uncomprehendingly. 'A good Christian family like that?'

'A good Christian family that has sent away its only daughter because she made one mistake. Is that what you would do to me if I fell?'

'I suspect that if I have to have you committed, Jeannie,' he said bitterly, 'it will be for an entirely different reason.' He stood up. 'What would you prefer? That we ignore the Bible and allow women to fornicate at will?'

'No, let's just stick to casting the first stone, shall we?' Jeannie stood up, too, and threw her napkin on to the table.

'Because that's the only type of Christianity you seem to understand!' She walked out and went up the stairs, pushing past Fiona. Back in her room she lay down on her bed, wondering why Innes couldn't see what he had done wrong.

Jeannie yawned and rubbed her eyes as she noted down the last of the results of the skin tests. There was a particularly bad outbreak of scabies, but a scientist from the university in Edinburgh wanted some skin samples, which would earn some money for the clinic. Although what might happen when he discovered they were all contaminated was anyone's guess.

'Hello, Jeannie.' It was Ross, smiling broadly as he walked in. 'Just thought I'd tell you that I've finished the lobby . . .'

'The lobby?'

'The hallway,' he corrected himself. 'And I'd like you to see it, since you helped with it. And the dining room is—'

'I'm really busy,' Jeannie rested her head in her hands. 'I'm sorry, it's just . . .'

'It's all right Jeannie, I understand.' But his voice was clipped, sharp and more than a little to the point. She could feel him looking at her, but she kept her eyes on the microscope. She didn't have time to look at a hallway, and she had promised to visit Angus for a chat and a game of chess. She never won, he was a much better player, but he asked how her day had been and always showed an interest in the surgery, suggesting ways to earn money, and even occasionally finding her a small benefactor. It was how she enjoyed spending her evenings, and Angus was unable to go out since he was in mourning. It meant they had time to be together. And that was something she had begun increasingly to think of.

She worked late the next evening, and with Christmas drawing close, only a few were able to sneak an hour to come and see her. Soon she'd have to go home to the silence, to Hamish, who was more withdrawn than ever, although his periods of lucidity were more frequent now, and Fiona, who was acting as if she was drunk or on drugs, although Jeannie knew that it wasn't so.

'Are you going, then?' Charlie said, as he shuffled about in the waiting room.

'No, I've some notes to write and—'

'All right, I don't want to know the details.' He grinned cheekily. 'Just tell me if you need me.'

'I'll be some time, Charlie, but I'm not planning on going anywhere except home. Shouldn't you be going home?'

'I'm waiting for my da. He said he'd some business to do, but once he was finished he was coming to see me.' Charlie waved his damaged hand and walked away, whistling to Buster as he went out of the door.

It was late when she finished and put the last of the notes into their buff-coloured sleeves. She locked the door, got into her car and tried to start it. Nothing happened. She tried again, but the engine just wouldn't ignite. Cursing, she got out and began to walk – through the wrong side of town on the wrong side of midnight. She decided to head past the back of Baxter's Court: there was a police station not far away and she could call Innes or a cab.

But ten minutes later when she was resolutely marching through an ever-increasing maze of low, covered alleys, her shoes crunching on the half-frozen mud that encrusted the cobbles, panic began to take hold. It was dark without gas lighting and she knew she was somewhere by Baxter's Court, but she had no idea where. She sensed rather than saw the drunks sleeping in the shadows, and heard the scuttle of claws on the cobbles. But she had to keep going: she would come to an end, eventually.

'What d'yeh want?' a belligerent female voice demanded.

'I'm looking for the police station,' Jeannie returned briskly.

'Ye'll no find the polis around here, hen.' The woman came up to Jeannie, breathing alcohol fumes in her face.

'Then I'll be on my way.' Jeannie went to move past her, but the woman reached out, grabbing her, forcing her back against the alley wall.

'Let me go!' Jeannie shouted, and struggled, but her opponent was too strong and knocked her back against a wall.

'And why should we do that?' a male voice added.

'If you don't let me go—'

'No one will hear you.' The woman held up Jeannie's wrist, ripping off her gloves and taking her ring and watch from her.

'Don't you know who I am? I'm the doctor.' Jeannie pushed against the heavy stinking woman, but she was thrown against the opposite wall and landed in a dazed heap in a half-frozen puddle.

'Gie us yer coat.'

Fighting to keep her bearings, Jeannie felt the thick winter coat being pulled off her.

'This is ridiculous,' she protested, and received a slap that cut her lip. 'Just let me go on my way.' She stopped as the cameo brooch was torn from the top of her blouse.

'Have yeh anything else?' the woman demanded.

'No, you've got everything. Just let me go.' Jeannie's anger was turning into fear.

'What do ye think, Bernie?' The woman laughed.

'I could think of a few things I'd like tae do.' He groped at Jeannie's chest.

'Mind out, Bernie!' The woman glared fearsomely, and as he let her go, Jeannie took to her heels and ran back the way she had come.

Ross and Tam walked back towards their office, quietly contented with another successful deal.

'Off home?' Tam asked, as he muffled his throat against the night.

'Aye, I'm finished,' Ross agreed. 'And what the hell is her car still doing there?'

'Who?' Tam shoved his hands into his pockets.

'Jeannie. My Jeannie Macdonald. What does she think she's doing at this time of night?' He walked up to the window of the clinic and hammered on it.

'Jeannie, it's Ross. Let me in!' he shouted, but to no avail.

'She's no there, mister.' A boy — it was Charlie — appeared from the shadows. 'Her motor-car wasnae working so she walked up the road.'

'When?'

'Not long.'

'Where could she have been going?' Ross said, mainly to himself. 'Just Baxter's Court up there.'

'Mebbe she had a job to do,' Tam muttered.

'No, she was going home,' Charlie said confidently. 'She told me.'

'I think I ought to take a wee look.' Ross's footsteps quickened automatically. Then all three saw a figure stumbling out of an alleyway and heading towards them.

'Jeannie!' Ross shouted. They saw the figure stop, then put its hands to its head.

'What the hell happened?' Ross said angrily, as he reached her.

'They stole my coat and my jewellery,' she babbled, her breath turning the air into tiny puffs of smoke. 'And they got the keys to the clinic. They'll break in — we've opiates in there.'

Ross dabbed her bleeding mouth with a handkerchief. 'You went to Baxter's Court on your own at night?'

'I got lost.' She took the handkerchief and pressed it hard to her mouth. 'But we have to get a policeman. If they get to the surgery—'

'How the hell could you be so stupid?" He grabbed her arms. 'Did you get a look at them?'

'She called the man Bernie. She smelt terrible and had no front teeth. A very big woman.'

'Wait here.' Ross gestured to Tam and they headed on in the direction of Baxter's Court.

Jeannie shuddered and looked around in the gathering gloom. Then she wrapped her arms round her and walked slowly towards the surgery. She sat down on the steps, feeling cold, alone and beaten.

Ross stared down the darkened street. Where had the bloody woman got to now?

'I told you to wait where you were,' he said, a few minutes later, as they walked into the surgery tenement.

'I'm sorry, I didn't think,' she said. 'I didn't feel very safe where I was.'

'Don't you listen to anything I say?' Ross snapped. 'Here.' He handed her the ring, watch and cameo brooch. 'The keys are in the pocket but I'm afraid your coat got torn.' He held it up. It was filthy and little more than a rag now.

'I don't want it after that awful woman's had it on.' She shivered. 'I just want to go home and pretend today never happened.' Exhausted and not knowing which way to turn, Jeannie burst into tears.

Ross stood and watched her. It seemed so out of character for her to cry: she had always struck him as a strong woman. 'Come on.' He put his arm round her. 'No permanent damage done. Not like you to do this, Jeannie.'

'I'm sorry,' she said, into his jacket. 'It's been a bad day.'

'Well, it's all over now,' he said. 'I'll take you home while Tam sorts out your car.'

They drove in silence, but as Ross saw her into her house, she turned to him. 'Please don't tell Innes,' she said quietly. 'He'll insist I stop working.'

'You need protection in that part of town,' he answered shortly. 'It's no place for a lady.'

'But if I stop working who will take my place?' She smiled briefly. 'Thank you. Proper knight in shining armour, aren't you?'

He touched her face gently. 'Goodnight, Jeannie. Sleep well, and try to have a bit more common sense.'

Jeannie watched him drive away, knowing that, deep down, she hadn't wanted him to leave. It was a frightening revelation.

'Angus is coming for lunch,' Fiona said, as Innes, Jeannie and Hamish arrived back from church. She had cried off with her customary Sunday-morning headache. 'He called while you were out.'

'Can't see why he doesn't attend church any more,' Innes complained, as he put his hat and coat on the hat-stand and placed his umbrella in the elephant's foot.

'Apparently he's fallen out with Sir Justin,' Jeannie said, 'so he worships at his local church. And pays into their coffers instead of yours.'

'I don't care about the money,' Innes said. 'Angus needs guidance, now more than ever. Guidance from people who care for him.'

'But Angus is successful, and we still see him.'

'I can be the friend to him that Hamish once was,' Innes went on. 'And when we do see him he just wants to talk to you about the clinic.'

Jeannie blushed. ' Margaret was interested. He feels so much responsibility. Honouring her memory.'

'It would be a mistake to read another meaning into the man's need for companionship, Jeannie,' he said.

'I'm not reading anything into it,' Jeannie assured him. 'I enjoy the company of an old friend. But I would enjoy it far more if Margaret were here to share in it.'

'I just can't sway you from your path, can I?' Innes said thoughtfully.

'As little as I can you from yours.' She smiled politely, then left. Trust Innes to meddle.

*

Christmas came and went, and as Jim had pleurisy, Jeannie hardly saw her family. It was even difficult to enjoy the few hours she had off, and as she drove to and from the surgery, Jeannie began to wonder if she would ever have a chance to have the kind of fun that Fiona and the others enjoyed. Relax with Angus in front of the fire. Or with . . . Another man's face washed traitorously into her mind. The man who had danced with her before he had been bewitched by Fiona, the man who straddled both worlds . . . Ross Macintosh.

'Don't be silly, woman!' But she wanted to be silly. With him.

'Happy New Year, Doctor!'

Jeannie looked up from her seat on the floor where she had been making a list of the contents of the medical cabinet to see Tam standing beside her.

'Tam!' she exclaimed. 'How did you get in? I mean, Happy New Year, and how did you get in?'

'The door was open. That lock isn't very good, you know.' He frowned. 'Someone like you, alone in this place, well, it isn't proper, now, is it?'

'Someone tried to break in a few nights ago, but Jim's ill and I haven't had time to fix it.' She closed the door of the medical cabinet. 'Not that we've much here to steal. We lost another benefactor because of my clinic.'

'Come on now, Doctor,' Tam said cheerfully. 'Not like you to be miserable.' He put out a hand to help her to her feet. 'All you have to do is ask your friends. Tell you what,' he scratched his stubbly chin, 'you stick the kettle on and I'll sort the door. Just needs a few screws tightened and mebbe a bit of wood fixing to it. Then it'll keep till I can come back with a new one tomorrow.'

'I don't have the money for a new door. Not until Dr Martin starts his new investigation.'

Tam chuckled. 'You don't need to pay me, I've a spare one

back at the yard.' He looked about the bare little room. 'Where do you keep your tools?'

'A few in there.' She pointed under the sink. 'How do you take your tea?'

'Four sugars, please.' He grinned. 'Got to keep myself sweet.'

By the time the kettle had boiled, Tam had stripped down the lock and was putting it back together with an ease that amazed Jeannie. 'Are you a locksmith?' she asked.

'I know a bit about them,' he said amiably.

Twenty minutes later, he had finished and the lock was almost as good as new.

'I'm off to first-foot Ross now,' Tam said casually. 'Are you coming?'

Jeannie blushed a little. 'It's a little awkward,' she began, 'just to call on him.'

'It's New Year,' Tam cried. 'Auld lang syne and all that!'

Jeannie hesitated. It was late and she had been working for over twenty-four hours. 'All right,' she said. 'I will.'

Tam offered her his arm.

Chapter 16

'Thought you said you wouldn't come back here,' Ross said, as he lay in bed, watching smoke-rings from his cigarette drift towards the ceiling.

'Well, you were so rude to me last night that I couldn't let it go.' Fiona pouted. 'You didn't dance with me once.'

'You were with Hamish. What was I supposed to do? March up to him and ask him if I could have a quick waltz with you, then take you off to the summer-house for a good hard ride?'

Fiona exhaled petulantly. 'He wouldn't have noticed, he hardly spoke a word all night. If you hadn't stopped escorting Jeannie, you could have taken her to the dances, and we could have seen a bit more of each other,' she said. 'I had to lie to Hamish to get here tonight.'

'I didn't ask you to come. In fact I had plans for tonight. An old friend was coming round for drinks. And Jeannie prefers to spend time at the surgery, which is why she doesn't accompany me.'

'That isn't true, Ross, and we both know it.' Fiona laughed. 'But who is coming to see you? A female friend?' Her eyes narrowed. 'Surely you'd rather be with me than anyone else?'

'You just like the idea of me leaving someone like Jeannie to have you.'

'And what of it?'

'The only thing I desperately want,' Ross said, 'is a drink.' He got up and pulled on his trousers and shirt.

'You need to get all your house decorated, Ross,' Fiona said tetchily. 'There is a difference between a rustic idyll and a hovel, you know.'

Ross headed downstairs and saw two heads appear behind the elegant stained glass of his front door.

'Happy New Year!'

As Ross opened the door, he was greeted by Tam, proffering a bottle of whisky. 'And look who I picked up along the way!'

'Happy New Year, Ross,' Jeannie said shyly, staring at her hands when he said nothing back.

'Happy New Year,' he replied slowly. 'Into the drawing-room, please.' He pushed them in none too gently.

'Goodness!' Jeannie took in the near-identical copy of her own house.

'I liked it,' Ross muttered, as he walked towards the drinks cabinet.

'It suits this room,' she said. 'You have a lovely house, Ross.'

'There's so much still to be done.'

'Can't expect to do everything overnight,' she said. He handed her a glass and she held it up in a silent toast.

Ross made an excuse and pulled Tam away out of the room. 'Why is she here?' he whispered urgently.

'I asked her if she wanted to come,' Tam replied. 'You and her make a good couple. I like her.'

'I'm a bit busy on the female front.' Ross stifled a laugh. 'The lovely Fiona just turned up, ripped off her clothes and jumped on my bones. I must smell like a dog.'

'But we had business!'

'Aye, but you know what it's like,' Ross smirked. 'There are some invitations you just don't turn down. Now, I'll go in there and be nice for five minutes, then I want you and her gone.'

Both men returned to the drawing room where Jeannie was looking at the porcelain figures on the mantelpiece.

'Does this mean we're friends again?' He cocked his head to catch her eye.

Jeannie nodded. 'Perhaps we get on better than either of us would like to admit,' she murmured.

'I can honestly say, Dr Macdonald, that I've missed your company. You look tired out.'

Jeannie stretched her neck. 'I am. I started twenty-six hours ago and will be back at work at seven o'clock tomorrow morning.'

'Then you ought to go home and get some sleep. We can catch up with each other's news later.'

Jeannie nodded. 'I think you may be right. If I spend any more time in this warm room I may fall asleep where I stand.' She drained her glass.

'Happy New Year, Jeannie.' He took the glass from her, then kissed her cheek.

'Happy New Year, Ross.' As she steadied herself with her hands on his shoulders, ready to kiss him back, she felt his arms round her. She stiffened slightly. As he continued to hold her, Jeannie laid her head on his broad shoulder, feeling the comfort of strong arms. Safe arms. His arms. And smelt the distinctive aroma of ladies' perfume, heavy perfume. Not the kind a man would use. Not the kind a dancer would use. The kind that the fast set at the club would use.

Ross closed his eyes as he breathed in the scent of carbolic soap that always seemed to pervade Jeannie. A clean, homely smell that reminded him of his mother. Suddenly she pulled away. 'I'll take my leave of you.' She backed out of the room. Ross heard the sound of a door closing upstairs. 'Happy New Year.' She was gone.

'How sweet!' Fiona said, as she descended the stairs clad in one of Ross's shirts. 'Chasing after you like that.' She came over to him and wrapped herself round him. 'Now, make me a drink and think how much more fun you can have with me than with Jeannie!' She looked over her shoulder to admire herself in the heavy gilt mirror that was the sole adornment in the hall and screamed.

'What?' Ross looked round and there was Tam, looking curiously at Fiona's slender body.

He shrugged and walked past them to the door.

'You can't let a horrible little man like that out of the front door,' Fiona said, aghast. 'People might think you were friends.'

Tam stared at Ross. 'Aye, Ross,' he said, in his broadest, harshest accent. 'Couldn't let anyone think that, now, could yeh?'

'He's staring at me!' She shrieked.

'Just wondering how much you charge, luv,' Tam replied, ''cause with the tits of a twelve-year-old boy, you'll not earn much.' He looked at each of them in turn, then walked out, slamming the door behind him.

'I can't believe you let him say that!' Fiona glared at him. 'He insulted me.'

'I'll talk to him later.'

'Take me home,' she ordered.

'No.' Ross turned and went upstairs. 'You wouldn't want to be seen driving with me, and you wouldn't want to be going home dressed like that.' He gestured to the shirt. 'So I suggest you get your clothes on, then walk to the bus stop. Or call a motor-cab.' Somehow he couldn't rouse himself to care about Fiona any more. She was too much effort for too little return.

Later that week, as the others had dinner with friends, Jeannie curled up in the old study, a fire in the grate, a book in her hands. She was wearing her oldest clothes and, fresh from the bath, had loosely plaited her long fox-red hair.

'The housekeeper let me in.' Ross stood in the doorway. 'You look as if you're enjoying yourself.'

'All I need is some hot chocolate and maybe some toast.'

She stretched. 'I won't be going to the club tonight. All this work is just too much. But Angus has agreed to propose you for membership of the club, and Innes will second it.'

'That's good news.' He moved towards her.

'All that relentless social climbing has paid off.' She laughed quietly. 'You don't need me any more. Perhaps you can introduce me to your new friends as I seem to have developed the skill of losing mine.'

'I have one thing to ask you,' he sat down next to her, 'but it can wait.'

'Would you like a drink?' She stood up. 'I'm working my way through this indecently fine brandy, or I can go next door—'

'Brandy will be fine.' He looked around. 'I've never been in here.'

'It was my grandfather's study. My father studied for his engineering degree here, and when I was at university, I spent hours here in the holidays.' She handed him a large brandy.

'I never thought of you as an academic. Why did you spend so much time here?'

'This is my home,' she said simply.

'So the family took you in?'

Jeannie laughed. 'I own this house or, rather, it's in trust for me.'

Ross digested the information. 'Tell me about growing up here.' He sat back and listened as Jeannie told him about the kind of life he could only dream about. Of ponies and nannies, schools and fun.

'You never had a care in the world, did you?' he said quietly.

'I suppose not.' She giggled with the brandy that, between them, they had almost finished. 'Your turn. Tell me about growing up in the Macintosh household.'

'You don't want to know,' he said wryly.

'Yes, I do,' she insisted. 'I want to know what turned you into the man you are.'

Her face was framed by her long red hair, and she looked

180

like a wife, the kind of woman any man would want to come home to. The kind of woman he wanted to come home to. 'It's not something I like talking about,' he said quietly.

'You know I won't tell anyone.' She put her hand on his arm.

Ross smiled. 'I was born and brought up in Lochgelly,' he began. 'My father worked down the pit, as did my two brothers. I was the youngest, and they moved heaven and earth for me to go to school. Then, when I got to fourteen, I joined the others. I knew eventually I'd get a clerk's job at the pit, but I wanted more. Most of the men there did a bit of boxing, and I used to organise the matches. Then I met the kind of people that need a bit of muscle . . .'

'You've got muscles.' She looked at him curiously.

'You're looking at me very closely.' He touched her nose.

'The study of the body is my trade.' She laughed a little. 'So, Mr Macintosh, what you're trying to say is that you have a troupe of men who threaten people.'

'No. The men would labour on building sites, ensure there was no trouble at dances or card games. Then I moved into rent- and debt-collecting, which was how I got involved in with the courts. Angus has sold Seaton's Court to me. I'm having new water-pipes put in and looking at how I can stop the drains flooding. It's still a hole in the ground. But it will get better.' He looked down almost shyly. 'Since then, well, I've been doing my best to establish myself in business and socially.'

'Which is where I come in.' She made a face. 'You're a disreputable man, Mr Macintosh.'

'Perhaps that's why we get on so well,' he replied. 'I don't have a reputation and you seem intent on losing yours.'

'Throwing it away on the burghers of Pathhead,' she said. 'Sometimes I think they're worth more than all those respectable people in the tennis club put together. They're honest, there's no hiding behind social niceties. What you see is what you get.'

'The club set have a far more pleasant life than anyone in Pathhead.'

'Do you miss anything about your old life?' Jeannie asked.

'My family,' Ross replied, without hesitation.

'I miss mine too,' Jeannie admitted. 'I miss having someone who believes in you, who's on your side no matter what.'

'You have Innes and Hamish.'

'It's not the same.' She sighed. 'I shouldn't be telling you all this, it's just tiredness talking.'

'A friend in need,' Ross murmured. He bent close to her and drew a finger down her cheek. 'Has anyone ever told you just how lovely you are?'

'Only my father, and that hardly counts.' Then she stopped. And waited.

Ross sat implacably, the clock ticking, the fire crackling. Jeannie waited for him to kiss her – he had to do it soon, she wanted him to so much that if he didn't she would explode with a longing that seemed to have sprung up on her. Her fingers itched to touch the planes of his face, to run down to the buttons on his shirt. And she wanted him to do the same to her. 'Oh, my goodness!' she said, as she put a hand to her chest. 'Oh, my goodness.'

'What are you thinking about?' he teased. 'Is it the same as I am?'

She shook her head in panic. 'I doubt it,' she said shakily.

'Why?' He gestured with his head for her to come closer. She could feel her chest heaving, then heard Ross chuckle as he moved towards her and rubbed his face against her. 'I love your scent,' he whispered.

'I smell of hospitals.'

'You smell of home, of mothers looking after children, of safe, warm places.'

'I'm not your mother,' she replied, but his words echoed in her head. Jim had accused her of being a nanny, and she knew that she liked to organise Innes. Was that what she was to Ross

Macintosh? Why else would he want to be here with her? She knew she wasn't the kind of woman to whom men were attracted. 'I'm just your friend.'

'Would you want to be anything more?' His voice had an edge to it.

'I don't think I can be.' Her words were hurried – she had to get them out before she said something she would regret. Such as how she would like him to think of her. 'I have no time for pointless romantic entanglements,' she continued, 'much as you have no time for romantic entanglements that involve decent women, who might expect you to act like the gentleman you wish you were.'

'This may come as a shock to you, Dr Macdonald,' he said, 'but my women enjoy it as much as I do.'

'Then stick to your kind, Mr Macintosh,' she replied quickly. 'I have no desire to be tarred by the harlot's brush.'

'But you said we were friends.' He reached out to her but she moved away.

'Not that kind. Just friends. I don't want a lover.'

'Then I'm sorry if I've put you in an awkward situation,' he murmured.

'You haven't.' She couldn't bear it any longer and touched his hands. 'It's just that I spend so much time with men that sometimes I forget I'm a woman and people read things into it.'

'That must have been it,' he said. 'And, as you noticed, I'm hardly in a position to offer for a wife.'

'Yes,' she replied, in a stilted tone. 'A few more years and you'll be sufficiently established to choose from among the kingdom's beauties.'

'And I promise I'll call on you for your advice.'

'Good,' she replied awkwardly, half of her wishing he would go and half still fighting the urge to throw herself on him.

'And if you need any help in finding a husband . . .'

Jeannie laughed. 'I did consider it once, but I'm not disposed to be someone's obedient little wife. I shall descend into disgraceful old age answerable to no one but myself.'

Ross chuckled, the tension finally broken.

'I think you'll fill that role admirably, Dr Macdonald.' He bent and kissed her cheek one last time. 'See you next week at the club?'

She nodded. 'It'll take a few weeks for your membership to go through but till then you can be our guest.'

She watched him leave. Despite the fire it seemed colder. Suddenly she wanted to weep.

'I wasn't expecting to see you here, Fiona,' Ross said, as he opened his door to her the following afternoon. 'I was about to go out.'

'I've just had a pleasant lunch, Ross.' Fiona came in and headed for the drawing room and the drinks cabinet. 'Don't spoil it by reminding me how much of a chore my company is to you.'

'Haven't you had enough?' he asked as she poured herself a martini.

'Why don't you take me to bed and enjoy the afternoon with Hamish Macdonald's wife?'

Ross strode towards her and grabbed her wrist. 'Watch your mouth, Fiona,' he warned her. 'You've far more to lose than I have.'

'What would Jeannie say,' she mocked, 'if she knew you'd been cuckolding her beloved cousin?'

Ross let go of her.

'I think you should go home, Fiona. There's nothing quite as unattractive as a woman under the influence of alcohol.'

'Oh, do I upset your puritanical working-class morals, Ross?' Fiona looked down at her reddening wrist. 'I used to have a life, something to do other than bother with nobodies like yourself.' She swung away from him alarmingly. 'Once I had the most eligible bachelor in Fife chasing after me. Hamish was

the man every woman wanted for their husband and I got him.'
She laughed drily. 'And now look at me. I got what I wanted,
and I'm paying the price. I'll be Jeannie's charity case till the
day I die.' A sob burst from her.

'Come on.' Ross took Fiona in his arms and rocked her
gently. 'It isn't that bad.'

'It's worse, Ross.' She wept into his jacket. 'Look at me. All I
have to look forward to is growing old.' She reached up and
began to kiss his neck. 'Make love to me, Ross. You want me,'
she sought his jaw then his lips, 'you know I'm still beautiful.'

Ross felt himself stir, but in a curiously detached way. 'No,
Fiona.' He gently put her from him. 'It's over, you know that.'

'You can't say that to me!' she wailed, then ran her fingers
down his spine. 'Please, Ross, you can't treat me like this.'

Ross stared at her for a moment. 'Go back to your husband,
Fiona,' he said eventually. 'I don't want you.'

'You can't just discard me!' she screamed. 'You will do as I
say.'

'Not without ruining you, Mrs Macdonald,' he replied
smoothly. 'If you speak a word of this, it will be your reputation that suffers, not mine.' He took the drink from her. 'I
suggest that you find another nobody to amuse yourself with
because I'm not interested in you any more.' He opened the
door.

'Since when did you occupy the moral high ground?' she
said, with a sneer.

'Since I discovered the truth about people like you. Now, get
out of my house and if you breathe a word of scandal about
me, I'll tell the world how dull it is to make love to a scrawny
madam like yourself.'

Fiona stood on the step. 'Was I not old enough for you?' she
asked nastily.

'There isn't anything interesting about you. I'd take Enid
Baker or Louisa MacLean over you any day. Goodbye.' He
closed the door in her face.

Fiona stood on the step, the anger on her face turning into drunken self-pity. 'She doesn't want you, you know,' she shouted. 'She's got someone else in her sights now.'

But the door remained closed.

'And so have I.' She crossed her arms resolutely. 'You'll learn, Ross Macintosh. This isn't finished until I say so.'

'You've had a long day,' Charlie said, as he watched Jeannie close the door on the last patient. 'You'll be glad when Dr Jim comes back.'

'I can't deny that,' she returned, as she walked back into the surgery. 'Just get tidied up, then it's home for the night.' She stopped as she heard a knock on the door.

'We could pretend we've left,' Charlie suggested.

'Open it.' Jeannie yawned. 'And let's hope it's a quick one.'

Charlie opened the door, and a scrawny young girl pushed past him and ran into the surgery. 'Please, Doctor,' she said, 'you have to come now.'

'What's wrong?'

'She's bleeding to death. It won't stop.' The girl grabbed her hand.

'All right, but I have to get my bag.' Jeannie picked it up, then followed the child.

'Where do you live?' she said, as they trotted along the rain-washed streets.

'Over there.' The girl pointed to a tiny pawn-broker. 'Hurry!'

Jeannie walked into an Aladdin's cave of foul-smelling clothes and broken furniture and went up the back stairs. In the flat above a young girl lay groaning on a mattress in the kitchen.

'Hello, I'm Dr Macdonald,' Jeannie said, as she pulled off her gloves and put a hand on the girl's forehead. 'What's wrong with you?'

The girl, her face grey and wet with cold sweat, couldn't reply. 'Have you been to an abortionist?' Jeannie eased away the sheet from the girl's body, and saw the padding between her legs. Bright scarlet with blood.

'Go and get an ambulance wagon,' she said to the child who had guided her there, then turned back to the girl. 'You've lost a lot of blood, but if we get you to hospital . . .' Even as she said it she knew there was no hope. From the amount of haemorrhaging, the girl's womb was obviously perforated.

'When did you have the abortion?' Jeannie tried, but the girl was slipping into unconsciousness.

Where was the ambulance?

Eventually it arrived and as she was climbing into the back with the girl she saw a thick-set man run down the street. 'What the hell—' He stopped, and Jeannie noticed how smart he looked in a cheap way.

'It's Betty, Da,' the child said. 'She got someone to take the baby away and now she's sick.'

The doors of the ambulance closed as they made their way to hospital. Jeannie breathed a sigh of relief. The man had looked like a nasty character and she'd had her fill of those.

Chapter 17

'And as a result,' Innes addressed the select group in the dining room, 'we now have enough money to put heating into the church, so there'll be no cold hands or hearts on a Sunday morning.'

'Bravo.' Angus led the applause, with his grim-faced father-in-law and the others, including Ross, following suit. 'Jolly good cause, Innes.'

'One attempts to serve God in the way he would like.' Innes almost blushed.

'I thought you were going to introduce me to some important people,' Ross whispered, in an undertone, to Jeannie.

'The Balliols are here, and the Wallaces. I never said you'd enjoy yourself, just that you'd meet important people and buy boilers for Innes's church.' She didn't mention that Innes had taken some persuading to allow him to come for dinner, even with the financial inducement.

'Reverend Macdonald,' the maid had come in. 'There's a police inspector at the door asking for Dr Macdonald.'

Everyone turned to look at Jeannie.

'Tell them it's not a convenient time,' Angus said angrily.

'He has an arrest warrant.'

Jeannie stood up. 'But I haven't done anything wrong.'

'I'll come too – you'll need representation,' Angus said quickly. He and Jeannie went into the drawing room.

'Miss Macdonald, Mr Fleming.' Detective Inspector Pullen nodded to them.

'It's Dr Macdonald,' she retorted. 'If you've come to arrest me, I hope you have it correct on the warrant.'

'Now, Jeannie,' Angus said, 'don't upset yourself. It will be a misunderstanding.'

'You took a Miss Elizabeth Houston into the Victoria Infirmary yesterday afternoon,' he began.

'She was suffering from what appeared to be a ruptured womb, which was causing massive haemorrhaging.'

'Her father has complained that she had an abortion and that you carried it out.'

'What utter nonsense!' Angus exploded. 'Dr Macdonald does not perform illegal operations.'

'She's died, hasn't she?' Jeannie said. 'Why do these girls insist on going to those places?'

The policeman nodded. 'I need you to come to the station and answer a few questions.'

'I'm in the middle of a dinner party.'

'And I'm in the middle of an investigation of a young girl's death.' He stared at her. 'Now, will you come or will I have to arrest you?'

'I'll come with you.' Angus squeezed her arm. 'I am Dr Macdonald's legal representative.'

'But I didn't perform the abortion,' Jeannie insisted. 'I administered first aid, as is my duty as a doctor.'

'There are a few questions that require answers, Dr Macdonald.'

The police station smelt of damp and old sweat. Jeannie and Angus were an incongruous sight in their expensive clothes next to the scarred wooden furniture and shabby constables.

'For the last time, I was brought to the house when the child came to me and told me her sister was dying!' Jeannie put her head in her hands.

'The girl's father is a nasty piece of work. Local pawn-broker. And from what everyone round here believes, you're the local abortionist.'

'I do all I can to save life, not end it. My God, man, have you any idea what happens during an abortion? It goes against my every belief, both medical and religious.'

'But it is a common way for women to rid themselves of unwanted children.'

'Which is why I instigated my family-planning clinic. To stop women getting into that situation.'

Angus looked at Jeannie, concern written all over his face.

'How can she prove that she was not the abortionist?'

'An alibi.'

'I was at the clinic, I saw twenty people, I wrote the notes down in the log. Each person paid roughly a shilling to see me.'

'And this can be verified in your records?'

'Of course.' She stood up. 'Now, can I go, please? I'm beginning to smell of this awful place.'

After she had shown them the records that stated she had been in attendance at the clinic in the hours before the girl's admission to hospital, Jeannie was free to go and Angus drove her home. Somehow she could tell that he was letting her collect her thoughts, and wouldn't say anything until she asked him to. At the house, they went into the study.

'I can't believe that these people are doing this,' she said, her voice betraying her exhaustion and exasperation. 'Why can't they just let me help them?'

Angus took her hand. 'Sometimes the people who most need our help, my dear, are those least willing to accept it.'

Jeannie gave a wobbly smile. 'Thank you, Angus,' she said shakily. 'I don't know what I'd have done without you there.'

'It's good to be useful instead of the recipient of charity and pity,' he mumbled.

'But—'

'You've been so kind to me since I lost Margaret,' he said. 'Particularly since Sir Justin seems intent on blaming me for her death. So many people I considered friends have turned out to be anything but.'

'Your friendship means a lot to me, Angus.' She looked at their entwined hands.

'As much as it does to me?' He stroked her fingers. Jeannie willed herself to look at him, but she couldn't in case she was mistaken.

'Everything sorted out?' Innes said, as he walked into the room. 'I presume you haven't been charged with anything.'

'No.' Angus pulled away his hand and stood up. 'They're satisfied that Jeannie was the second person to attend to the girl and she has been formally exonerated.'

'That's something,' Innes said. 'Well, thank you, Angus, you've been kept up long past your bedtime.'

'I'll be in touch.' Angus held Jeannie's gaze for a little longer than he should have, then left.

He was an attractive man, Jeannie thought, everything she should want. And he wanted her. But she knew, as sure as she was breathing, that something was holding her back. Margaret.

That Sunday, Jeannie dreamed through Innes's interminable sermon, wondering about a time when she could simply have kept house, lived with her husband and raised some children. But that would never happen now. Because the one man who had expressed an interest would for ever be Margaret's in her heart. To think of him in that way seemed like a betrayal of her friend, but he was kind, gentle and witty, and her only chance of a husband. Angus would be a good husband to her, the way he had been devoted to Margaret. But could she live with her conscience if she married him?

A little later she walked out of the church and waited for Innes to come to be congratulated on his service. But as the congregation wandered away, enjoying the sharp sunshine,

Jeannie heard an accent that was rarely heard in that part of Kinross.

'Murderer!' It was Houston, the pawn-broker. 'You murdered my daughter and my grandchild. Abortionist!' He rushed over to her. 'You'll not hear the end of this, madam!' And spat in her face.

'Now.' An off-duty chief inspector – only that grade of policeman and above had the money to worship at Innes's church – grabbed Houston and wrestled him to the ground. 'I am arresting you for breach of the peace.'

'She's the abortionist! She's the murderer! Arrest her!' As Houston was dragged away by some of the younger congregation, Jeannie could feel everyone's eyes on her. She got out her lace-edged handkerchief and wiped away his spittle. And waited for someone to begin chatting again.

'I've been cleared by the police, Innes, what more can I say?' she said, as they sat down for dinner that evening. 'If I keep denying it I'm simply drawing attention to the allegations.'

'You're destroying our good name in these parts,' Innes replied. 'And I'm trying to do my ministry here.'

'But I'm not doing it purposefully!' Jeannie took a deep breath. 'If it happens what can I do? It's only because that awful man turned up at church that anyone heard of it. But I can't help it if no one ever listens to me, if they just believe what people shout at them. I've tried, Innes, but if people would rather listen to gossip than the truth there's nothing I can do.'

'Defiance is appropriate in certain circumstances,' Innes said quietly, 'but there are also times when compromise is necessary.'

'How can I compromise?' she asked.

'By giving up your work with women. That's the choice, Jeannie. Our family's good name or your stubbornness.' He left Jeannie alone with her guilt.

Jeannie spent the rest of the afternoon walking over the hills, trying to find some peace. When she arrived back at the house, Fiona was fussing in the drawing room, already dressed for the club.

'You're going out already?' Jeannie asked. 'I thought we might stay in, and Hamish isn't having a good day.'

'There's no point in sitting here moping,' Fiona picked up the bottle of gin. 'Martini?'

'No, I need to get ready.' Jeannie left her and got dressed in her best clothes. At least at the club she wouldn't see Houston. She could dance away her problems, forget about the poor and unfortunate — be like Fiona for a few hours. She smiled in the mirror, a bright false smile that started and ended with her even white teeth. She felt as if she was drowning.

'Marjorie!' As soon as they arrived Fiona headed for her friends, pointedly ignoring her family. At least Hamish wasn't there to see it, thought Jeannie.

As she watched Innes drift away, she felt a sudden panic. She didn't want to face the people who had watched her being accused and spat at that morning. But they were all around her. She headed for the patio. Angus was there, staring out into the dark night. The sadness on his face tore at her. 'You look like I feel,' she said gently.

'You feel as bad as I do?'

She shook her head. 'It's that clinic of mine again,' she said wistfully.

'I'm rather good at listening,' he said.

Gradually the whole story spilled out, the people, the illnesses and the ever-present struggle for money.

'Let me worry about finding sponsors for your clinic.' He patted her on the arm. 'I'll have it organised by the end of next week.'

'What would I do without you?'

'Bully someone else into it?' He grinned. 'Do you want to dance?'

'I just want to go to bed and sleep.'

'Fiona has a very eclectic circle doesn't she,' Angus remarked. 'Unlike boring old us, friends for years.'

'Fiona likes to collect admirers,' Jeannie grimaced. 'You must be the only man alive who's blind to her charms.'

'I was Hamish's best man,' Angus said, as he stared up at the sky. 'So much has changed since then. And not for the better.'

'Perhaps it'll change tomorrow,' she said gently.

'Perhaps.' He looked up into the sky, then walked away, into the darkness that surrounded the clubhouse. Part of Jeannie wanted to go with him, to comfort him, but another part wanted to leave him to his grief. To let him come to himself.

'I heard you had a run-in with Houston,' Ross said, when he found her on the patio. 'To say nothing of the newspaper report that you were questioned by the police.'

'He blames me for his daughter's death. And, unfortunately, mud sticks.'

'What do you mean?'

'To say I'm being cut is an understatement. Even the waiters won't speak to me.'

'I thought you didn't care what people said about you?'

'I don't care what they say if they say it to my face, but they only say it behind my back.'

'Come and dance.' He held out his hand.

'I don't want to. You know I'm an awful dancer.'

'Coward.'

She held out her work-reddened hand. As she walked to the dance-floor, she heard the murmurs.

'Just ignore them.' Ross looked straight ahead.

'It's a disgrace.' That was a female voice.

'Just ignore them,' he murmured again.

'I want to run away and hide,' she whispered.

'Thank you.' He swept her up and began to dance with considerably more grace than she. 'You'd leave me standing here for everyone to laugh at?'

'What?' Jeannie burst out laughing.

'You heard me.' He chuckled. 'And just this once, Jeannie, let the man lead.'

They danced three quicksteps, then Jeannie couldn't stand the stares any longer. 'Please, let's go.'

'You wouldn't last a second in my life, Jeannie Macdonald.' He escorted her back to the table at which the rest of the family were sitting.

'Why not?'

He shook his head.

As she drove home that night, she found her family's coolness towards her as distressing as the hostility of those at the club.

'Well, I'd better be going,' Ross said, as he finished a late-night sherry with Innes and Jeannie.

'No, stay,' Jeannie said.

'I have to be up early and I've little taste for company after today.' Innes put down his glass and left the room.

'It will all blow over, won't it?'

'They're your friends,' Ross said mercilessly.

'I'm glad you were there tonight.' She walked over to him and laid a hand on his arm. 'At least you know what I'm doing.'

'Or I'm so desperate to ingratiate myself into your circle that I'll ignore anything?' He looked keenly at her.

'No,' she said firmly. 'Whether you admit it or not, Mr Macintosh, you think I'm doing a good job.'

'I do.' He smiled. 'But in a ham-fisted way.' For a moment he hovered.

'Is there something you want?' Jeannie said hopefully. Nowadays it seemed to her that only Ross knew how to make her feel better. And she wanted him to stay. There was something about him that made her feel she could talk to him all night and listen to him too. He was the most interesting person she knew.

'Goodnight.' For a moment, she saw uncertainty pass over Ross's face. He bent towards her and she turned to him and their noses banged together.

'Sorry.' She giggled with nervousness. Had he been about to kiss her?

'My mistake. Goodnight.' He picked up his coat and hat in a single fluid movement.

An icy winter turned into a bitter spring and Jeannie found her practice busier than ever. Jim's weak chest coupled with his need to earn extra money by doing more shifts at the hospital, often kept him from the surgery. Days and nights merged into one long waiting room full of people. And as spring dripped into a chill wet summer, the passing weeks were only discernible by the increase in daylight that she never saw.

'So, what do you think of our financial situation?' she asked, as she sat in Angus's drawing room late one evening, sipping sherry as she sought his advice on funds for the clinic.

'Pretty dire,' Angus said. 'Are you sure there are no more charitable foundations you can approach?'

'I've tried everything.' She shook her head despairingly. 'There just aren't enough hours in the day. I can't be a doctor and a bookkeeper.'

'If I could have a look at your trust fund, I might find a way to get some money from it. All you have to do is tell Innes that I'm now your legal counsel.'

'Why would I do that, Angus? I thought I might approach Ross Macintosh for money. He's always been sympathetic to what I'm trying to do and has never refused to help me when I needed him.'

'But he's not far from those he left behind, Jeannie. Men like Ross aren't fussy about how they make their money, you know.'

'That's just snobbery, Angus, because he didn't inherit it.' She took her glass from his hands. 'I'd thought better of you.'

'You jump to his defence very quickly, Jeannie,' Angus said, his voice sounding strained.

'I've just found that he isn't the man I thought he was.' She smiled. 'Angus, I have two cousins, but thank you for the avuncular interest.'

'A woman needs the protection of a man, so I will become the administrator of your surgery. If you give me power of attorney over your business dealings, I can look at ways to make the best use of your money.'

'Would you?' She clapped her hands in delight. 'I don't deserve you.' She felt the weight of her financial anxieties lift from her shoulders.

Angus looked as if he had something else to say – she could see it was on the tip of his tongue – but he swallowed it. 'I'll send you the papers. Take care, Jeannie, and call in to tell me how you get on.' He bent and kissed her cheek.

'I will. Goodbye.'

Angus was more than a friend to her, Jeannie knew. Perhaps she ought to forget her concerns about Margaret. They got along so well together – and surely that was the foundation of a good marriage. Together they would find a way to pay for the clinic.

'If only people knew what I'm really doing,' she murmured. Then she stopped. 'Why didn't I think of it before? My side of the story.' And walked to the telephone.

'When will the interview be published?' Jeannie asked.

Robert Birse exhaled deeply. 'Difficult to say. You're a controversial woman, Dr Macdonald. I have to be cautious not to shock our readers.'

'A man is blaming me for his daughter's death, and she died at the hands of an abortionist.' She stared at the journalist sitting impassively in front of her. 'All my good work is disappearing because people now believe I'm the kind of person who'll perform these operations.'

'Well, you'd hardly be the first doctor in these parts to undertake them,' Robert said. 'I'm sure you're as aware of them as I am.'

'I don't know what you're talking about,' she replied. 'And I'm not the guardian of anyone's morals but my own.'

'Jeannie!' Hamish walked in. 'Oh, I'm sorry, I didn't know you were consulting.'

'Robert Birse, the *Courier*.' Robert offered his hand. 'Dr Macdonald is giving me an interview.'

'The *Courier*?' Hamish echoed. 'Jeannie, are you sure?'

'It's the only way to stop the gossips, Hamish,' she said. 'I'm going to tell my story, and let everyone know the truth.' She chuckled. 'My cousin Hamish, Mr Birse.'

'Are you also in the medical profession?' Robert asked politely.

'Oh, no.' Hamish shook his head. 'I'm busy with my crosswords most days.'

'Have we published any?' Robert put away his notebook.

'Not yet.' Jeannie opened a drawer. 'But there's no reason why you can't.' She took out a set of grids.

'Jeannie—' Hamish began.

'Hamish,' Jeannie said challengingly, 'I've some here.'

Hamish went over to her and looked at them. Then he smiled nervously at Robert. 'That one.' He pointed at it. 'It's a good one.' He handed the grid to the journalist and backed out of the room.

'Get it in the paper.' She stood up, and gestured for Robert to do the same.

'I can't make any promises,' he began.

'Don't let me down, Mr Birse. You may need me – because I've a lot more to say.'

After a week of quiet asides and disapproving looks, the

surgery lost its last charitable grant. Now they had only enough money to survive for a few months. And Jim had no income, except from his hospital work.

'What will we do?' she said, as they looked over the letter for the thirtieth time.

'We attend to these sick people in there,' Jim replied, gesticulating at the waiting room. 'And I'll talk to the hospital, see if I can get a few more shifts there till this blows over.'

'I'm sorry, Jim,' she said. 'It's your life's work and I've ruined it.'

Jim laughed drily. 'We all make mistakes, Jeannie, and we all have to live with them.' He patted her hand. 'And one day you'll come into your own. You'll be proved right because the truth will out.'

'My crossword.' Hamish was smiling broadly as he looked at it. 'They printed it.'

'Congratulations.' Jeannie hugged him. 'You're famous now.'

'Should I send them another?'

'Why not write to Robert Birse and ask him?' She smiled. 'If the readers like this one the paper should want to publish your others.'

Hamish smiled and Jeannie saw a shadow of the man he had once been. Perhaps this was who Hamish was now, she thought, this quiet, rather diffident man. And they would have to get used to it, as they would have adjusted to a blind Hamish.

Chapter 18

'Ross!'

'Jeannie!' Ross was standing eyeball to eyeball with a large man who smelt strongly of hair oil.

'I really need to talk to you—' She stopped as she sensed the atmosphere in the room.

'It's all right,' Ross growled. 'He's just leaving.'

'I'll see you later,' the man snarled, and stormed out of the room, slamming the door.

'He didn't look happy,' Jeannie remarked, as she perched on Ross's desk.

'No, he didn't.' Ross stared after him.

The door opened and Tam walked in. 'Cup of tea for the lady.'

'Thank you. How's the knee?'

'Still giving me some gyp, but not as much as before. That castor oil tastes foul, though.'

'Is your knee playing you up again?' Ross was discomfited that Tam had seen Jeannie without telling him.

'The doctor knows her stuff,' Tam said.

'Did you make me some tea?' Ross asked.

'If you want me to be your maid, I suggest you buy me a pinny,' Tam retorted.

'You made her one!'

'She's a guest.'

'Tam,' Jeannie jumped off the desk and went over to him,

'I have to ask him a favour. And he has to be in a good mood for that.'

Tam grinned, showing the spaces where his teeth had been. 'All right, Doctor,' he said, 'but I'm doing it for you, not him.' He went off to fetch it.

'What do you want?' Ross said.

'Money.'

'Here's twenty quid,' Ross said, and opened the box on his desk.

'Thank you.' She folded the notes, trying not to stroke them. 'But it isn't enough. No matter how much anyone gives us, it isn't enough. I wondered if you could bring some in from local business and the like.'

'How much?' He sat on the desk next to her.

'I need the money to keep the surgery open.' She cleared her throat. 'Since my clinic opened, the surgery has suffered from my association with it. It's my responsibility to make up the difference.'

'I can try. I admire you, Dr Macdonald. Not many would bother with this.'

'We'll be taking part in a study of pulmonary disease among the folk of Kirkcaldy in a few months,' Jeannie told him. 'If I can keep the surgery open till then, we'll be able to continue until I can find another way to keep my clinic open. I might be able to persuade the hospital to take it on.' She took his arm. 'I overreached myself, I understand that now, people weren't ready for the clinic. If it's run from the hospital, they'll be able to ignore the public outcry. There's talk that the government will give them money to do it soon.'

'But you'll have lost your clinic,' Ross said.

'I don't know what else to do. I've run out of options and I don't have the energy to find another way.' She traced a scratch on the desk with her finger. 'I've made a mess of things, and I can't fight any more.'

'Things have a habit of working themselves out.'

'You don't understand,' she protested. 'Since I got it into my mind that I wanted to be a doctor, I thought that the only battle would be to complete my degree.' She laughed. 'Then it was a battle to find a job and be accepted as a physician, and another to find a way to help people, and then to make everyone understand what I was doing.' She sighed, a deep sigh that seemed to come from her soul. 'I just don't think I have any fight left in me.'

'Jeannie,' Ross cupped her face in his hands. 'Don't let them win. I was pulling myself out of my background for years before I met you, when it suddenly got a lot easier. You've always treated me as an equal, unlike some of the others. You just took me as a man. And that, Dr Macdonald, is the measure of who you are.'

Jeannie stared at him – a man who respected and wanted to help her. A man who liked her just for being her.

At that moment Tam walked in. 'Sorry! You never said you were busy with a woman, Ross.'

'I'm not,' Ross said, as Jeannie moved away. 'Think about what I said. I'm willing to help you in any way I can. And there might be a better way to help than just giving money.'

Jeannie shrugged. 'At least we can try.'

He did more than try. Every day there was a letter addressed to her with a donation, or sometimes just an envelope stuffed with money. The amounts were never large enough to make a difference on their own, but she knew that Ross was keeping his word. And that made the world of difference to her.

'That's the first time I've seen you smile in months, Jeannie,' Hamish remarked as they had breakfast together one morning.

'Just thinking about the future, Hamish.' She folded the letter carefully and put it down on the pristine tablecloth. 'And wondering why it never does what we want it to.'

'Because we hope for the wrong things, Jeannie,' he said.

'Because we think we can make God go along with what we want, instead of the other way round.'

Suddenly Jeannie saw a new Hamish, neither the happy-go-lucky man he had been nor the nervous, introspective man he had become. He was thoughtful, perceptive. 'I've no idea what God has planned for me,' she said.

'You help people, Jeannie.' He actually winked at her over his cup. 'You've helped me. I've been given a contract by the *Courier* to write their crosswords. Finally I've a real job. I can pay you back for everything.'

Jeannie saw now that he had shed the bitterness. He'd found his place. He wasn't the business success he had thought he would be, and he certainly wasn't the man everyone had imagined he would be, but he was still Hamish.

'I don't need anything back, Hamish,' she said. 'Just to see you like this is all the thanks I could ever ask.' She excused herself from the table, got ready for work and left the house, trying to push away the jealousy inside her: everyone else was moving on with their lives and leaving her behind. Innes was moving on, and Hamish no longer needed her support. She'd been discarded, like a nanny they'd grown out of.

But even with the ever-reliable Angus in charge of the accounts, things were far from easy.

'We have enough money to run the women's clinic till the end of the month,' he said, late one Friday night. 'Why don't you ask Innes to break your fund? You're bound to have enough in it.'

'I can get to my money when I marry or turn thirty,' she replied. 'The trustees, one of whom is Innes, have been immovable about it.'

'You have bills to pay, Jeannie, and if you don't break your fund, you might find yourself out of a job. I can't work miracles, but if I had your fund I'm sure I could do something useful with it. Innes isn't a broker and I am.'

He handed her the books. 'Read them for yourself, my dear. Now I have to see some of my other clients.' He bent to kiss her swiftly and left the sunny conservatory where they had been sitting.

Jeannie spent hours looking at the accounts. The last of Margaret's money had gone and there would be no more. Did she really have the nerve to speak to Sir Justin and ask for some of Margaret's legacy?

'Eugenia.' Sir Justin welcomed her into his study, a shrine to his hunting trophies. It was lined with leatherbound books that would never be read. 'It's lovely to see you. I hear about you, of course, but rarely have a chance to talk to you.'

'I know,' she said wryly. 'I've become rather notorious lately.'

'How's that clinic of yours? Margaret was so enthusiastic about what you were doing there.'

'It's going well.' She smiled as he handed her a sherry. 'But we're running out of money.' She looked up at Sir Justin. 'I know this sounds a bit heartless, but Margaret came to see the clinic before she had her accident. She mentioned that she was changing her will, and making a bequest to the clinic. I wouldn't ask but the situation is desperate.'

Sir Justin was silent. Eventually he said, 'I had hoped that it wouldn't come to this, Eugenia, but Margaret's will is being contested.'

'Contested?' Jeannie repeated. 'By whom?'

'Angus.' Sir Justin's face darkened. 'My daughter changed her will two days before she died, and he's contesting the new will on the grounds that she was not of sound mind when she made it.'

'Margaret was perfectly sane.' Jeannie jumped to her friend's defence. 'I spoke to her just before she died – she came to the surgery to see how we worked. I can't believe Angus is putting you through this.'

'The more I learn about him, the less he surprises me.'

'He's always been such a decent man – he's helped me so much with my recent troubles.'

'Be careful with Angus. I found out too late that he's not the gentleman he appears.' He pulled open a drawer and took out his chequebook. 'How much do you need?'

'Anything would be useful. I'll have to close the clinic soon, and the surgery itself is under threat since we lost two of our charitable grants from religious foundations.' Jeannie winced.

'Have this.' He held out a cheque. 'It'll keep you going till all this unpleasantness is sorted out.' He paused. 'You've been spending a lot of time with Angus, haven't you?'

'I told you that he's been helpful through my recent problems.'

'Don't allow yourself to become involved with him personally,' Sir Justin warned her.

'Angus has been a friend for years.'

'I mean romantically, Eugenia.' He considered his words carefully. 'It would not be to your benefit. It might even be dangerous.'

'Of course. Thank you.' She kissed his cheek and bade him goodbye.

'Angus!' Jeannie welcomed him with more reticence than usual when he appeared in the drawing room. 'Thank you for coming.'

'Anything for my favourite girl.' He held her gaze for rather too long.

She handed him a glass of whisky. 'There is something I want to know.'

'You can ask me anything.' He patted the seat next to him.

'You told me about our financial troubles. And I cannot get the bequest Margaret left to the clinic because you are contesting it.'

Angus's face darkened. 'So, he's trying to get you on his side now, is he?' He looked at her in a way that made her almost afraid.

'It isn't that. It's just me being selfish.' She took his hands. 'We need the money desperately.'

'Well, there's nothing I can do. Her father's trying to ruin me – he's spoken to my clients.' His lips closed and she could see he would say no more on the matter.

'I don't want to fall out with you over something as vulgar as money,' Jeannie murmured.

'You were the one who brought it up.' Angus got up and crossed to the window. 'Perhaps I should leave.'

'No!' She ran over to him. 'I mean, I'd like you to stay, if you want to,' she added. How could she have suspected that Angus would do anything to hurt her? He was simply trying to protect himself. Margaret had told her often enough that her father didn't like Angus.

Angus turned to her with an almost wicked look on his face. 'Why would you like me to stay, Jeannie?' He put a hand to her face and rubbed his thumb over her lips.

'I have so few friends left,' she muttered.

'Is that what I am to you? A friend? I'd thought we were more than friends, Jeannie.' He stroked her neck.

'Margaret,' she whispered.

'Margaret is gone, and life must continue for us. We can be together.' He kissed her neck.

'But you were happy with Margaret.'

'She was my consolation prize. I made her happy and I tried to be a good husband. But since you returned, it was becoming more and more difficult to ignore my feelings.'

'So why marry her in the first place?' Jeannie closed her eyes. It was difficult to ignore the waves of pleasure his lips were giving her, but something worried her.

'I wanted to marry and I knew she'd make a suitable wife, passive and obedient. Not like you.'

'Not interrupting anything, am I?' Fiona's brittle tone interrupted Angus's hand's journey southwards. 'Angus, darling, you're looking simply divine. Quite the most handsome man in the district.' She came across to kiss him. 'Come and amuse me. I lack male company and that's not a situation I enjoy.'

To Jeannie's chagrin, Angus moved away from her to sit with Fiona. But it was a relief too. Angus had told her that Margaret, who had been like a sister to her, had been in a sham of a marriage. As she watched Fiona enchant him in her own stylish way, Jeannie battled with her feelings. Angus had all but declared his love for her, but Margaret, the woman who had died while pregnant with his child, stood between them. The woman who had supported everything Jeannie had done. Her dearest friend, his wife. But there he was, talking to Fiona. He had lost weight since Margaret had died, and his friendly face had a strong, lean look about it. Fiona was right, Angus was a handsome man, an eligible widower in a land now devoid of suitable men.

Jeannie was distracted for the rest of the evening, unable to concentrate on what Angus had told her about Margaret's will because of what he had said about their relationship. She had always wanted a husband, and to be the same as everyone else. She wanted a handsome, urbane man, who was a respected member of their society. A man she liked, cared for and trusted. But Angus was still, in her mind, Margaret's husband.

'Hopefully we'll be quiet for the next few days,' Jim said, as she arrived the next day. 'It's amazing how people recover when there's a game of pitch and toss going.'

'I haven't been to the Links Fair for years,' she said. 'Uncle Gordon used to take us, but Daddy complained that he was leading us astray, mainly because he spent most of his time in the gambling tents while Hamish and I wandered around on our own. Innes stayed at home with his stamp collection. I remember they used to sell bright pink candy.'

'Guaranteed to rot your teeth in an afternoon.' Jim smiled.

'Aye – if the germs all over it don't kill you first!'

'And I was going to buy you some,' Jim said teasingly.

'You're that desperate to get rid of me?'

'Dr Jim!' Charlie ran in from the waiting room. 'It's Midden Pete. They've found him, and he's deid!'

Jim picked up his bag. 'Sorry to leave you with the list, Jeannie . . .' He pulled on his coat.

'Away you go, and remember to wash your hands. No man has ever been as well named.'

'It'll have to be another night for me at the fair,' Jim said. 'See you later.'

The waiting room was groaning with people, many of whom smelt sweet with the rot that the wet weather had brought. 'I'll still be here tomorrow by the looks of it,' she said. 'First, please.'

She worked through the morning, but the long line of patients didn't diminish. Jim hadn't returned and Jeannie was tempted to send them home, but what would be the point? She would only see them again a few hours later. So she worked on. When Jim returned for a few hours before his shift at the hospital, they had hardly time to greet each other before it was time for her to leave.

Jeannie had put on her coat and stepped out of the building when she paused. She could go home, have dinner and go to bed. Or she could have an adventure. She rifled in her bag for a penny, then threw it into the air. 'Heads home, tails the fair.' The coin landed in the gutter. She looked down at it. 'Tails it is,' she said triumphantly. The coin was lodged in a suspiciously solid piece of mud.

'You want that, Doctor?' Charlie said, as he appeared beside her. 'Wouldn't have thought you'd want to put your hand in that shite.'

'Something tells me you put it there just in case, Charlie. Of course you can have it. Less money for me to waste at the fair.'

Chapter 19

They walked together along the steep road that wound down towards the seafront. Jeannie detected the tang of salt in the air, mixed with the faint burning of the lights strung up everywhere and the smoke from the makeshift braziers that were cooking sausages and hunks of fatty meat.

'Smell that!' Charlie sniffed appreciatively.

'Only if I have to,' Jeannie replied, as they were carried along by the crowd to where the tents were hoisted. The attractions. 'Come on.' She took Charlie's damaged hand and marched purposefully through the crowds.

'I know the way, Doctor,' Charlie whispered, as they stood outside the Cavern of Curiosities – a striped dirty tent guarded by a shabby man with a handlebar moustache, promising them the mysteries of the Orient. 'This way.' The pair went round to the back of the tent where wires and drums were piled up. 'Come on.' He held up the edge.

'Charlie!' Her hands flew to her mouth.

'Now!'

They scrambled under the filthy tarpaulin but as they emerged into the dim gas-light they heard a man shout, 'Oi!'

Jeannie felt Charlie grab her by the coat and they disappeared back the way they had come. Then they ran, as fast as they could, through the fair until they came to a halt near the bottom outside a large beer tent, laughing as if neither had a care in the world.

'Look at your hair!' Charlie chortled. 'You look like a wild woman out of the tent.'

'I'm filthy!' She tried to brush the mud off her clothing, but it was too damp. She giggled.

'What on earth happened to you?' Ross Macintosh's voice floated to them over the hubbub.

'What are you doing here?' She squinted at him.

'The beer tent is mine.' He beckoned her over. 'You look like you've been in a fight.'

'Charlie's been teaching me how to find alternative entrances.' She smiled proudly.

'Leading you astray, eh?' Ross glanced down at the lad. 'Come on, I'll give you the tour.' He stared at Charlie as he ushered her away from him, and threw him a coin with a wink. 'A wee drink, perhaps?' he suggested to Jeannie.

'Maybe later. Now I want to see what's going on.'

Ross took her elbow and they walked together through the fair. They tried their luck on the hoopla stall and watched children duck for apples in a barrel. She stood beside Ross as he didn't quite manage to ring the bell with the strong-man hammer, and laughed as they paraded themselves through the hall of mirrors.

'Not much more down here,' he said, as they came to the end. 'Just a fortune-teller . . . and if the lady wanted to find out what was in store for her?'

'I shouldn't, you know, Innes would be most upset.' She grinned.

'Since when has upsetting him stopped you doing anything?' he asked, and held up a sixpence.

Jeannie took the coin and went into the tent. It was dark and smelt of sacking, straw and musk. A rather fat middle-aged woman sat over a crystal ball. 'Sit,' she said.

Jeannie sat.

'Cross my palm with silver.'

Jeannie handed over the coin as the oil lamp spluttered in

the evening breeze. The woman took her hand and ran a pudgy finger over the rough palm. 'You're at a crossroads in your life.' She glanced up meaningfully. 'And there's a man, a man who cares for you but you don't see it. A tall, dark, handsome man, who you don't want to love. But you do.'

'What's his name?' Jeannie said breathlessly.

'The signs are dim.' The woman looked into her eyes, and Jeannie had the uncomfortable feeling she was being examined in the way she examined her patients.

'You have money problems, working beneath your station, but your problems will be over with this marriage.'

'Is his name Angus?' she asked.

'Aye.' The woman nodded. 'He's the one for you. He's the key to all your worries. But beware of false love.'

Jeannie smiled. Angus was her saviour.

'Thank you.' She got up, walked out and saw him there. A tall, dark, handsome man. Called Ross. Her face fell.

'Well?' he said, as he came up to her. 'Did she tell you about your tall, dark, handsome stranger?'

'You know it's all rubbish,' she replied. 'And, yes, she did.'

'You don't look very happy with what you learned,' he remarked mildly.

'What she told me isn't in my plans. I'm tired. I think I'll head for home. Thank you for your company, Ross.' She walked away, trying to understand how a sixpenny fortune-teller could upset her so much.

Ross checked himself in the mirror one last time. He looked successful, a man of means. But would Hamish see him like that? Or would he just see the miner, the boy from Lochgelly who had charmed, schemed and bullied his way into their circle? There was nothing for it. He'd just have to go and find out.

'I'll see if Mr Hamish is in to visitors.' As the housekeeper left him, Ross steeled himself to be told that he wasn't in.

'Ross!' Hamish walked out of the conservatory. 'This is unexpected. Have you visited our home before?'

'A few times.'

'Jeannie isn't here. So much to do, you know.' He ushered Ross towards the drawing room. 'She's considering asking the infirmary to own and run the ladies' clinic. It's just too much for one woman on her own, even with Angus helping her. Funds are never easy to come by, especially for controversial causes like hers.' He opened the drawing-room door.

'What are you doing here?' Fiona paled as they walked into the room.

'I've come to talk to Hamish,' Ross said politely. Fiona left him cold now, despite her beauty, because he could see her as she was: a porcelain doll, beautiful to look at but cold and empty inside.

'What about?' Fiona asked.

'A business matter,' he returned.

'Why don't you take him into the conservatory, Hamish?' Fiona suggested.

'Perhaps that would be best,' Hamish said. When they had sat down, he went on, 'I know about you and my wife. She's difficult to resist.'

'I don't know what you're talking about.'

'Fiona has needs that I cannot meet. She ought to be more discreet, though. She was seen going to your home.'

'I haven't spoken to her for over six months,' Ross said slowly. 'I'm sorry.'

Hamish shrugged. 'Men tire of her. It's the chase and initial conquest that engage them.' Hamish gave a little smile. 'Afterwards it's just a sordid little affair . . . She'll never leave me, she's got the protection of a husband, and none of her other men would be foolish enough to marry a woman who was so consistently unfaithful. But I can't make her happy.' Hamish paused. 'So what is it? Photographs, or simply letters?'

Ross shook his head. 'I came to talk to you about Jeannie.'

'What about her?'

'I have come to ask your permission to marry her.' He spoke quickly, betraying his nervousness.

Hamish began to laugh. 'You, a vain social climber who thought nothing of sleeping with another man's wife, want to become Jeannie's husband? What makes you think you could be faithful to her?'

'I would,' he replied stiffly. 'I can provide for her and I can help her with the clinic . . .'

'So you'd have no objections to her keeping on with the work, even after you had children?'

'Of course not, if that was what she wanted,' Ross said. 'What's wrong with a woman working?'

'A lot of men would disagree with you. Go away and think about what being married would mean. One woman, Jeannie, for the rest of your life. If you aren't sure, we'll say no more about it. But if you are sure it's what you want, I'll not stop you.'

'Thank you.' Ross attempted to shake his hand but Hamish walked past him.

'I have forgiven my wife, Mr Macintosh, but not you. And I don't think you're good enough for my cousin, although that is her decision to make and not mine.'

As Ross left, Hamish returned to the drawing room and Fiona.

'What did he want?' she asked fearfully.

Hamish sat down. 'Has Jeannie accepted Angus yet?' he asked.

Fiona arched an eyebrow.

'Macintosh wants to marry her too.' He squeezed Fiona's hand. 'Let's hope she chooses the right man.'

'I never thought she was attractive enough to collect two suitors,' Fiona sniped.

'Jeannie is a special woman, not of the kind men fall in love with, but whom they love for ever.'

Fiona said nothing.

'Thank you for coming, Angus,' Jeannie said, as he walked into the surgery. The waiting patients gazed at him with something approaching worship. He looked so out of place: his clothes and bearing didn't belong with the small, hunched people surrounding him.

'I thought it was about time I saw the place I administer.' He cast an eye over the small waiting room. 'Why are there no seats?'

'They disappear and become firewood,' she said wryly. 'At this time of year we don't bother replacing them. We tried a long bench once, but it didn't last the morning. Charlie had already told them.'

Angus looked around suspiciously, as if he was waiting for someone to attempt to steal his watch.

'Why don't we talk in my room?' Jeannie said. But when she opened the door and Angus walked in, she felt her natural defensive instinct take over. 'Sorry, but we don't have the funds for niceties.'

'I know.' Angus was preoccupied, and it showed. 'I wanted to talk about another matter.' He went over to Jeannie's desk and picked up her stethoscope. 'A matter we had begun to discuss when Fiona came in.' He wrapped the tubing round his fist.

'Please don't snap it – the rubber is perished enough as it is.' Jeannie tried to take it from him, but Angus grasped her fingers. 'And I don't have the funds for a new one,' she continued.

'Let me take care of those things, Jeannie,' he said quietly. 'Be my wife and let me take care of everything.'

'Angus,' she murmured, and closed her eyes.

'Jeannie,' he whispered, 'I know that Margaret was your closest friend but this is what she would want. For both of us to be happy.'

'Angus, I don't know what to say.' It was a lie. She knew what she wanted to say. But she couldn't. She couldn't turn down a marriage proposal. Not at her age.

She arrived home cold and tired after the drive home and an exhausting day at the surgery. As she walked through the house, she was met by Hamish, grinning broadly.

'I'm so happy for you, Jeannie,' he said, as he embraced her. 'My two favourite people in the world. And now I'll have you both here. Together.' He held her tightly. 'I was so happy when Angus told me he had asked you. It means the world to me to know that you're happy.'

Jeannie's heart sank. Everything about Angus should make her want to marry him. And Hamish would be happy – everyone would, except her. He belonged to Margaret, but he had betrayed her. She knew it in her heart. The way he talked about her, the way he was contesting her will. How could she trust what he claimed to feel about her?

After dinner Hamish and Fiona went for a walk, and Jeannie retired to the study, to listen to the clock ticking and watch the fire. Fate had offered her a handsome, successful, popular husband. Why did it feel so wrong?

'The housekeeper let me in,' Ross said, then cleared his throat. 'In your bolt-hole again?'

'Sit down.' She indicated the chair across from her. 'You have a habit of catching me with my guard down.'

'You have the same habit, my dear Jeannie.' Ross cleared his throat again and pulled at his coat sleeve. 'I came here to ask you something.'

'Ask away.' She swept a hair off her face as he sat down next to her on the sofa.

'I need a wife.'

Jeannie remembered: she had promised to help him. She swallowed hard. 'And you want me to find you one?'

'Yes. Whoever you think is the most suitable partner for me, I'll propose to her.'

'Someone decorative?' Jeannie's voice was vaguely bitter. 'Appearances are everything to you, aren't they?'

'Ideally someone who didn't give me nightmares.' A smile curled his lips. 'Someone I could look at without getting bored.'

'You're cutting down the field, you know,' she said. 'And I suppose someone who is just out of their Season?'

'No, someone nearer my own age. Late twenties.' He waved to get it over and done with, but she didn't seem to understand what he was talking about.

'Rich?' She looked up at him.

'Definitely.' He grinned, but then, having seen she was not amused, grimaced.

'Would you accept a widow?' Jeannie bit her lip.

'No, I don't want someone else's wife, I want my own.'

'Anything else?' For some reason – she suspected the tiredness – there was a sinking feeling in her stomach.

'She should be interesting, and know her own mind. But not too much work.' He put his lips close to her ear. 'And she has to enjoy the bedroom.'

'Good.'

'She'll be spending a lot of time there.'

Jeannie nodded, almost in resignation. 'I'll try to find someone suitable.' She stood up and moved towards the fire. 'I'm getting married too.' She was wringing her hands. 'Pity, or I could have put myself forward for the position. Although I don't think I'd qualify on most counts.' She laughed without emotion.

'You're getting married?' Shock was written all over his face.

'It's not that surprising.' It came out louder than she intended. 'Someone might like me enough.'

'Who?' Ross trawled his memory for someone who had shown an interest in her.

'Angus Carmichael.' She smiled shyly. 'He's in mourning for another month or so, but he has declared himself. Don't tell anyone, please, there's been no official announcement yet.' She was babbling now and didn't know why.

'Why is he marrying you?' Ross said quietly.

'He doesn't mind that I'm a big fat lump, or that I work with poor people, or that I dance like a barnyard animal.' She laughed shrilly.

'I've never seen you together.'

'Well, he's a good friend of Hamish. They met at university and when he came to stay in the holidays he became part of our set. He's been a member of the family, more or less, for years.'

Ross was silent for what seemed like hours. 'My wife must be able to dance,' he said eventually. 'I forgot that. Congratulations, Jeannie.' He stood up. 'And since you're now engaged to someone else, perhaps I ought to go.'

'I shall try to find you a wife,' she said, as he walked away. 'Someone much better than me, don't worry about that—' Her voice wavered and she had to stop. And realised he had already closed the front door behind him.

Chapter 20

'What are you up to?' Tam said, as he came into Ross's office the next day.

Ross was playing with a small box. 'Nothing.'

He tried to put it away, but Tam was too quick for him. He grabbed it and opened it. 'Bloody hell!' He took out the ring, a large sapphire mounted on a thick gold band. 'That must have cost you a fortune!'

'Got it in Edinburgh.'

'Who's the unlucky woman?' Tam grinned.

'No one.' He looked up. 'I forgot my bloody place again, didn't I?'

Tam thought briefly. 'Someone turned you down?'

Ross nodded. 'She's marrying someone else.' He stood up. 'Well, the rent won't collect itself.' He walked past Tam. 'And I don't want to hear another word about that other matter, right?'

'All right.' Tam followed behind him. 'Who was it anyway?'

'No one you'd know,' Ross replied.

Tam wasn't so sure.

From then on Jeannie saw little or nothing of Ross, but spent increasing amounts of time with Angus. She enjoyed his company, and Hamish felt at ease, so the four became a firm fixture at the Sunday-night dances at the club, to which Ross never went now. She had accepted an offer for the clinic from the hospital board. That way she and Jim would still have jobs. Jeannie sighed as she looked once more at the agreement. The board would take over her clinic, and she would work for them in the area of women's health, to include family planning, gynaecology and infants. It was a good deal, and two years ago she would have jumped at it. But now, to hand over the clinic seemed like an admission that she had failed. That she, a woman, couldn't run a clinic and needed a man to do it for her. Angus didn't understand – but no one had ever told him he couldn't do as he wanted because of who he was. Her eyes strayed to the window. As always she wondered where Ross was, and wished he would come and talk to her, make her feel better, angry and alive.

'He's not here, Dr Macdonald,' Tam said, as he opened the office door. 'He's at home.'

'Can you tell me where his house is? I just know that he lives over by Raith Park.'

'No, hen – sorry, Doctor,' Tam corrected himself. 'He's at home with his mam, in Lochgelly.'

'I really need to see him,' she said. 'I wanted to tell him about my clinic.' It was a feeble excuse and they both knew it.

'You got your car?'

It didn't take long to get to the little mining village, but even in the warm dusk it was a revelation to Jeannie. The village, with its pretty name, was a grim place, covered in the dust of the mine's dark bounty. Jeannie drove past the tiny cottages, wondering which was Ross's family home.

'They live up at the end,' said Tam.

The houses were getting a little larger, until they turned a corner and came to a row of cottages, each with its own little garden.

'Ross bought his mother a house here so she could move

out of the colliery houses,' Tam murmured. 'My mother still lives down there.'

They stopped outside a tiny cottage, and Tam got out.

'Come on, then,' he said happily. 'Mrs Macintosh will be in for a real surprise.'

'It's hardly polite, just turning up at her door without an invitation,' Jeannie worried.

'This isn't your posh folk now,' he told her. 'Round here, folk don't stand on ceremony.' He went up and knocked on the door, then shouted, 'Hello! It's me!'

'Tam!' An older woman, with familiar twinkling green eyes, opened the door. 'And . . . ?' She put a hand to her mouth. 'You have to be Jeannie.'

'Yes,' Jeannie replied uncertainly. 'But how did you know?'

'Just as my Ross described.' Mrs Macintosh ushered them both into a tiny front room.

'I know this is terribly rude—' Jeannie began.

'Not at all,' Mrs Macintosh interrupted. 'He's down at the pub. Come in for a cup of tea while I force poor Tam to get himself down there and fetch him back.'

'If you insist.' Tam tipped his cap and walked away.

'I told him he should bring you for a visit,' Mrs Macintosh said, as they went into the kitchen, 'but I know Ross. He prefers to have a bit of mystery about him.' She stopped as she opened the kitchen door. 'Betty, Mary, this is Jeannie,' she said, to the two young women present. She turned back to Jeannie. 'They're my daughters-in-law and the wee monsters trailing mud in and out of the place are my grandchildren.' She pointed to a horde of little boys and girls running in and out as they played in the garden. 'This is the newest arrival.' An infant lay sleeping by the fire in a wooden cradle. 'Mary's third and last.'

'You'll be able to tell me how to manage that,' Mary grinned. 'Ross said you're an expert on women's matters.'

As Mrs Macintosh pulled out a wooden chair and put the kettle on again, all four women shared a smile.

'Oh, hang,' Mrs Macintosh said quickly. 'Anyone fancy a wee stout?'

'Mam?' Ross walked straight in at the back door, followed by three other men. 'Tam was spouting some nonsense about . . .' He tailed off. His mother and his two sisters-in-law were sitting by the stove, as they had when he had left them. But with them, on a chair, with a sleeping baby in her arms, was Jeannie Macdonald. 'What are you doing here?' He stared at her as if she had returned from the dead.

'I needed to talk to you.' Suddenly Jeannie realised she had made a terrible mistake in coming.

'Perhaps it would be easier if you went into the front room, Ross,' his mother said. 'We'll make a bite of supper.'

Mary took her baby from Jeannie.

The front room was tiny, little more than two armchairs and a little table, with a fire in the grate.

'What do you want?' Ross said quietly.

'The hospital is taking over the women's clinic,' she said. 'I can't keep it open any more. I can't manage the money and the hospital can expand the clinic and help more women.'

'And you came here to tell me this?'

'No,' she said slowly. 'I came to ask why you aren't my friend any more.'

Ross smiled. 'You know, most people would have worked it out.'

'I'm not most people. I want to know why you never come and talk to me, tell me what I'm doing wrong, even when I'm right.' She smiled back at him.

'Really?' He bent and rubbed his nose against hers. 'I think you should leave.'

'Why?' There was something about his smell, the feel of his skin.

'Because you know what will happen if you don't,' he murmured. 'And you're getting married, remember?'

'I'm not. I want to turn him down,' she whispered.

'You know what you're saying, don't you?' he asked urgently.

She nodded and he kissed her. She kissed him back, pulling his head closer to her, greedy for him. She felt his hands, first round her waist, then on her back.

'Do you want—' Mary ended a high-pitched giggle as the two sprang apart. 'I see you're busy.'

'Yes, we are,' he said. And he took Jeannie's hand. 'Close the door behind you, Mary.'

'What must she think of me?' Jeannie wondered.

'She knows I love you.' He kissed her nose as he pulled her gently to the chair. 'Never thought I'd find you here.'

'Well, you never even mentioned you had a mother.' She played with his fingers. 'Not forgetting all those nephews and nieces.'

'I told you where I was from.'

'You made it sound as if they were dead.'

'Well, they'd hardly fit into my life now.' Ross chewed his lip. 'Can you see people like Fiona having tea here?'

'We're the most terrible snobs, but my father was in trade, and many of the people at the tennis club still see me in that way. We're only accepted because my grandfather was a solici-tor.'

'But Sir Justin and the like?'

'All clients of my grandfather.' She shrugged. 'And people like Sir Justin are so rich that they aren't bothered about little things like where others come from. Won't your mother be wondering what we're doing?'

Ross chuckled. 'I doubt it.' He kissed her again. 'But if your sensibilities are offended, we can go next door and eat cake.'

Jeannie nodded. 'She seems to know a lot about me.'

'I've mentioned you once or twice,' he responded, then took her hand and walked through the door.

Perched on a settle next to him, Jeannie drank tea as the

family gossiped and played with the children. Jeannie could see the looks that Ross's mother was exchanging with him, and it excited her. She didn't want the night to end, but eventually Ross's brothers and their families drifted away, till only Jeannie, Ross and his mother were left in the kitchen.

'Well, I'm away to bed now,' Mrs Macintosh said. 'You'll be staying tonight, Jeannie, so I'll put some blankets in the front room for Ross. You can have his bed.'

'I couldn't do that,' she said, shocked.

'Nonsense,' Mrs Macintosh replied. 'It's far too late for a lady like yourself to be out. Goodnight, both of you.' She smiled broadly then went upstairs.

'I can't stay,' Jeannie repeated quietly.

'Why not?' Ross said. 'Innes will be at the Kirk and the others, well, you're hardly answerable to them.'

'You know why.' Ross took her fingers and made a steeple with them.

'Don't worry about your virtue, Dr Macdonald,' he murmured. 'I'll be sleeping down here.' He led her out of the kitchen. 'It's not terribly comfortable, but it's a bed,' he said, as they reached the small, barely furnished room, with its single bed and chest of drawers. 'I'll say goodnight now, I think. There are a few matters you should sleep on. We can talk tomorrow.' He tried to move away, but Jeannie did not let go of his hand until their arms were stretched to their full length. More than anything, she didn't want him to leave. Didn't want the night to end.

'You know what this will mean, don't you?' Ross murmured. Jeannie nodded slowly.

'Oh, God, Jeannie.' He pulled her into his arms as she closed her eyes, enjoying his touch, the way he was opening her clothes, helping her pull off his own. She felt his lips on her neck, felt his skin warm on hers, and knew she was right. She'd never felt like this with Angus – she liked him, but as a friend. She wanted Ross, with a passion that both frightened and excited her. He laid her on the tiny narrow bed, and suddenly she was shy, covering herself with her hands.

'Don't, Jeannie,' he said softly. 'I want to look at you.' He sat down and moved her hands away gently, replacing them with his own. 'You're lovely,' he said.

And she believed that she was.

But as he removed the last of his clothing, she looked away, cursing herself. She'd seen hundreds of men naked, but this was different.

'Don't be nervous.' He lay on the bed next to her and kissed her again. 'We've all the time in the world.'

She giggled. It all seemed so absurd, both of them in the tiny bed in the tiny room.

'And please don't laugh at me.'

'There's not much room,' she remarked.

He moved so that he was on top of her. 'I've waited so long for this.' He kissed her neck and licked down to her collarbone.

'I don't know what to do,' she whispered, as she pulled his head away from her. 'I mean, I know what's supposed to happen, but . . .'

'But you're the local expert on making love!' he said incredulously. 'Are you telling me you're a virgin?'

Jeannie nodded, and expected to see shock on his face, but he seemed proud that she had chosen him as her first lover, and more than a little amused. 'Sorry, I'll probably do it all wrong,' she muttered.

'Just do what comes naturally, Jeannie, and you can't go wrong.'

She felt him nudge against her thigh and suddenly everything changed. 'I can't do this,' she hissed, and pushed him aside. 'You don't understand.' She sat up and clutched the sheet to her.

'What are you doing?' Ross raised his hand to touch her face but she flinched away from him.

'Just go away and leave me alone.' Jeannie could feel a

thousand emotions running through her. How could she have forgotten her beliefs, her morals, and thrown herself at Ross, a known seducer of vulnerable women? She watched as he left the room, then picked up her clothes from the faded rug and went to the nightstand where there was a jug of water and a bowl. She could smell him on her, a hard, masculine smell that was at odds with the soft lace and frills of the undergarments she was stepping into.

Jeannie ran her fingers through her hair, trying to pull it back into its simple bun. She hadn't been herself, she had been some man-hungry virago. And she was reminded of the women she had turned away when they had asked for abortions, all the lectures she had given about being careful. The first time a man had looked at her, she had thrown caution to the winds. What kind of a woman was she?

'Think, woman,' she told herself. Ross had said he loved her. Had he said the same to the others? How could she have chosen him over Angus, a friend of their family for years and the widower of Margaret? She had run to him, offered him her body, willingly betrayed Angus for a man who had asked her to find him a wife. That was how much he thought of her: a diversion for a night.

'What's wrong?' Ross said, as he opened the door to find her putting on her lisle stockings. 'What are you doing, Jeannie?'

'I have to get back,' she said avoiding his eyes.

'Stay. It's after midnight,' he said, in a matter-of-fact voice. 'My mother's expecting to see you in the morning.'

Jeannie stepped into her skirt and threw her arms into her blouse. She buttoned it as quickly as she could. 'This was a mistake, Mr Macintosh, a terrible mistake, and I'll thank you not to make the situation any worse.' She put on her sensible shoes. 'Please give your mother my apologies.'

'Jeannie, no!' Ross's voice was strident.

'Cover yourself up, please,' she said unsteadily, as she picked up her bag and coat.

'At least let me drive you back.' Ross pulled his trousers over his long johns.

'I'll find my own way home.' Jeannie slipped out of the room, ran down the stairs and out of the house. She took gulps of the chill night air to calm her nerves.

But then Ross was at her side, wearing only trousers and his shirt thrown over his shoulders. A thousand stars sprinkled their light on to the rainwashed track next to the cottage.

'Don't leave, Jeannie, please.' His arms slipped round her shoulders. 'You came to me, remember?'

'Yes. But you wouldn't have come to me. And now I'm walking away.' She shrugged off his hand and got into her car.

Ross knew Jeannie well enough to understand that she needed to be alone. 'I came to you,' he murmured, 'but you never noticed me.' She'll calm down, he thought. There was no way she would marry Angus Carmichael, but deep down he feared that she wouldn't even consider himself.

Jeannie drove home and went into the drawing room, unable to face her lonely bed after sharing one with Ross. Innes was sitting in a corner in the darkness, staring into the fire. 'Hello, Jeannie,' he said. 'Don't mind me, I'm just trying to make sense of my day. I'm sure you know what that's like.' Jeannie didn't answer. 'I spent the evening with the Hendersons. Bess wrote to me that she wants to come home, but they won't accept her even though she's given up the child for adoption. Been trying to . . . Hate the sin but love the sinner.' He exhaled loudly.

'Oh, Innes,' Jeannie collapsed on to the sofa, 'I can't marry Angus.'

'It's just nerves, Jeannie,' he said. 'Angus is a decent enough fellow and you'll be a steadying influence on him.' He put a hand on her shoulder. 'And you need to be married.'

'But I'm in love with someone else,' she said. A tear rolled down her cheek. 'And tonight I . . .' She couldn't bring herself to go on.

'Now, Jeannie, as a doctor, people tell you medical problems that they wouldn't dream of mentioning to anyone else. As a minister I deal with moral problems. Tell me as your minister, not as your cousin. Please.' He sat down next to her.

Jeannie cast her eyes down. 'I thought I should marry Angus because he's a friend, because it's a good match, because I might not get another proposal at my age and because Hamish was so happy at the prospect.' She picked at a loose thread in her skirt. 'But all the time I knew there ought to be something more to it than suitability.' She laughed. 'I suppose that's straight out of the penny dreadfuls.'

Innes patted her hand.

'Well, there was another man. Someone I didn't like at first but then I found I respected him, and he was so attractive and sure of himself. And he was always there when I needed him.' She swallowed. 'And I threw myself at him.'

'And he didn't reject you. He didn't behave like a gentleman, knowing you were considering committing yourself to another?' Innes said.

'No, he didn't.' She looked up into the dark warmth of the room, the shadows playing at the back of the dying fire. 'And I've let myself down, let down Angus, and I still know that I want Ross more than I want anything else.'

'Ross Macintosh?' Innes exploded, grabbing her arm. 'You fool, Jeannie! You complete and utter fool!'

'I love him. I thought he loved me,' she replied trying to defend herself from the onslaught.

'As much as he loved Enid Baker when he was sleeping with her? Fifty-two-year-old Enid Baker, who introduced him into the club? As much as he loved Fiona when he was sleeping with her?'

'He slept with Fiona?' Her head snapped round and she met Innes's eyes.

'They had an affair, until he tired of her. That man collects lonely women. I always had my suspicions that he was pursuing you for your trust fund, but you went to him. Can you imagine what would happen if it got out? We'd be ruined socially, and you'd be humiliated every time you saw him in the club now. And Angus by association.' He stood up. 'Anyone but Ross Macintosh. He's an acknowledged rake.'

Jeannie pushed back the wail that was at her lips. She knew that Innes was right. Ross had used her, and even now, if he tried to again, she'd let him.

'I can't marry Angus,' she said stiffly. 'I couldn't before and I can't now. Especially now.'

'You like Angus, and without him you'll never marry. We all make mistakes, Jeannie. I suggest you pray for the strength to put your indiscretions behind you. And we'll never speak of that man again!'

Innes's stern expression cowed her. She nodded and left the room. As she walked up the stairs she relived her time with Ross. She was as bad as the women she had lectured to at her clinic – because she still wanted him. She was no different from any other woman. Which, for Jeannie, was indeed a humbling thought.

Chapter 21

'You don't look very pleased with yourself,' said Tam, as Ross walked in the next morning. 'For someone with a new doctor to play with.'

Ross smiled grimly. 'That's not quite the case. Got a few complications to work out.'

'Someone playing you at your own game, Ross?' the older man mocked. 'It's a turn-up for the books for you not to know where you stand with a wench.'

'Aye, well, it's different this time.' He sat down and opened a letter that had arrived that morning.

'What's wrong?' Tam asked.

'Carmichael!' He threw the letter at Tam's bulky figure. 'After all he said, he's backed out of the deal to sell Paton's Court!' He stood at the window. 'He's taken everything that mattered from me. And I'm not going to tug my bloody forelock any more!'

'What can you do?' Tam returned curiously.

'I'm going to talk to Sir Justin Fleming. I've heard Carmichael hasn't a penny to live off so he must have got his money from Fleming, because no one else would dare lend him any. He's useless.'

Jeannie spent the morning with a long list of patients, the damp weather having brought out the usual complaints of lung and chest congestion and, of course, various nasty, foul-smelling skin fungi. Eventually she was left with only her sputum samples to send off. But there was something else too.

'I didn't think you'd be showing your face here,' Ross said, as she walked into his office. 'Or have you decided that you want a bit more rough?'

'Save your compliments for your dancers,' she spat back at him. 'You are no gentleman, Mr Macintosh, and my only regret is that I let myself be taken in by you.'

'I've never lied to you. You just let your innate snobbery get the better of you.'

'Like Enid Baker let hers? Like Fiona let hers?' she goaded him.

'I don't know what you're talking about,' he said.

'You had affairs with both of them,' she said. 'Enid, a woman old enough to be your mother – and Fiona! How could you do that to Hamish?' Her anger spent, she willed herself to understand him.

'Enid was helping me become established,' he said slowly. 'She had to have something in return.'

'Couldn't you have walked her dog?' she asked.

'Enid is a better negotiator than that.'

'I can see why you spend so much time with dancers,' she interrupted. 'But with Enid you were a gigolo. When did you and Fiona find each other?'

'Last year. She was all over me like a rash.'

'Didn't you ever think about Hamish?' Her voice was quieter now.

'I was flattered by the attention. Good God, Jeannie, I'd defy any man with blood in his veins to ignore Fiona when she's on heat.'

Jeannie took a deep breath.

'You must have thought I was such a fool.' She shook her head. 'Was it Fiona who told you how much I was worth?'

'No. She told me her husband couldn't make love to her any more.'

'So you stepped into the breach? What a charitable man you are to make such a sacrifice.'

'She meant nothing to me.'

'And you, Mr Macintosh, mean nothing to me. And now you're a member of the club, there is no need for you to bother me any more. Goodbye.' She walked out and slammed the door. Ross wrenched it open and raced after her into the rain-washed street.

'I love you,' he said, as he grabbed her arm.

'You don't know what love is!' She pulled away from him so violently that her coat ripped at the seams. She hurried off down the street, ignoring the curious looks of passers-by.

Ross scowled at the young men lounging against the wall, and went back into his office. He stood and stared at the wall, the damp and the broken furniture. 'Didn't take you long Jeannie Macdonald, did it?' he said bitterly. 'Didn't take you long to change your bloody mind about me.'

It was early afternoon when she made her way to the surgery near to the elegance of Raith Park. She knocked on the door, and the maid showed her in immediately.

'Dr Macdonald!' Gordon McLeod greeted her. Jeannie started.

'What?' he said, in an amused voice. 'That is your title, isn't it?'

'Just surprised that you used it,' she said. Gordon ushered her into the laboratory. 'I had your note but was unable to leave earlier.'

'Before I begin, I just want to say that I admire what you've been doing in Pathhead,' he said. 'And your women's clinic was a daring but hopefully effective experiment to help those poor unfortunates.'

'I'm signing it over to the infirmary,' she said. 'Unfortunately you can't run a clinic on admiration.'

'I know. And now I'm about to break some of my deepest held beliefs.'

'I don't understand.' But the hairs on the back of her neck rose.

'I've always admired you, Jeannie, from the moment I delivered you. You're intelligent, committed and with more life in you than a barrel of monkeys. And that is why it pains me so to tell you this.'

'What, Gordon?'

'There are many diseases today that seem to be little more than a curse on humanity.'

'One of the four horsemen,' she murmured.

'Some we can put down to bad water or bad air, and some we can blame on an intemperate lifestyle.' He picked up a textbook and opened it. 'Recognise this?'

'Of course.' She bridled. 'It's a chancre.'

'The first sign of syphilis.' He blew out the breath in his lungs. 'And this disease, like so many others, pays no attention to the circumstances of the person it affects.'

'We all know why a certain physician got knighted, Gordon. Services to the Crown, wasn't it?' She looked at him keenly. 'Spit it out. I'm not one for subtlety.'

'When Mrs Margaret Carmichael visited me so that I might confirm her pregnancy, she was presenting symptoms of the disease.'

'No!' Jeannie shook her head vehemently. 'Not Margaret. She was sweet and gentle and—'

'Jeannie, please.' Gordon put a hand on her arm. 'Think rationally. She was pregnant and the child would have been born with congenital syphilis.'

Jeannie stared at him. 'My God, she didn't—'

Gordon MacLeod looked down. 'She was in the stables. It was never established how she came to fall, but she undoubt-edly fell from a great height. Sir Justin was anxious you should know before you made your decision.'

Jeannie nodded. She felt the bile rise into her mouth. Margaret had been betrayed by a man who had sworn to cherish and protect her. She had been condemned to death by his actions. 'But syphilis can be curable, with the right treatment,' she said.

'The discovery of her condition temporarily unhinged her mind, I imagine. Or the knowledge that her child would be born with the syphilitic stigmata and die a horrible death.'

'And Angus is contesting the will on the same grounds.' It was difficult to think of anything other than that her dearest friend had borne this horrifying knowledge and hadn't been able to tell her.

Gordon swallowed. 'Mr Carmichael visited me prior to his wife's pregnancy. He was in the second stage and wanted to know if it was possible for him to have a child. I informed him that he should seek treatment and that it would take two years at least. He declined to do so. And since then he has denied that he ever sought my advice on the matter. His army records state he was clear of it when he joined up. I can only imagine that the disease is now in its latent stage, no longer contagious but still inside him. Eventually the final stage will take hold and he'll die.'

Jeannie nodded. 'It's easy for someone to ignore what's wrong with them when they don't have any symptoms. But what kind of man would put his wife through that and risk his child's life?'

'We both know he's not the first, nor likely to be the last.' He cleared his throat awkwardly. 'It may be wise for you to consider a test,' he added.

'I haven't had relations with him.' She smiled. 'I'm sorry, but you are my doctor.'

'I need hardly tell you that this conversation never occurred,' he said. 'And don't forget that it's possible you're condemning him out of hand. She might have taken a lover.'

'I knew Margaret.' Jeannie's embarrassment was swept away

by the mention of her name. 'There was only him.' She stood up. 'Thank you for your honesty, Gordon.' She held out her hand.

'Thank you, Jeannie.' He gripped her hand and shook it. 'Fortune favours the bold, you know.' He sat back in his chair. 'And of all the qualities you lack, boldness is not one of them.'

Jeannie sat in her bedroom, looking out at the old oak tree, standing bare against her window. How long had Margaret known, she wondered. Then she remembered: her friend had tried to tell her. She had come to the surgery and asked about syphilis. And Jeannie had dismissed her questions as those of a nervous pregnant lady. If only she had listened to what Margaret was trying to tell her, she might have been able to persuade her that there was another way. But Jeannie had been too wrapped up in her own problems, her own life, and had failed Margaret in her hour of need.

She curled up in her armchair, tears flowing down her face. 'Margaret, I'm sorry,' she said aloud. 'If only I'd listened to you. if only I'd been the friend to you that you were to me.'

The next day, when she was working at the surgery, Angus arrived. 'I thought I'd look at the books,' he said cheerfully, and bent to kiss her cheek. 'Actually I just wanted to see you yet I have to sing for my supper.' He wore that appealing, quizzical look that asked her silently if she had made a final decision.

How easily he wore his guilt, Jeannie thought. Did he really think he was not to blame for Margaret's death?

'I'm busy,' she said. 'One of my patients has syphilis.' She noticed that Angus didn't flinch.

'Never mind. Once we're married, you won't be working here any more,' he said.

Jeannie felt disgust, hatred and many other emotions rise in her. 'This is where I belong, Angus, and I will not leave. Ever.'

It was late on Friday night when she made her way to the Fleming house, set back in the hills. When she arrived a maid took her hat and coat and the butler poured her some sherry. Sir Justin came in. 'Eugenia.' His face was sad, the laughter lines now just age creases. 'Gordon has talked to you?'

She nodded.

'I would like to have told you myself, but I was her father.' He blinked away a tear.

'I will be breaking off every connection with Mr Carmichael,' Jeannie said, 'when I have a chance to talk to him.' She waited as Sir Justin composed himself. 'But I would like to know the rest of the facts, if I may.'

Sir Justin went to the window, looking out on the darkness of the gathering autumn. 'I always enjoyed Carmichael's company – he's engaging – but I never for a moment thought he'd set his cap at Margaret.' He shrugged. 'I wanted someone else for her, but she wanted him, so they married.' He took a gulp of his whisky.

'But then the war came and when he returned he wanted to prove himself as a broker, so I recommended some clients to him. He made a mess of everything, and even ran off to Glasgow when it became too much, leaving me to sort them out. But Margaret wanted him back, so I had to persuade him to return. I told him I wouldn't let him manage any of my friends' money, but Margaret signed over everything she had. And he lost most of it.'

Jeannie could see he was trying hard to keep himself in check.

'Then when she told me she was with child, I could have forgiven him everything. But a few weeks later she was dead. And the post-mortem revealed something else we didn't know about Angus Carmichael. He had obviously broken his marriage vows with the lowest kind of woman.' He threw his glass against the fireplace with a passion that was much more like the Sir Justin Jeannie knew.

'But Margaret had changed her will, cutting him out. And he's contesting it, blackmailing me. Unless I defer to him he will tell the world that she committed suicide. And that she had what she had.'

'So he would force you to move her grave to unconsecrated ground?' Jeannie moved to stand beside him. 'And ruin her reputation, shame those who loved her?'

'I've no idea what he's doing now, Jeannie.' He looked her straight in the eye. 'But I would warn you against any dealings with him, business or personal. I have received information that he has recently acquired sufficient money to pay off his debts.'

'He's been in charge of the finances for the clinic for some time!' she exclaimed. 'And we've less money than ever.'

'Bring your books to me. We'll take that man for everything.'

'Will that make you feel better?' she asked numbly.

'No, but it'll stop him in his tracks. You had a lucky escape, Jeannie. I'm glad, for your sake and your family's.'

It all became too much for Jeannie: she found herself sobbing into Sir Justin's shoulder, weeping like a child for her friend who had been betrayed. Sir Justin wanted revenge, but Jeannie wanted someone to comfort her.

After she left Sir Justin, she went to see Innes. She knew he would be less than sympathetic but she had to talk to someone.

'Jeannie?' He looked at her in surprise. 'Aren't you working today?'

'I need to talk to you, Innes.' She strode through the door. 'I think I've just made a pact with the devil.'

'Is this something to do with Ross Macintosh?' he said, with trepidation.

'No,' she replied. 'I've told him I want nothing more to do with him, despite his protestations of love.' She tucked her hair behind her ear. 'But I'm on my way back from showing the clinic books to Sir Justin. We suspect that Angus has been defrauding the clinic.'

'Why would he do that?'

'Because he has no money. Because he was such a success at looking after other investments in his broking business that he lost most of his clients and Sir Justin banned him from using Margaret's name to prospect for more.'

'That makes him incompetent, not a thief.'

'Then perhaps he just wants to fund a lifestyle he cannot afford. Perhaps the temptation of complete trust was too much for him. Only he can tell us. But I can't have him steal another thing from my patients. They have little enough as it is.'

Innes nodded slowly. 'I always thought that Angus was an adventurer, but he comes from a good family and he was at St Andrews with Hamish.'

'That's not all.' Her voice shook. 'He gave Margaret syphilis.'

'And he told you?'

'No, I found out from a mutual friend. Would he ever have told me or waited until I had given birth to a dying child? Until I had it too?'

'I will talk to him immediately.'

'That's the least of my worries, Innes,' she replied. 'I'm going to have it out with Angus, and then I'm going to the police. He's going to prison, whether it shames us or not.'

'This is not for you to do, Jeannie,' he warned her.

'Then if you want to stop me killing him, Innes,' she said carefully, 'I suggest you get yourself an army.'

It was late but she decided to go back to the surgery. She had work to do, which wouldn't keep.

She was looking at the cultures of skin fungus she had grown when Jim came in.

'Has he been back?' he asked conversationally.

'No.'

237

'He was in earlier looking for the books. And he wasn't best pleased when I told him you had them. He'd have been even angrier if I'd told him where you'd taken them.' He smiled grimly.

'Well, I said I'd do the calls tonight.' She began to leaf through the notes on people who needed a visit. Then she packed her bag and headed for the courts with Charlie and Buster.

'I'm looking for Mr Ross Macintosh,' Innes said politely.

Tam looked at him warily. 'And who might you be?' he said loudly, so that Ross could hear him.

'The Reverend Innes Macdonald.'

The door opened and Ross came out. 'What is this, Innes?' he asked bitterly. 'My official notification to stay away from the lot of you?'

'Quite the reverse, actually,' Innes replied. 'I think Jeannie's going to need your help.'

'I've helped her till I'm blue in the face.' Ross stared at him.

'You gained enough from our patronage, Mr Macintosh,' Innes replied shortly, 'and after your appalling conduct with a member of my family, you have a debt to us.'

'Jeannie came to me. As you well know, I had spoken to your brother. I did not set out to take advantage of her.'

'No. This is about your continuing affair with Fiona.'

'Whoever's putting a smile on her face it isn't me,' Ross told him. 'I haven't been with her since January.'

Innes hadn't been expecting such candour. 'Jeannie has discovered something about Angus Carmichael that would lead us to believe he is not as he seems. Information that if she acts upon it might endanger her.'

'Call the police.'

'Due to its nature, it would not be a good idea to make things official. But I've heard that you might be the person to help on an unofficial basis.'

'You want me to warn him off?' Ross said.

'Carmichael has been defrauding the clinic. Jeannie is set on having it out with him, and I'm concerned about his reaction.'

'Trust Jeannie to rush in.' Ross shook his head.

'Then will you help?'

'Only if she wants me to,' Ross said. 'I'll want to talk to her first.'

'Where are the books?' Angus was back at the surgery, unusually agitated.

'I don't know,' Jim said warily.

'How can I be expected to do anything when what I need isn't here?' Angus continued.

'Do your best,' Jim snapped. 'Which is what we have to do without enough equipment or funds.' He turned away.

'I need the books,' Angus repeated.

'Jeannie's got them.' Jim looked him up and down. 'We've hardly a penny left. She's trying to find a way to save money.'

'Smillie!' Angus said. 'You have to understand it from my position. I need the books.'

'Come back tomorrow,' Jim said tartly, as he turned away. 'And while you're at it, bring some of our money with you.' Without saying anything more Angus left.

'Doctor.' A young woman walked in.

'Not just yet, dearie,' Jim said wearily. 'I have to make a house call.'

'I need to talk to Jeannie,' Ross said, as he faced the housekeeper at the door.

'Everyone's in the drawing room,' she said, and ushered him towards the door.

Ross walked in to find Jim Smillie talking to Jeannie and Sir Justin Fleming.

'So it's true,' Ross said grimly, as he took in the scene.

'It's just got worse,' Sir Justin said. 'Carmichael has been to the surgery and discovered the books are gone. That means he will run.'

'What's happened to Angus?' Hamish's voice floated over them. Ross and Jeannie looked round. Hamish was standing in the doorway in his dressing-gown and slippers.

'He's been defrauding the surgery,' Sir Justin told him.

'No!' Hamish sat down heavily. 'He can't have been, not Angus.'

'Don't upset yourself,' Jeannie walked over to him and took his hands, 'not when you're getting better.'

'He's a good man,' Hamish whispered, 'weak, but a good man nevertheless.'

'Have you any idea where we may find him?' Ross persisted.

Hamish took a deep breath. 'I'm so sorry to do this to you, Jeannie,' he said slowly, 'but I think I know where he is.'

'I don't care what you have to say, Hamish,' Jeannie declared. 'I just want what's mine.'

'Wherever he is,' Hamish said, into his chest, 'he'll be with Fiona. People don't realise how small this world is until they try to hide in it. I saw them together a few times, when they thought everyone was in another room. And have you noticed that when Fiona goes to Edinburgh to visit her family he's often away on business?'

'This isn't helping us find them,' Sir Justin said quietly. 'Where could they be?'

'I have a good idea,' Ross said grimly. 'Fiona was a creature of habit.'

They got into two cars – Sir Justin and Innes in one, Ross, Hamish and Jeannie in the other – and Jim returned to the surgery. They drove out into the countryside, and as dusk began to fall, they reached a quiet country house, used by walkers and, as they now knew, by lovers. Ross had been there often with Fiona. He went in first, followed by the others. 'I'm looking for Mr Carmichael,' he said to the man at the reception desk.

'Mr Carmichael?' The man paled as he saw the assembly in front of him.

'I suggest that you tell us,' Sir Justin said, with quiet authority, 'unless you want it public knowledge what this place is used for.'

'We do not wish any trouble, sir.' The man took a deep breath and swallowed. 'Room six.' His eyes held recognition when they strayed to Ross.

They went up the stairs, walking silently along the thick carpet to the door. Ross knocked quietly, the polite knock of a servant.

Angus opened it. His face fell when he saw who was outside, but it was too late. Ross pushed open the door and everyone rushed in, to discover Fiona draped over the bed, drinking champagne and smoking a cigarette. She screamed, and wrapped her négligé round her slender body.

'You've some explaining to do, Carmichael,' Sir Justin said. 'Let's start with where you've hidden Eugenia's funds.'

'Jeannie, this isn't what you think—' Angus began.

'Isn't it?' Her voice wobbled. It was one thing to confront Angus with his fraud, but another to see his blatant affair with his best friend's wife. 'You aren't who I thought you were.' She pressed her lips together to stop herself screaming at him.

'What have you done with the money?' Innes asked.

Angus looked down.

'My lawyers are applying to the courts to have your assets seized,' Sir Justin said calmly. 'If you want to avoid the indignity, I would advise that the money is returned.'

'I have invested it to get a better return—' Angus began.

'That money was to be used on the poorest in Fife, not to buy you champagne!' Jeannie roared.

'Just give me a few days—'

'Your time has run out,' Sir Justin informed him.

Angus looked at each of them in turn. 'It's just a misunderstanding,' he said. 'In a few days we'll all be laughing about it.' He tried a smile, but it set on his face.

'In a few days you'll be in gaol, unless you can come up with all the monies you have stolen from us.' Sir Justin put a hand on his shoulder. 'If you'll come with me—'

'Hamish,' Fiona said, as she got off the bed. 'Oh, Hamish.' She dissolved in tears, but Hamish moved away.

'How could you, Fiona?' he said. 'Of all people, how could you do it with Angus?'

'I don't know,' Fiona replied. 'Please don't leave me, Hamish. Please!'

'I suggest you get dressed and find your way back to your family in Edinburgh, my dear,' Sir Justin said coldly. 'Then you should consult a physician.'

'A physician?' Fiona said faintly.

'I'm perfectly fit and healthy!' Angus burst out.

Fiona put her hands to her mouth. 'What's wrong with you?' she asked him fearfully.

'No!' Jeannie said forcefully, and walked over to Fiona. She turned to face the grim assembly. 'Gentlemen, I must ask you to leave.' Her tone brooked no argument. A moment later she and Fiona were alone.

'It's something awful, isn't it?' Fiona said quietly.

Jeannie nodded.

'And he may have given it to me?'

'He has syphilis. It seems to be in the third stage, and for a while he won't be capable of infecting anyone else.'

'Have you got it?' Fiona's voice trembled.

'He hasn't had relations with me.' It seemed so natural to discuss this with Fiona now. A few short weeks ago, Jeannie would never have dreamed she could.

'Will you examine me?' Fiona put her hand on Jeannie's.

'If you wish. But it won't tell you for sure.'

Fiona lay back on the bed as Jeannie got out her gloves and put them on. 'You don't appear to exhibit any of the symptoms,' she said slowly, 'but you won't know for certain until you have a blood test.'

'Thank you, Jeannie.' Fiona sat up and looked away as Jeannie threw the gloves into the wastepaper basket. 'I didn't think you'd be the one to help me.'

'If you have it, the cure takes at least two years,' Jeannie said. 'And you'll have to give up the idea of having children.'

'But he never told me,' she said softly. 'Why would he lie to me?'

'Because that's who he is,' Jeannie felt a curious sense of responsibility for her. 'He lied to all of us.' She waited as Fiona dressed and packed her little evening case. Then she opened the door. The men were waiting outside.

'Angus left a few things in here that he needs,' Hamish said, as he walked into the room.

'Of course.' Jeannie closed her bag.

Angus and the others walked in. He made no effort to speak, but smiled winningly at both white-faced women. 'That seems to be all in order,' he said, as he picked up his watch and a few oddments.

'One more thing, Angus,' Jeannie said.

'What?' Angus's face showed that he thought he was being given another chance.

'This!' She swung her fist at him with all her might, catching him squarely on his chiselled chin. He went down like a stone.

'Jeannie!' Innes moved towards her but Ross had grabbed her round the waist.

'You're bloody lucky she did that, Carmichael,' Ross said, as he rubbed Jeannie's hot knuckles, 'because if she hadn't I would have. And I'd have killed you!' He laughed at the man stumbling to his feet. 'Now I think it's about time you left. I'm proud of you, Dr Macdonald. You'd have made a good boxer.'

'I think I've cracked a knuckle,' she whispered. 'My hand really hurts.'

'Come on.' Ross gave her a quick hug. 'Let's get you home.'

They drove away with a silent Fiona and Hamish. When they arrived Hamish took his wife to her rooms.

'They've a lot to talk about,' Jeannie said wistfully. 'I hope, for her sake, that she isn't infected.'

'And what about you?' Ross said quietly. 'What if you are?'

'He was so busy sleeping with Fiona he never approached me,' she said. 'I didn't think of it at the time, but I should have realised . . .' She watched as he poured them both a drink.

'I've given Fiona some of my sleeping-draught.' Hamish had come into the drawing room, interrupting them, and warmed his hands by the fire. 'Tomorrow will be time enough to talk.'

'If you require a witness, I'll testify for you,' Ross said gruffly. 'Save the other details coming out.'

'Thank you, but there's no need,' Hamish said. 'I have no intention of divorcing Fiona, particularly if she's ill. She'll need nursing.'

'But after what she's done, Hamish?' Jeannie exclaimed, as she went to the drinks cabinet and poured some whisky.

'I love her.' Hamish looked at the floor. 'I'm the only person she's ever talked to.'

'But—' Jeannie tried to speak, and Hamish put up his hand.

'No one took her seriously. She was like a doll in a cabinet, taken out and played with for a few hours, but no one bothered to listen to a word she said. Even the men tired of her because she needed constant reassurance that she was something special. What kind of life did she have once you had taken off the wrapping paper?'

'I wish I could do something to help you, Hamish,' Jeannie said.

'You've given me shelter, patience, companionship and even a new profession. I am Kirkcaldy's premier crossword inventor, but I'll understand if she isn't welcome in your home.' He glanced at Ross, who was watching the proceedings thoughtfully. 'Still want to be one of us?'

'I'll stick with being myself, I think.' He watched as Hamish kissed Jeannie's forehead and went to the door.

'You can stay here, Hamish,' she said impulsively. 'She may need my nursing too.'

'You want to cure the world, don't you?' he said tenderly. 'Goodnight.'

Jeannie picked up the two tumblers on the drinks table and went to the faded sofa. She set them down, then crumpled into it, sobbing like a child.

Then she felt Ross's arms cradling her. 'I'm so sorry,' she sobbed. 'I've ruined everything.'

'Now, that's not the Jeannie Macdonald I know,' he murmured. 'Let it all out. My shoulders are broad enough, even for your worries.'

'Will everything be better in the morning?' she asked, in a worn-out voice.

'It'll take longer than that but, yes, everything will be fine.' He warmed her hands in his. 'Sir Justin will get every penny out of Carmichael, and he'll disappear back to Glasgow where he belongs. And Hamish and Fiona, well, who knows how long their future will be or where it will take them? But he'll be there as long as she needs him.'

'And will you be here?' Her voice was a little more hesitant.

'I'll be here as long as you want me, Jeannie Macdonald,' Ross assured her. 'You cause far too much trouble to be let out alone again.'

'Is that a promise?' She laid her head on his shoulder.

'It's a guarantee. I love you, Jeannie. I know I'm just a miner's son, with new shoes and a motor-car, but I love you. Whatever you do, I'll be right behind you.'

'I don't want you behind me, Ross,' she replied, 'I want you next to me.'

'You know me, Jeannie!' He raised his eyebrows. 'I've never stood at the back for anything. Though I'd hate to think what my mother will say when she finds out I send you to work.' He shrugged. 'Although, there'll be talk because of my past.'

'It doesn't seem to matter any more,' she said softly.

'Aye, let's just think about the future,' he said tenderly. 'Because that's what we can do something about.'